THE HAND THAT TAKES

FALL OF THE COWARD, BOOK ONE

TAYLOR O'CONNELL

TAYLOR O'CONNELL BOOKS

The Hand That Takes
Fall of the Coward, Book One
Taylor O'Connell

For Anika,
The love of my life.
Thank you for all of your support and encouragement through this process.

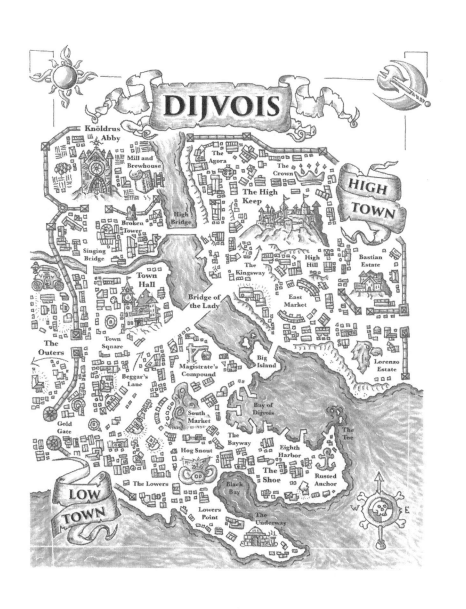

I

THE LOCKET

Lo, men, harken a tale for thee, of a man and a man's desires, this song I shall sing.
—Balliel the Bard

Those who want naught, have all.
—Kellenvadra

THE HEIST

Pale beams of moonlight shone through the black clouds of the storm-wracked sky. Rain fell sidelong, slapping flesh and cobblestones alike, soaking cloth clean through and sending a chill to the bone.

Bartley cried out in pain, a wordless curse that hardly carried over the tumult of the storm.

"Quiet," Sal warned. "If those steel caps hear you, we're dead."

Bartley said something about a Sacrull damned quarrel but was cut short by a boom of thunder. He was always talking, Bartley was, even when he didn't have a crossbow quarrel jutting from his leg, but that's the way Yahdrish were. Yabbers, Sal's uncle called them, but Sal had never dared tell that to Bartley.

"Just try to stay quiet," Sal said, grunting as his friend leaned more weight on his shoulders.

Bartley's limp had worsened. There had been no time to stop and examine the injury, but Sal could tell the leg was hurting him. He only hoped it was a quarrel and not a bolt. There was nothing worse than digging out a broadhead.

Bartley began to whimper with each step. His pace slowed as he shifted even more of his weight onto Sal. Had it not been for the ankle-high water in the streets, Sal might have carried him, but with the storm in full swing it was out of the question.

"Don't let them put me in the crow-cages," Bartley said, his teeth chattering. "Please, I couldn't—I wouldn't last."

"No one is going to the crow-cages. You just keep quiet. Focus on walking."

Bartley gritted his teeth. "They knew. The whole time, they knew."

"They couldn't have known," Sal said. Hoping it was true.

"I'm telling you, they knew. They were waiting for us."

"Right. Well, try and keep your voice down," Sal said. He didn't want to think about it, didn't even want to consider what the presence of the City Watch implied. "Did you see what happened to Vinny?" he asked, trying to change the subject.

Bartley shook his head. "Not after we crossed the outer wall. I was with Anton."

Anton. That son of a bitch had some explaining to do. Sal ran a hand over the bump in his jerkin pocket, if only to make certain the locket was still there. From the moment he'd first laid hands on it, he had known there was something wrong with the thing, something strange in the way it felt, something otherworldly. He found himself torn between outright repulsion and an irresistible attraction to it, but the instant he saw Anton, willing or not, Sal would be rid of the locket.

When they neared the alley mouth, Sal put a hand on Bartley's chest, signaling for the Yahdrish to stop. He poked his head from the alley and looked up and down the flooded street for any signs of steel caps. He searched the rooftops, though in this rain the threat of crossbowmen was well diminished. Catgut didn't hold up to the wet.

Nonetheless, Sal kept his ears open for the click of a crossbow crank or the clatter of steel on chain mail. As the Lady's luck had it, he heard neither, nor any sounds that would indicate the presence of the City Watch.

"When did you last see Vinny?" Sal whispered as they crossed the street and slipped into the next alley.

"We split up once we were inside. Vinny was with Odie. I went with Anton. Bloody steel caps ambushed us before we met back up." Bartley hesitated for a moment before he went on. "Anton didn't make it."

Sal stopped short. "What do you—didn't make—" Sal swallowed and took a deep breath. "What do you mean, Anton didn't make it?"

"There was nothing I could do. Took this Sacrull damned bolt and I could hardly think straight."

"What happened to Anton?" Sal asked, his heart in his throat, tears coming unbidden to his eyes.

"Poleaxe," Bartley said, shaking his head. "Steel caps came out of nowhere while we were on the bailey wall. It's like they were waiting for us all along."

"Anton, he's—"

Bartley nodded. "I'm sorry, Sal, there was nothing I could do."

"What about the others?" Sal asked. He swallowed and wiped at his eyes. "Did you see what happened to anyone else?"

"Sacrull's balls," Barley cursed, "how should I know? After I got hit by the quarrel, I fell off the wall. If I hadn't landed in that hedge, they'd have killed me, sure as spit."

Sal took a breath to center himself. It was a lot to take in. A steel cap ambush in the High Keep, and now Anton was dead—but this wasn't the time to think on it. They needed to get out of the open. He could worry about what to do with the locket later.

"Right. Well, you can rest your mouth for a turn. Let's just focus on getting you to the safe house," Sal said.

High Hill was as far from the Lowers as anywhere in Dijvois, a long walk even had they both been healthy. As they trudged along, Sal expected to see a pack of steel caps around every corner and a crossbowman on every rooftop. Yet the Lady's luck held. From time to time Sal's hand slipped into the pocket of his jerkin, but it was hard enough to keep Bartley upright with both hands free, so his fingers never remained on the locket for long.

Still, each time he brushed the smooth gold, tendrils of energy surged up his arm and through his body, filling him with a sensation that was equal parts elation and dread.

Bartley let out another cry of pain. "I don't think—I can't go on much longer."

"It's not much farther now," Sal said. "Just up ahead."

Bartley let out something halfway between a laugh and a whimper. "Don't lie to me. I'm hurt, not simple. We haven't even crossed the bridge."

The Yahdrish was right, of course, but Sal needed to keep his friend's mind off the distance and the quarrel jutting from his leg.

"What bridge would that be?" Sal asked.

"Suppose that doesn't matter," said Bartley. "Though I'd rather not cross at the Bridge of the Lady. Bound to be steel caps waiting."

"I think we're best off taking the ferryman's way," Sal said.

"In this rain? The Tamber will be flooded. I doubt if the ferry is even crossing. More than like, the ferryman is done for the season. Besides, what coin do you plan to pay him with?"

"If we can't cross by ferry, we'll double back to South Bridge."

"South Bridge is bound to be guarded as well," Bartley said. "I'm telling you, the City Watch knew we were coming."

Sal shook his head, but he was starting to wonder whether that was true. The steel caps had set an ambush, after all.

The walk to the Ferryman's Ford didn't take as long as Sal had expected, though the downhill slope seemed to hurt Bartley more than walking on level ground. Still, with the lack of interference from the City Watch, it almost seemed their night had taken a turn for the better.

The ferry was moored to the Tamber's eastern bank, the High Town side of the river. Even better, there were no signs of steel caps waiting for them at the ford. Sal considered this irrefutable evidence that luck had joined their cause at last.

"I told you the river would be near flooded," Bartley whined. "The dock is underwater, and look at that chop. I don't much fancy a swim. Not with this quarrel sticking out from my leg."

"Should we stop and pull it out?" Sal asked with a smirk. "Swimming would save us the cost of a ferry ride."

Bartley reddened, his face pinched with irritation. "Go and knock. I'll wait here." Bartley had always been prickly. It stemmed from being small, and the inevitable japes about his size.

As the ferryman wasn't on the river or the dock, it stood to reason he was shut up in the shack, keeping himself dry from the rain.

After the fifth knock, a wizened little man swung the door open. "Gods be dammed, I heard you the first time," the old man said, jabbing a knobby finger into Sal's chest. "You mean to bring down my door, boy?"

"We need a crossing."

The ferryman scowled. "And so you'd better, if you come banging on my door at the hour of the wolf. But you're not going to get no crossing, not this late in the season, not in no storm, and not when she's near flooded."

"We're willing to pay."

"I should think you were, but that don't make a lick of difference. Like I done told you, ferry's through for the season."

"One last crossing, that's all we ask. We are more than willing to compensate for the additional risk."

The ferryman squinted at the river as though gauging the peril. Then he turned his wrinkled visage on Sal and gave a smile that showed far too many teeth. "Nine krom."

Sal nearly had to bite his tongue, but he dared not balk, no matter how excessive the rate. He nodded. There was no time to waste; they needed to cross the river before the City Watch thought to pay a visit to the Ferryman's Ford.

"Nine it is."

The ferryman held up a hand, his palm yellow and callused from years of poling his raft across the Tamber. "And another four krom for the boy. In this storm, I'll need the extra hands on the pole to keep from going bottom up."

Sal nodded once more.

"And two," the man said shrewdly, "for waking me at this Sacrull damned hour."

Sal nodded a third time. To think, people called *him* a thief.

"Silver is good, and gold's better. If you'd like to pay in gold, I can do it for ten, but don't think you'll get away shimming no coppers, neither. Hard krom, or you can swim your way across."

Shimming the ferryman fifteen coppers was precisely what Sal had intended to do. Instead, he assured the old man he would receive his silver in full.

The ferryman's smile crept ear to ear. Clearly he was pleased with himself. He held out a hand palm up.

When Sal didn't respond, the ferryman rubbed thumb and forefinger together in the universal gesture of expected payment.

Sal steeled his nerve, cleared his throat, and nestled his boot firmly beside the door frame. "We don't have the coin—not now, that is, or rather, not here—but I assure you we're good for—"

The ferryman flung the door shut, and his scowl turned malevolent as it bounced off Sal's planted boot.

"No coin, no crossing!" the ferryman shouted. "Begone, or I'll send the boy to fetch the City Watch. I will."

"There's no need for that. We can pay you the coin. We just need to cross back to Low Town to get it."

"Cross back to Low Town so you can scamper off and short me my fair pay, is more like. Mayhap you'll have better luck with the bridges."

They would have no such luck, a fact the ferryman would soon learn should any steel caps show.

No doubt the news of an attempted burglary in the High Keep would already have circulated through every regiment of the City Watch. No one would be crossing the bridges before morning. If they tried, the steel caps would likely have Sal and Bartley thrown into crow-cages the moment they set foot on any one of the bridges.

Sal put a hand over his pocket. The gold locket within felt abnormally heavy for such a small thing. He considered a possible trade, but immediately dismissed the idea. "Twenty krom, and you'll have your pay by morning. My word is my bond."

"Keep your bond. No coin, no crossing. Now move that boot, or I'll wake the boy. He'll get the City Watch here, and them'll move the boot for you."

Sal stood up straight and did his best to feign confidence. Wet and bedraggled as he was, he doubted it was all that convincing. "Don't go making threats you won't carry out."

The ferryman's eyes narrowed, his weathered face shriveling up like a prune. "Don't think I would?" the old man snarled.

Sal kept his boot firmly planted and tilted his head slightly, smiling as though they were having a pleasant chat. "We both know you're not sending for any steel caps. Now drop the act."

"Oh, and why is that?"

"Because I know what you move upriver, and if the City Watch shows up, they just might go looking in that shed there," Sal said, pointing.

"Don't go threatening me, boy," the ferryman said. "Have you any idea the people—"

"What do you think would kill you first?" Sal said. "One of the magistrate's crow-cages, or Don Moretti's hired knives?"

The ferryman remained stone-faced. "Get gone. This is your last—"

Sal slipped a leather throng up and over his head. He pinched the silver ring that dangled from the throng and held it so close to the ferryman's nose that the old man's eyes went crossed as he backed a step away from the door.

"I take it you know this sigil?" Sal asked.

The ferryman gave only the slightest of nods, the apple in his throat bobbing as he swallowed whatever words had come to mind.

"And you know he is good for the coin should my associate and I not return on the morrow to pay?"

At the mention of coin, the fear drained from the old man's face. "I ferry you over, you'd best pay my due."

Sal reassured him, holding the ring out like a shield.

The ring bore the crest of the Commission. Each of the four quarters, and the center circle, was a different color, each color representing one of the five families of the Commission: black for Svoboda, blue for Moretti, white for Scarvini, red for Dvorak, and gold for Novotny. In the center of the crest was a falcon, a sigil that belonged to only one man in Dijvois, the underboss of the Svoboda crime family, Stefano Lorenzo.

The ferryman stared at the ring as though he wanted nothing more than to slap the thing from Sal's hand. He stared for some time, his nostrils twitching. In the end he agreed to take them across, for eight krom, though not without some form of collateral. He insisted on the ring, and after a moment of hesitation, Sal agreed to hand it over.

Once they'd shaken on the deal, the old man went back inside the shack, shouting for the boy to get out of bed.

The boy was a head and a half taller than Sal, and the pole he retrieved was as tall as three men stacked head to toe. He was lean, with long sinewy muscles like wound rope. Unlike his employer, the boy seemed entirely untroubled by the rain.

"Bloody hell," said Bartley, as Sal and the boy joined him near the dock, the ferryman a couple of steps behind. "I thought you'd taken a wrong turn into the river, or did that old man coerce you into a payment of flesh for his services?"

Sal made a face to show his distaste for the jape.

"Best get on that raft if you're wanting crossing," growled the ferryman. "I'll not suffer this wet all night."

Sal helped Bartley limp across the dock and onto the rocking raft. The boy followed, planting his pole into the river to keep the ferry from straining at the cord as the ferryman untied the moorings.

The Ferryman's Ford was one of the shallowest and widest segments of the Tamber. The width helped to reduce the speed of the current, making for a smoother, safer crossing. Despite that, the boy had his work cut out for him, as this late into autumn the current was strong. To Sal it seemed the boy was doing all the work, poling the raft across, while the old ferryman moaned about the rain.

"Catch the rope there!" the old man yelled as the raft reached the west bank.

Sal obliged and nearly slipped from the raft as he reached over the edge.

The ferryman roughly took the rope from Sal and secured the raft to the dock. "I'll be expecting my due at sunup. Eight krom silver."

"Eight krom," Sal said, as he helped Bartley limp onto the dock.

Without looking back, the pair made their slow trek across the dock, slogged through mud that sucked at their boots, and eventually found themselves on the slick cobblestones of Beggar's Lane. They followed Beggar's Lane and cut through a series of alleyways until they reached the outer edge of the Lowers.

Sal pushed through the door of the safe house and sighed with relief as the smell of rosemary and rushes wafted over him. The rushes were not woven into proper mats; rather, they'd been scattered about the floor like straw in a stable. A single candle burned atop the lone table, and the flame flickered, casting dancing shadows throughout the room until the door was closed.

The back door was locked and barred. No one would be coming in through the cellar.

Bartley moaned as Sal lowered him into a chair.

Then Sal took a seat, propped his elbows on the table, and put his face in his hands.

"First back?" Bartley asked.

Sal lifted his head from his hands and had opened his mouth to speak when he heard a rustling noise behind him.

Bartley cried out.

Sal dropped from his chair to one knee and drew his pigsticker from his boot sheath. He squinted. His eyes struggled to adjust to the dark, but faintly he could make out a man sitting on a cot in the far corner. The man coughed, stood, and approached the table at a leisurely pace.

"Sacrull's balls," said Bartley. "Luca, you trying to stop my heart?"

"The fuck happened?" Luca asked. "Where's the rest?"

Luca wasn't a big man, nor was he particularly fast or strong. To look at him, one might take him for an average nobody, just another Pairgu on the streets of Dijvois. But nobody crossed Luca Vrana.

Luca was a made man. He ran his own crew, a legitimate,

Commission-sanctioned crew, which answered to Don Moretti himself. Even without the patronage of the Moretti family, the name Luca Vrana carried a threat in its own right.

"No one else came back?" Bartley asked, as Sal slipped the pigsticker back into his boot.

Just then the safe house door swung open and a gust of humid air swept into the room. Three people staggered in. Valla and Dellan each had one of Anton's arms over their shoulders. It looked as if they'd carried him all the way from High Hill.

The toes of Anton's boots dragged across the floorboards, plowing furrows through the scattered rushes.

Sal put a hand over his pocket. His heart raced at the sight of Anton. "Is he dead?"

"Move the fucking candle," Valla snapped, her voice cracking like a whip. "Yahdrish, get out of the bloody way."

Sal snatched the candle from the table and Bartley toppled over in his chair as the big Vordin, Dellan, shoved him aside.

"We need to get him stripped so we can put pressure on the fucking wound," said Valla as she laid Anton on the table.

Valla looked soaked as much with blood as with water. Sal could see she had taken a few cuts, but nothing that called for immediate attention. Most of the blood on Valla belonged to Anton.

Anton lay on the table, silent and motionless, a wicked gash between his neck and shoulder that cleaved clean through the collarbone, deep into his chest. The wound bled profusely, although, from what Sal could tell, he was breathing, faint and raspy as it was.

Bartley had been wrong. Anton had survived the blow from the poleaxe—thus far.

With both hands, Valla was pressing a blood-sodden shirt into the wound.

"Someone give me another shirt," Valla said.

Sal dropped his cloak to the floor. He hesitated for an instant, his hand going to his pocket before he slipped out of his jerkin and shirt. The shirt dripped rainwater as Sal pushed it into Valla's hand. She tossed the blood-soaked linens over a shoulder, wrung out the clean shirt, and pressed it onto the wound.

Sal slipped back into his jerkin and cloak, and looked up to see Dellan staring him down.

Dellan was a Vordin. Tall and lean, he wore all black wool and boiled leather. He claimed to be Kalfi-born, though with his shaved head and face it was impossible to tell if he had the peppered blonde hair the clan was famous for. Dellan's teeth were filed to sharp points, like a shark's. His skin was not pale, but maggot white, and so heavily tattooed it looked to be marbled with veins of black. Still, neither the tattoos nor the filed teeth intimidated Sal nearly so much as the man's eyes. They were not the dark eyes typical of the Kalfi clansmen, but piercing blue, cold and hollow. Predatory eyes— the eyes of a killer.

"Where were you?" Dellan asked, his stare locked on Sal. His hands were at his sides, where Sal knew he kept his daggers, two ugly pieces of steel that had tasted enough blood to sate a river.

"Steel caps," Sal said, "cut me off in the courtyard. I had to run. I found Bartley, and when I saw he was shot, we went for the safe house."

"Shot, were you?" Valla said, turning on Bartley. "Is that why you left him up there to fucking die? Where were you shot, Yahdr-ish? The slit between your legs?"

"I took a quarrel to the leg," Bartley said, sullen as a spoiled maiden. "What in Sacrull's hell was I supposed to do, crawl after Anton on all fours? I thought he was dead."

Without a word Dellan closed the distance to Bartley, and with one hand on Bartley's back forced him facedown on the table next to Anton. Bartley thrashed and squealed as the big Vordin pulled the broken quarrel shaft from his leg. No matter how hard Bartley fought, he couldn't squirm loose; Dellan was too strong. Corded muscles bulged beneath his pale, tattooed skin. Slowly the bloody remains of the quarrel came free.

"Someone get a mender!" Bartley cried out, grasping at his lower leg where the quarrel had been, blood running between his fingers.

Dellan examined the quarrel, spat, and threw the bloody haft to the rushes.

"No one is fetching a mender," Luca said. "No one is leaving this room."

"It missed the bone," Dellan said with a sneer.

"Weakling," Valla spat. "Craven, and a fucking Yahdrish."

Bartley merely hunched lower and clutched his leg all the tighter.

Valla snarled at Bartley. "Left him to die like——"

"Enough!" said Luca. "I want to know what happened."

"Someone talked," said Valla, still pressing on Anton's wound. "They knew, the whole time they knew. They ambushed us. They were fucking waiting."

Luca's eyes began to burn with a murderous fire.

"Wasn't the High Keep's guards, either," said Valla. "Steel caps —bloody steel caps, Luca."

Luca's glare swept over all of them, resting momentarily on each in turn until it settled on Sal.

"Why would someone have talked?" Sal asked, Luca's stare unsettling him. "Look, we came back. Clearly, we didn't rat——"

"You saying it was the big man or that pretty flower Vincenzo?" Dellan said, baring his filed teeth.

"What?" Sal said, taken aback. "No, I'm not suggesting anyone talked. I'm saying we're here, and that should be good enough. Now, did anyone see Vinny or Odie?"

"They would have been on the far side——"

Luca slammed a fist on the table, and everyone went quiet.

Anton spluttered, his limbs flailing.

"Fuck's sake," said Valla through gritted teeth. "Someone help me hold him down. Yahdrish, give me your jerkin!"

Sal and Dellan moved to help, while Bartley stripped out of his jerkin and doublet.

"Dammit," Valla cursed, "I can't get the bleeding to slow. Luca, if we don't——"

"We need a mender," said Bartley, handing Valla his jerkin. "The bleeding isn't going to stop if we don't get him a mender, and if he doesn't bleed out, I will."

"You're not getting no bloody mender in here, you understand me?" Luca said, a vein in his neck bulging. "If he dies, he dies. I want to know what the fuck happened out there. Where's the parchment, where's the ring?"

"We never got the ring," Dellan said, still staring at Sal, his filed teeth bared as though he might take a bite out of Sal at any moment. "This tunnel rat never met me at the door."

Luca's attention turned back to Sal.

"Like I said, the steel caps cut me off in the courtyard," Sal said. "When I jumped into a hedge to hide, I found Bartley was already there. We waited for the steel caps to go by, and we got out of there. I don't know what else you expected of me."

"You ran," said Dellan. "Tail tucked between your legs, you ran and left the rest of us to die."

"Were we going to fight off the whole City Watch?" asked Bartley.

"And the parchment?" Luca said, turning to face Bartley. "What did you do with the parchment?"

"We were ambushed on the bailey wall," said Bartley. "Vinny and the big man never showed up, and when Anton took that poleaxe—he had the letter, they must have taken—"

"Anton has it," said Valla. "Told me as we carried him out of there."

"Where?" said Luca, crowding in on the group around the table.

"Dammit, Luca," Valla spat, "give me your shirt and back off."

The door swung open with a bang. A gust of wind scattered the rushes and set the candle flame to dancing.

The big man stepped in, followed by Vinny. They dripped rainwater on the floorboards. Neither looked particularly pleased, and yet they were alive.

The big man was named Odie, and he was, in fact, the biggest man Sal had ever seen. He was at least half Norsic, the other half only the gods knew what. Odie had a war hammer slung on his back, the iron head forged in the shape of a man's fist.

The other half-Norsic, Vinny, looked ragged at best. His long hair was matted down on his face like wet straw. His eyes widened when he saw Anton lying on the table, bleeding and writhing under the combined restraint of Valla, Dellan, and Sal.

"What happened to him?" Vinny asked.

"Poleaxe," said Sal. "Steel caps caught them on the bailey wall."

Vinny shook his head. "They stopped us in the gatehouse. We couldn't have gotten there. Odie had to take two of them out just to get us free of the outer wall."

That caught Luca's attention. "Told you, I didn't want any guards killed, City Watch or otherwise. This was supposed to be a clean job."

"Killed two on the bailey wall when we came on Anton. Two more on South Bridge," said Dellan with a shrug. "Don't know how else we could have gotten back."

"We took the ferry," Sal said in an offhand manner.

Dellan and Valla shared a look as though they'd not even considered the ferryman's way.

"Thought it was too late in the season for that," said Vinny.

"This was meant to be a clean job," said Luca. "That means no dead steel caps."

The big man stepped forward, crossing his thickly muscled arms over his chest. "Couldn't be avoided." Had it been anyone else in the party that dared contradict him, Luca might have ripped into them, berated them mercilessly, but no one chided the big man.

Odie wasn't officially a made man, as Luca was, but he was an acting enforcer, a leg-breaker that collected overdue debts on behalf of Alonzo Amato, which made him virtually untouchable without the express permission of Don Moretti or one of the other four bosses of the Commission.

"We need to get out of here," said Luca, his voice flat. "Dead steel caps means the magistrate is going to be out for blood. We need to get out and separate."

"If we try and move him, he'll die," said Valla. "We need to get the bleeding stopped so we can bandage the wound."

Luca looked down at Anton without a trace of pity in his eyes. "If the bleeding hasn't stopped by now, he's dead already. Drop him in the Tamber, or the bay, or throw him in the fucking gutter. Just make sure he doesn't die here."

With that said, Luca shoved Sal out of the way and began rifling through Anton's blood-soaked pockets. By the time he'd found what he was looking for, Luca's arms were red to the elbows. In his bloody hand he held a crumpled piece of parchment.

Luca swept his gaze over the seven. "Get gone. We're done here. You'll have your shares on the morrow."

Sal and Vinny exchanged a look, then wordlessly helped Bartley to his feet. Each of them shouldered one of Bartley's arms and helped him walk. Bartley whimpered with every step but managed not to cry out. Odie scooped Anton into his arms as though the injured man were a child. Dellan and Valla fell into the big man's wake, with Luca in the rear. Sal pushed open the door and once again found himself out in the rain.

2

A RIDE ON LIGHTNING

Bartley's limp had only worsened since Dellan had removed the quarrel. He seemed to wince more, and whimper louder, than he had on the walk down from High Hill.

Vinny was a head taller than Sal and outweighed him by a good three stone. To Sal's relief, Vinny shouldered most of Bartley's weight.

The others separated from the trio along the way. Dellan slipped into the shadows of the first alleyway off Vixen Road, alone and without warning. Odie stumbled off down Patcher's Way, cradling Anton in his arms and muttering something about finding a mender. Valla had followed at the big man's heels, a concerned look on her usually coquettish face. Sal considered going with them to help, but what could he do for Anton that Odie and Valla could not?

Sal still had the locket. If Anton lived, Sal would be rid of the thing. If he didn't—well, Sal could worry about what to do with it then. He wished Valla and Odie well and called on the Lady White to keep Anton breathing, though there was only a slip of a chance Valla and the big man would even find someone capable of treating Anton in his state. He had been a step away from death's door when they had dragged him into Luca's safe house.

When Luca finally went his own way, Sal breathed a sigh of relief and felt as though a hand had unclenched from his throat.

"I'm just glad we're still alive," Sal said, once he felt they were far enough out of earshot that Luca wouldn't hear. "When everyone split off but Luca, I thought he might make three new corpses out of us."

Vinny sighed. "You're telling me. I didn't think he'd let anyone leave the safe house alive after he decided one of us was a rat."

"Hold on, you—the both of you thought we were going to die," Bartley said, "and neither of you said a bloody word?"

"And when should I have voiced this concern? asked Vinny. "When Luca had us cornered in the safe house, or when he was following behind us through the quiet, empty street?"

"Anytime before the knife was in my back would have been good," said Bartley.

"You learned nothing after what happened to Fabian?" Vinny asked. "You never really know what Luca is going to do."

"What ever happened to Fabian?" said Bartley.

"Strange though, wasn't it?" Sal said, ignoring Bartley's question. "Someone must have talked. Elsewise, how did the City Watch know we would be at the High Keep?"

"No one would have talked," said Vinny. "You said that yourself."

"No one that went to the High Keep," Sal said. "But there were others who could have put together what we were planning—blast powder, flash oil, wards, counter-wards, grappling irons, masked cloaks. That's a lot of gear. If I had to guess, I'd say it was someone involved on the supply end."

"Makes sense," said Vinny.

"And what if it *was* someone who worked the job?" asked Bartley. "What if it was one of Luca's crew that set all of us up?"

"Doubtful," said Sal. "What would they have to gain by botching the job?"

"Isn't it obvious?" said Bartley.

"Who would have set us up?" asked Vinny. "It doesn't make sense."

"Doesn't it?" said Bartley.

"Let's hear it," said Sal. "What was there for any of us to gain by telling the steel caps we would be hitting the High Keep?"

"The score," said Bartley, arms wide, palms up, as though what he said was the only possible answer. "Someone wanted the score."

"And so they told the steel caps to stop us from stealing it?" said Sal. "What sense does that make?"

"I'm with Salvatori," said Vinny. "Besides, what score are you referring to? We left the High Keep with nothing to show but a bloody piece of parchment. Have to say, I don't see the upside in anyone telling the steel caps about the job unless they are on the City Watch's payroll."

Bartley shrugged, signaling he was finished arguing for the time being. They had reached the Hog Snout, the inn where Bartley kept a room. The Hog Snout was far from the city's most reputable inn, as the beer was flat and the wine was oily, the tables were less than clean, and the privy stank of—of an unwashed privy.

Despite its faults, the Hog Snout was always warm, dry, and welcoming. Morning or night the Hog always had a fire burning in the hearth and a gaggle of fun-loving patrons more than willing to play a hand of cards, roll the knuckles, or start a song around the taproom.

"Either of you gents want to come up for a cap or two?" Bartley asked with a wicked smile. "I could really use one after the night I've had."

Vinny shook his head. "I think I'll be heading home. My da' has to be drunk enough to need help into bed by now."

"Sure you don't want to warm yourself by the fire?" asked Sal. "You could dry out some before heading home."

"I'd only get wet again," said Vinny, looking up at the black-clouded sky. "No sense waiting it out, I don't think it'll be letting up anytime soon."

"Be safe," said Sal.

"See any steel caps, you'd best go the other way," said Bartley.

Vinny winked, brushed long, wet hair from his face, and went on down the road.

Sal followed Bartley inside and was hit with the scent of meadowsweet. The smell was one thing he loved about the Hog Snout.

The pair passed by the taproom, going directly for the stairs. A singer was some ways into "When Pigs Don Armor," and it seemed half the patrons in the taproom had joined in the singing.

Bartley had occupied the first room on the left for nearly three years, long enough that the inn's help had ceased tidying up the room. Which was a real shame, because if there was one thing Bartley's room could have used it was a good tidying up.

After he'd helped Bartley into dry clothes and bandaged his leg wound with a clean linen shirt, Sal searched for a place to sit and decided on the bed. Once comfortable, Sal reached into the pocket of his jerkin and received a jolt of energy as his fingers closed around the locket. Cold tendrils coursed through his body, tingling in a tantalizing way. For an instant he thought he heard a faint voice, words whispered in the wind.

He considered telling Bartley about the locket then and there, but decided the Yahdrish really didn't need to know. With his mouth, it would only be a matter of time before half the city knew about it.

Bartley limped to the dresser and opened one of the drawers. He withdrew an ornately carved box. It was Bartley's most prized possession, a box Sal had seen many times before, made of ebony wood and jade. He'd gotten it from a trader out of Dahuan, and the carving on the lid was of a queer Dahuaneze goddess. According to Nabu Akkad, she was a goddess of the night or some such. From Nabu's descriptions, Sal had taken the goddess to be similar to the Lady White.

Bartley set the ebony box on the bed next to Sal.

"You're going to get the straw damp," Bartley said. "Come now, off the bed."

"Talk to me like your dog, and I'll find something to stick through that hole in your leg," Sal said, putting a fist up as though he meant to fight.

"Come at me, and I'll find a hole to stick my leg through," Bartley said with a smirk. "Now then, for the reason we have all gathered here today." Gingerly, as though he were unveiling a holy relic, Bartley lifted the lid of the ebony box. A damp, musty, almost footy smell filled the room. White silk lined the inside of the box. Within lay a wooden pipe and three caps of skeev, golden-brown mushroom caps that had been dried and cured until fit to crumble. Bartley removed the pipe and a cap and handed them to Sal.

"Why don't you do the honors. I've just remembered I want to write out a list for when the errand boy comes on the morrow."

"You have an errand boy?"

"He's the runner for the inn, but I've learned that if I hand him a list and enough coin, he'll get the goods without too much fuss."

As Bartley limped back over to the dresser, Sal began to crumble the cap between his thumb and forefinger and into the bowl of the wooden pipe. Beneath the golden-brown layer of skin was a brighter yellow, the meat of the mushroom. The cap crumbled like a clod of dirt and left a dull yellow residue on Sal's fingertips. He packed the skeev down in the bowl and waited for Bartley to finish writing out his list.

Bartley lit up a handlamp. Then he limped back to Sal and accepted the pipe.

A faint crackling and a smell like burning leather filled the air as Bartley put flame to the skeev and inhaled. He blew a cloud of white smoke in Sal's face and smiled impishly before handing the pipe back to Sal along with the handlamp.

Sal put the pipe to his lips and the flame to the skeev. When he inhaled, the acrid taste of smoke filled his mouth. He swallowed, holding the smoke in his chest while he set down the handlamp. He laid the pipe back in the ebony box and blew the white smoke full in Bartley's face.

"Oy," said Bartley, rubbing at his eyes. "What do you think you're doing?"

Sal only laughed. Everything slowed down, and at the same time everything grew brighter, the colors more alive. Sal felt a rush to his head, and then euphoria spread throughout his entire body.

Bartley waved him off, scooped up the ebony box, and limped

back to the dresser. "Could go for a full day of shut-eye," Bartley said, as he limped back to the bed and lay down.

"You ought to clean and re-dress that wound first," Sal said, his head spinning, his body weightless. "Here, I'll do the—"

Bartley snored. His eyes were closed, his arms folded across his chest, his mouth open wide as he slept.

Sal decided to see himself out.

He made his way downstairs, and walked quickly past the taproom as the singer started into the final verse of his song. Stepping out the inn door, Sal was thrilled to find that the rain had stopped falling.

In the east, a faint glimmer of pale orange light began to brighten the dawn sky. Merchants and stall vendors were coming out into the streets to start the new day. Sal didn't bother picking any pockets. Too tired for any more excitement, he walked in the shadows and stuck to the alleyways when possible.

———

Slowly he opened the door, willing it not to make noise as he slunk inside. The house was quiet and dark, apart from the dawn light that crept ever brighter, and the smoldering hearth that glowed a faint red. Sal spooned out a bite of pottage from the cauldron that hung over the hearth.

The pottage steamed in the morning air and smelled of baked apples and gravy. The taste was savory and a little sweet, though it burned Sal's tongue and the roof of his mouth something awful. He nearly spit the mouthful to the rushes but forced himself to swallow. The food was like a hot coal as it burned down his throat and sank into his stomach. He tried to stifle a cough, but the effort only made it worse. He went into a fit of coughing. He cursed himself for making so much noise and stood stock still, listening for any sounds of movement.

After a moment Sal assured himself he'd not woken her. He headed for the stairs, and as he put his hand on the railing, he looked up to see her standing at the top.

"Name of the Light, what are you doing skulking home at this hour?" Nicola stood with her hands on her hips, the same way their mother used to stand when she was scolding him. "And what is that smell? Salvatori, have you been smoking with those dock rats again?"

"Sweet sister, what brings you out of bed at such an early hour?"

"Not that I could have slept through your racket, but I'm headed out for the morning. I'm gathering wild herbs today. It'll mean a day out of the city walls, if you'd care to join me."

"I'd rather remain within, at the least for a few hours of shut-eye."

Nicola gave him a dark look, something else she'd inherited from their mother.

"I hope you haven't been getting into trouble."

"You know I would never cause trouble. Harmless as a nettled thresher, I am."

"Nettled threshers are poisonous."

"Are they, now?" Sal asked with a grin.

"I can smell the skeev from here," Nicola said, shaking her head.

Sal could still taste the acrid smoke on his breath and feel the residue on his fingertips. The skeev flowed through him like liquid euphoria. He shrugged, walked up the stairs, passed his sister, and slipped into his room, a small four-cornered space with a bed, a night table, and a window overlooking South Market.

Sal's eyes arrowed in on the bed. He wanted nothing more than to sink into the straw mattress and never wake, but before he lay down he saw something lying atop the blanket—a letter, folded in three parts, sealed with a dab of red wax, and stamped with the sigil of a dragon.

Feelings Sal could not quite name began to boil up within him.

"I found that on the floor, under your bed," Nicola said behind him. "I noticed you hadn't opened it."

Sal picked up the letter, walked to the door, and shoved it at Nicola before he slammed the door.

He lay down, the room spinning ever so slightly, his body melting into the bed. The urge to reach for his pocket was stronger than ever, as though the locket called to him, the words too faint to comprehend yet too urgent to ignore. He slipped a hand into his jerkin pocket and brushed the smooth surface of the gold with thumb and forefinger.

The locket was warm to the touch, almost hot—a sensation so unlike before. Rather than probing, the tendrils of energy seemed to pull Sal into a tight embrace. The contact stilled the throbbing in his head and slowed his beating heart from a gallop to a canter.

Then he heard thunder, smelled a storm coming in the air, but when he glanced out the window he saw a bright, sun-filled morning, not a dark cloud in the sky.

His entire body felt lighter, a surge of electricity coursing through his veins. He stood and walked toward the window. He could hear the storm, feel it in his very bones. Only, when he looked out the window, he could see no signs of a storm brewing. Down below, business in South Market was in full swing.

Sal opened the window and was hit by the crisp morning air as it rushed in, reeking of fish and humming with the music of a multitude of tongues. The market square was lined with stalls. Merchants cried their wares: "Cockles! Get your cockles here!" or "Bonefish! Fresh bonefish!" Old crones haggled over lampreys, and copper-skinned foreigners hauled wheelbarrows of walleye, crappie, and perch.

And nowhere did Sal see any sign of the storm that he felt.

Mayhap he was experiencing a side effect of the skeev. He considered sitting down at the foot of his bed, when his eyes were drawn to the Godstone.

Standing at the center of South Market, like a great gray pillar wrapped in ivy, the ancient Godstone remained the only piece of history in Dijvois that predated the First Empire. Before the armies of the First Empire occupied Pargeche and built the port city of Dijvois, the land was peopled by the ancestors of the Pairgu, nomadic tribes that moved around the country based on the seasons.

Sal had never given the stone much thought, despite the view he'd had from his room for some years. It might have been the skeev that caused him to wonder about the stone and what it had meant to the ancient peoples. A fruitless pursuit in any case, as no one alive truly knew what the Godstones were used for.

Locket in hand, he stared at the Godstone. There was a clap of thunder, a crack so loud Sal nearly jumped from his skin.

He was pulled off his feet by a force so jarring it felt as though he'd swallowed his tongue.

It was a sensation like riding a bolt of lightning: Whiplash as he tore through the air. Weightlessness, with a touch of vertigo.

Wind whipped at his face, and the next thing Sal knew he was tumbling headlong across the cobbles, coming to a halt at the foot of the Godstone.

Someone shouted in surprise. As Sal scrambled to his feet, people murmured. He looked about, taking in the shocked faces of the market-goers surrounding him. Like a hare fleeing for its life, Sal darted for the nearest alley mouth.

He ducked into an alcove and propped his head against the brick wall, his breath steaming before him like dragon smoke. Leaning his back against the wall, Sal slid to the ground and hugged his knees. He closed his eyes and tried to figure out what had happened.

He took some time to run over it in his mind, but it had happened so fast. It was all such a blur. He felt at the pocket of his jerkin. The locket was still there.

Shaking, Sal got back to his feet. He took the long way home, avoiding the crowd in the market. No matter how he tried to puzzle it out, nothing could explain what had happened.

Nothing—but magic.

3

END

The entire city bustled with the sort of excitement that came only with holidays. Sal had felt it from the moment he'd woken. It was the day of End, the day that signaled a change of seasons. More importantly, it marked the end of the duke's yearly pilgrimage.

Sal joined Bartley and Vinny outside the Hog Snout just before sunup. Sal had slept a day and a night through, and felt twice the man he had the morning before.

After a good sleep, he'd managed to think rationally on the incident with the window. Much of what he'd experienced in South Market, and with the Godstone, must have been a figment of his imagination. No doubt it had been that skeev. Bartley had gotten his hands on some bad skeev, which had caused Sal to hallucinate and fall out his window. He was lucky not to have been hurt by the fall.

Still, there was something strange about that locket. It wasn't much to look at, simply a piece of tarnished yellow gold. Old gold, his uncle would have called it. It was simply a locket with three vertical stripes etched into the surface. When Sal had nicked the thing, he could have sworn all three stripes were colorless, merely lines carved into the metal like some rune. Only, that morning Sal had seen that one of the lines was red—a vibrant blood red that he couldn't believe he'd not noticed before. There was also a change in the way the locket felt. It was no longer cold to the touch but luke-warm, inviting rather than repulsive.

Nevertheless, still uncertain what to do with the thing, Sal had decided to leave the locket in his dresser drawer when he made his way to the Hog Snout.

"How's Anton?" said Sal. "Any word?"

It seemed the botched heist, coupled with the news of a possible rat in the crew, had taken its toll on all of them. Vinny, who was usually irritatingly good-looking, had dark rings under his eyes. His fair Norsic skin was wan, his long blond mane matted and greasy.

"Spoke with Odie just this morning," Vinny said. "Anton is breathing. Hasn't woken up, but he's alive."

Sal felt a strange mix of emotions. Anton was alive. Just that morning, Sal had come to grips with the idea of Anton not living. Still, it was good news.

"Can't believe he lived," said Bartley, shaking his head. "I saw the blow he took. Thought he'd been split in two."

As rough as Vinny appeared, he looked ages better than Bartley. The little Yahdrish was outright pallid, his eyes bloodshot with heavy shadowed bags beneath them. He'd been on the pipe early. More than like, it was the first thing he'd done that morning, some-thing that was happening more often than not of late.

It hurt Sal to see him that way, but what could he do? There was no changing other people.

"Too bad he'll miss End," said Bartley. "A real shame, that."

"Who knows, there may be no day of End. Rumor is, the duke won't winter in Dijvois," said Vinny. "Gods know there are warmer places in Pargeche to spend a winter."

"I wouldn't blame the man," said Sal. "Come the first snows, I'll consider someplace more southerly myself."

"Nym and Krathus are supposed to be quite nice this time of year," said Vinny in a mock-pompous voice.

"I can't see us prospering in Nym," said Sal. "I imagine thieves either starve or hang on small islands. Though in Krathus I hear it's so warm a man could sleep naked on the streets."

"Don't know that I'd recommend it," said Vinny. "The women of Krathus get one look at your shriveled worm, and you'll wind up celibate for good and all."

"It'll never happen," said Bartley.

"It had better happen," said Vinny. "A worm's not used, it's liable to fall off."

"Not your worm," said Bartley. "The duke's court. They wouldn't move court. The duke has to winter in Dijvois."

"And why is that?" Vinny asked. "He's the duke. He can hold court wherever he damn well pleases."

"Haven't you heard?" Bartley asked. "The duke's health is failing. They say we'll have a new duke before the year is out."

"A new duke?" Sal asked. "Is it truly so bad as that? I've heard nothing of Tadej taking ill."

"It's been months now," said Bartley. "Almost didn't leave Krathus at the break of summer."

"Truly?" Vinny asked. "Might be I'll put my name forth. That Nelsigh king, he might have heard of me, you know?"

Sal laughed, but Bartley was in no fit state for japes.

"The bloody king of Nelgand?" said Bartley. "How would he have heard of you?"

"I suspect you're right, Bart," said Sal. "They'd never move the duke's court. It's just not plausible."

As the oldest and most significant city in all of Pargeche, Dijvois had always been the seat of the sovereign. Since the fall of the First Empire, the Pairgu kings had ruled their land from the throne of the High Keep.

"Well, gents, where shall it be?" said Bartley. "Gold Gate, or the Bridge of the Lady?"

Sal and Vinny exchanged a look, and they both began to laugh.

"What's so funny?" Bartley asked.

On the day of End, there were two places in Dijvois where the population gathered en masse, the Gold Gate and the Bridge of the

Lady, but the Gold Gate was as far from High Hill as anywhere in Dijvois, which made all the difference.

Sal shrugged. "Not really an option, the way I see it."

"But we go to the Bridge of the Lady every year," Bartley said, "and so does every other cutpurse in this city. Don't you think they've wised up on the bridge? Besides, there'll be thrice the steel caps on the bridge as there will be at the Gold Gate, you can count on that."

Sal and Vinny once again exchanged a look.

In order to reach the High Keep, the duke's retinue would be forced to enter the city through the Gold Gate, then make their way through Low Town, across the Bridge of the Lady, onto the Kingsway, and up High Hill.

Bartley turned an even brighter shade of red. "I swear on the blood of Sacrull, I'll kill you both if you don't explain what is so damn funny."

"You, my friend," said Vinny.

Bartley balled his hands into tight fists.

Sal smiled at the thought of little Yahdrish attacking Vinny with only his fists. Even sober, and without an injured leg, Bartley was outmatched. Vinny was built like a typical Norsic. He stood two heads taller than Bartley and outweighed him by a good six stone. Droll as the mismatched fight would be to watch, Sal couldn't allow it.

"Listen," Sal said, putting an arm around Bartley's shoulders. "The Gold Gate is in Low Town, yeah?" Bartley hesitated before he nodded. Clearly he still feared he was the butt of some jape. "Well, think on it. If the gentry and nobility have to make their merry way down from High Hill, cross the Bridge of the Lady and brave the *terrors* of Low Town, just to get down to the Gold Gate, where do you think they'll gather in greater numbers?"

Bartley gave him a sullen look. "More room at the Gold Gate for people to gather, and they will be less suspicious, seeing how every other thief in the city is going to be on the Bridge of the Lady."

Vinny sighed and spoke as if addressing a small child. "If we go picking at the Gold Gate we'll be lucky to get out of there with iron dingés and a few copper krom between the three of us."

"We'll be lucky to get away with our heads," said Bartley. "Or for that matter, unlucky, because if we go to the bridge, we will most like be hoisted up in crow-cages come evenfall."

It was Sal's turn to sigh. "None of us are going to the cages so long as we're careful. But it might be you'd rather sit this one out?"

The words cut just as Sal had intended. Bartley's chest puffed out, and his eyes narrowed.

"Well," said Vinny, "will you be joining us on the Lady, or should we expect to find you at the Gold Gate once our pockets are full to bursting?"

"I'm going in for a cap," Bartley said. "Anyone care to join me?"

"Best keep your wits about you," Sal cautioned, but Bartley was never one to listen to sense.

Instead, the Yahdrish went into the Hog Snout alone.

Vinny looked to Sal, worry plastered across his face. Sal merely shrugged.

When Bartley returned, a smile stretching cheek to cheek, he asked the other two if they should get drinks before making their way to the bridge.

Vinny cleared his throat.

"The vendors will have set up shop, and people will already be arriving," said Sal. "We'd do well to get our places now. Elsewise we're going to find ourselves out a day's pay."

Vinny motioned with his head, and they walked up the street, moving in conjunction with the crowds of revelers all making their way to wherever they planned to view the duke's retinue. The trio took alleyways as often as streets. The alleys were virtually deserted, offering a respite from the people bustling along the cobblestone streets like herds of cattle. When he did find himself in a crowd, Sal used the opportunity of close contact to pick a few pockets, but as they neared the Street of Rags, Sal kept his hands to himself.

"I noticed your limp has healed," said Sal.

Bartley gave him a sheepish look. "Went to a Talent. Same mender Odie took Anton to. She put it right as rain."

"Did you, now?" Sal asked. "

"Cost me six gold krom."

"You didn't go to no mender," Vinny scoffed.

"And how should you know?"

"Because you haven't got six krom," said Vinny. "Before Luca's job you told me you didn't have two iron dingés to rub together. So unless you went to the loan sharks again, you didn't see no Talent."

Bartley looked at his feet.

"You didn't," said Sal. "Lady's sake, Bartley, what's the interest?"

"None of your damned business is what it is."

"You should have come to me," Sal said. "I'd lend you the coin, and you'd get to keep your thumbs even if you couldn't pay me back by week's end."

"A man has his pride," Vinny mocked.

"A man has his needs," said Bartley. "Coming face to face with death gives a man a man's hungers."

"Ah," said Vinny, raising a finger. "And without coin or whore, our Bartley would starve for pleasure, this is known."

"What would either of you boys know of a man's pleasures?" said Bartley. "I have appetites that only a professional woman could satisfy."

"Only for want of a real profession would a woman satisfy your appetites," said Vinny.

"Would you claim courtesanship an unworthy profession?" Bartley asked.

"Courtesans? As well stuff a pig in armor and call him a knight," said Vinny. "You've never stuffed anything with more class than a two-bit streetwalker. This isn't Vinigre. You and I both know there are no courtesans in Pargeche."

"There are all sorts of exotic women working in Dijvois," Bartley said. "Yet all the different women from different places speak but the same tongue once I've laid them on their backs."

"The tongue of silence?" asked Vinny.

Sal laughed, and Bartley turned red as a coral crab.

"You wouldn't know a real woman if she slapped you in the face with her tit," said Bartley. "Tell him, Salvatori, there's nothing wrong with the working girls in Dijvois. They're as good as the whores anywhere else in the world."

Sal shrugged.

"Well, tell him, would you?"

"I wouldn't know," said Sal.

Bartley gave a short bark of laughter. "Now don't go acting as though you've never bought yourself a wench."

Sal tried to think of a way to change the subject. Instead he remained silent, not daring to look Bartley in the eyes lest he surmise the truth of things.

"How should you know what the whores are like in the rest of the world?" said Vinny. "You were born in Low Town and haven't left the city walls since you were weaned."

Bartley ignored the sally, unwilling to drop the issue concerning Sal's chastity. "Surely you've had a woman, Salvatori?"

Vinny stopped and looked at Sal, as a silent question played across his face.

Sal shrugged and kept walking.

"No?" said Bartley. "Is it possible?"

"Lay off," said Vinny. "Slaying whores by the hundreds is nothing to brag about. When's the last time you had a woman that didn't take your coin before your seed?"

"Not ever?" said Bartley, still ignoring Vinny. "Can it truly be that our little Salvatori is a maid?"

Sal flushed with embarrassment. He felt his palms grow clammy, his head faintly dizzy.

"How could this be?" said Bartley, an impish grin spreading across his face. "There must be at least one woman in the city who'd be willing to make a man out of you." Bartley had been about to say something else when he stopped short. It seemed he had finally realized the route they were traveling. "Not this way," Bartley said.

"Well, that shut him up right and good," said Vinny.

Sal cleared his throat. "It's the fastest way to the Bridge of the Lady, and you've already put us far enough behind."

Bartley planted his feet, crossed his arms, and shook his head. "I won't. There are other ways to reach the bridge."

"There are," Vinny allowed, "but we're taking the Street of Rags, Yahdrish, now get going."

Sal usually avoided the Street of Rags whenever possible; they all did, and not only because of the Magistrate's Compound. There was a time when the street had been referred to by its proper name, the Street of Justice, but when the new magistrate took over and erected the crow-cages, the citizens of Dijvois began to refer to it as the Street of Rags, because it was where, they said, the magistrate hung out his dirty laundry.

The crow-cages—six in all, forged of black iron and twisted steel, each just large enough to contain a man—hung from scaffolding and spanned the length of the street. They were a warning to the criminals of Dijvois, a warning Sal and his friends took to heart. They knew the risks of their chosen profession, and the crow-cages were the grimmest of reminders as to where it could end.

Inside four of the cages were prisoners. Three of them were slumped to the bottom of their cages, either dead or dying. One man remained standing. As he drew closer, Sal could see the prisoner was naked, his scalp crudely shaven, his red, sun-beaten skin peeling and blistered. The cage wouldn't allow him to stand up straight, so he hunched, fingers clenching the iron grate.

The prisoner mumbled something through cracked lips, but Sal and his friends pretended not to hear.

They were alone on the street, aside from the prisoners and two steel caps that stood sentry outside the Magistrate's Compound.

The steel caps were known for their visorless coned helms. They wore midnight blue tabards over chain brigandines, the white axe and crescent moon of the magistrate blazoned proudly on their chests. Each man carried a six-foot poleaxe and, scabbarded at either hip, a long knife and a single-edged sword.

As if the crow-cages weren't bad enough, Sal had heard rumors of the under-cells, a dungeon below the Magistrate's Compound where the magistrate's inquisitors kept devices far more terrible than the crow-cages. He prayed to all the gods he never found himself in that dungeon.

They pushed through the crowd on Beggar's Lane until the Low

Town bridge tower façade loomed before them. No fewer than three crossbowmen stood sentry atop the tower. Sal made mention of them to his friends. Should they need to run off the bridge, they would want to slip past the tower unnoticed.

Bartley nudged Sal with an elbow, then pointed to the six steel caps beneath the tower arches.

"No need to draw attention to ourselves," said Vinny. "Go on now."

They passed beneath the arches of the Low Town bridge tower and stepped onto the Bridge of the Lady. On their immediate right was an immense limestone statue carved in the likeness of the Lady White, goddess of the moon. The statue was what gave the bridge its name; it was the last physical representation of the Lady White left in Dijvois, the sole survivor of the iconoclasm that had followed the rise of the Vespian Order.

A scant few in Pargeche still worshiped the Lady White. She was an archaic goddess, not so old as the Godstone, perhaps, but one that rivaled the Lord that was Light himself.

It was she, the Lady White, who lit the night sky while Solus slept. When his eye would open and rise again into the sky of day, the Lady would flee until the next evenfall, when she could once again rise among the stars.

Sal brushed the hem of the Lady's limestone dress for luck. He had never been a pious man, but as the Lady White was the patron goddess of thieves, assassins, and their like, Sal had made her his own.

"What in the Light's name was that?" Vinny whispered in his ear. "What happened to not attracting attention?"

Sal shrugged and spoke with more confidence than he felt. "No one saw. Besides, it was just a little touch."

"And nobody knows what that touch means? Right in front of the bloody steel caps," Vinny said, incredulous. "Light's blessing, if I don't work with two of the most witless jackanapeses in the city."

"And what did I do?" Bartley asked.

Vinny only shook his head.

"Right. Should we get to work, then?" asked Sal.

"You lot go ahead. If you want to work deuces I'll be elsewhere," said Vinny. "I'm going to distance myself before one of you
does something that gets me thrown in a crow-cage."

At that, Vinny stalked off. Bartley looked at Sal and rolled his
eyes. They shared a smile and wordlessly went to work.

On a regular day the Bridge of the Lady was highly trafficked,
with one half designated for oxcarts, horse-drawn carriages, and the
smaller wagons pulled by mules, the other half for pedestrian traffic
crossing between Low Town and High Town.

On the day of End, the Bridge of the Lady was a veritable
marketplace, with merchant stalls crowding either side, and shoulder-to-shoulder foot traffic. No carriages, wagons, or oxcarts were
allowed to cross for the day.

The energy in the air was electric. Vendors cried their goods:
"Hotcakes, hot fresh hotcakes"; "Mince pies, get your mince pies!"

The Vespian monks, dressed in their dun brown habits, hoods
raised to protect their shaved pates from the morning sun, stood
beside a stack of kegs and filled mugs with frothing brown ale for a
copper krom a pint. Come Fitzen, the monks would be giving away
whatever they weren't able to sell on End, to make room for the
stock they would brew from the year's last barley harvest.

Beneath the massive bronze statue of King Bethelwold the
Great a band played, filling the air with the sweet sounds of lute,
pipes, and fiddle.

The statue of the long-dead king showed a handsome man, his
posture proud, his sword raised high, the crown of sovereignty his
brow. According to legend, it was only because of King Bethelwold
the Great that the citizens of Dijvois celebrated the day of End.

In times of old, the king's court had resided permanently within
the walls of the great port city of Dijvois, ruling from the throne
upon High Hill. The city had been abandoned by the First Empire,
and later became a key stronghold of the kingdom of Pargeche, but
as time moved on, more land was conquered and subjected to
Pairgu rule. As the kingdom grew, the kings of Pargeche began to
feel their grasp of their expanding nation slowly slipping through
their fingers. Rebellions arose, and neighboring kingdoms threat-

ened war. For a time, the future of Pargeche balanced on a sword's edge.

In a stroke of brilliance, or so the historians claimed, one king managed to quell the internal disputes and marshal his armies to batter back the invading hosts of both Nelgand in the west and Skjörund in the east. During his reign he had been known as Bethelwold the Third, but the historians had dubbed him Bethelwold the Great.

King Bethelwold ruled for twenty-seven years before he went to his sickbed with consumption, an illness from which he never recovered. During his reign he was responsible for not only the reunification of Pargeche but also the codification of Pairgu common law, the founding of the monastic university, and the establishment of the King's Pilgrimage.

Unlike those who came before him, Bethelwold the Great did not merely rule his kingdom from the throne in Dijvois. Instead, Bethelwold wintered in the great city, and, following the early rains of spring, traveled throughout his country. He held court in the keeps of his vassal lords and observed the entirety of his lands, until his eventual return to the throne in mid-autumn. The tradition was carried on by the successive rulers of the Pairgu, and Pargeche had remained one kingdom united. Since the first pilgrimage, the citizens of Dijvois had celebrated the day of the king's return, and eventually it became known as the day of End.

The singer was halfway through "Piddle on the Diddler." Sal weaved his way between the onlookers, slipping his hand into jerkin pockets and cutting purse strings with his finger-knife as he went.

> "For when a diddler diddles a dame,
> to his house there falls great shame.
> Piddle on the diddler if you know what's good.
> Piddle on the diddler as right you should.
> A diddler tries to shrug the blame,
> but all who know will curse his name.
> Piddle on the diddler, for all do see
> the diddler's ways bring infamy."

The fiddler stepped out in front of the rest and cut a jaunty tune on the fiddle strings while the singer stomped a foot in time.

> "And if the diddler diddles your sis,
> well, go on now, give the diddler a kiss.
> Don't piddle on the diddler, give him a pass.
> Don't piddle on the diddler, lest you keep the lass.
> Now, everyone knows there is no crime
> half so bad as a girl diddled in the blind.
> Though before you go piddle, consider you this:
> If not for that diddler, who'd diddle your sis?"

As the singer moved into the sixth verse, Sal's gaze lingered on one of the women watching the band.

She had long, raven-black hair and wore a blue silk dress imprinted with a subtle floral pattern. The blue was not the typical woad often used by Pairgu dyers, but lapis lazuli, like something right off a vellum page from the holy book. She sparkled like a sapphire in the sun.

Sal was drawn closer, like a moth to a flame. Gold glinted, and he noticed she wore gold teardrop earrings set with small sapphires.

The woman was intent on the band, laughing with the rest, as others clapped and the band played and sang their bawdy song.

Although she seemed entirely focused on the performance, the woman in the blue dress clutched her purse tight to her bosom. A prudent measure, as it rendered the purse virtually unattainable.

Sal thought he could get his hands on the sapphire earrings. They had to be worth a fistful, and they were hanging there like fruit, ripe for the taking.

> " 'Hypocrisy!' the diddler would scream,
> for diddling is not all diddling seems.
> He'd point the finger; they'd fall to their knees.
> The diddler would smile, for the diddler'd be
>   pleased.
> At long last, the diddler would be

vindicated and piddle free!
He'd hold up his hands, and he'd make a big scene.
Then out from his mouth would come the obscene.
'Everyone's a diddler, you fools, don't you see?
We all ought to piddle on you, not on me.' "

Sal moved up right behind the woman in the blue dress. She smelled good, sweet with an undercurrent of spice. He felt a pang of guilt as he moved his hand into position.

He reached out for the earring.

Trumpets sounded, cutting through the din of the crowd.

Sal was shoved in the back.

His hand slipped, and he clouted the woman on the ear.

Everyone was bustling. Sal was elbowed and shouldered, then shoved to the ground. When he got back up, he'd lost sight of the woman.

The music stopped. A blanket of tension fell over the jostling crowd.

Then there was cheering, another blast of trumpets, and the crowd began to settle as the standard of the crowned eagle flapped into view.

Even now, under the subjugation of Nelgand, Duke Tadej was allowed to continue the tradition as had his ancestors, the kings of old. The duke and his entourage would complete the year-long pilgrimage by making the climb up High Hill and onto the throne of the High Keep.

Today, Duke Tadej had returned to Dijvois at last.

The ducal standard was a golden eagle on a field of black. In one talon it grasped a scepter, in the other a scroll. Behind the standard bearer rode a host of ducal guards, each armored in a panoply of steel and armed with a lance, shield, and longsword.

Three men rode abreast just behind the guards. The man riding on the left flank had black hair and a scar that ran from his ear down to the corner of his mouth. Sal knew him to be Urek Shatterspear. The man was a war hero who had served as captain of the ducal guard as long as Sal could remember.

Prince Andrej rode in the center. His black stallion stood a good eighteen hands, an ill-tempered beast that reared and tossed its head as the prince drove his spurs into its ribs. The prince's long blond hair blew in the wind; his nose was upturned, his eyes forward as though the cheering crowd were invisible. Prince Andrej was the younger of the two princes of Pargeche, the heir presumptive. Though if the rumors were true, he was the more entitled of the pair.

Next to Andrej rode his older brother, Prince Matej, second son of Duke Tadej and the heir apparent. Matej rode a roan mare. Unlike his younger brother, Matej wore his hair short, yet his golden beard reached nearly to his breastbone. Matej waved, and the smallfolk cheered as the procession passed.

The crowd seemed to love Matej, the way they waved and shouted his name. Strange how much it reminded Sal of a time not so long ago, another day of End that he'd spent at the Gold Gate. He'd watched, standing beside his sister, as another prince had ridden past on a roan mare, just like the mare Matej rode. The other prince had looked much like Matej as well, only his beard had been cropped short, his golden hair just long enough to blow in the breeze.

Nicola had pointed him out to Sal, and he had waved excitedly with the rest of the smallfolk. They had cheered and shouted his name as he had waved and ridden past. "Jadrej," they had said, but that was then. Now they said "Matej." It was as though no one recalled the prince who had been. As though Jadrej had never been.

Following the princes was another host of guards marching afoot, dressed in the ducal colors and armed with pikes as well as longswords. Behind them a team of horses, eight strong, clopped across the paving stones of the bridge. They pulled a carriage—

A stinging, throbbing pain thudded though Sal's ear. Few things hurt like a clout to the ear, and the ringing that followed was nearly as bad as the pain. Sal spun around, fully ready to lay fists into whoever had smacked his ear, when he realized it was the woman in the blue dress standing before him.

She was younger than he'd thought, and quite striking now he'd had a look at her face. Her dress brought out the true blue in her eyes, like two depthless pools of lapis lazuli that he'd be happy to drown in. Her lips moved, but Sal didn't hear the words they formed. He was too distracted by the movement of her pink lips. They looked soft, apt for kissing.

She shouted something and slapped him on the ear once again. The slap jarred Sal back to the present, at least enough that he realized she was walking away through the crowd.

He went after her. His ear hurt like Sacrull's hell, and he should have been furious. Yet for all that, he couldn't think of anything but the fact that she was getting away, and he knew he didn't want that. Nothing in the world seemed so important as learning the woman's name, or anything that would help him to find her later.

When finally Sal spoke, his tongue felt clumsy, as though he'd not used it for so long that he'd forgotten how. He tried again, willing his tongue to do his bidding.

"Please, wait," Sal said, clapping a hand on the woman's shoulder. "My Lady, what—"

There was a crack of pain in his jaw. For an instant everything went black. Then Sal realized he was on his hands and knees. His jaw was on fire, throbbing hard enough to make him forget all about the pain in his ear.

"Keep your filthy hands off the lady," said a man standing over him. "Next time I take the hand."

The man was big, mustached, and wore a bastard sword slung on his back. He reached over a shoulder and unsheathed the blade just enough to show the glint of steel.

Sal coughed and spat a glob of blood onto the paving stones. He nodded to show his understanding, and the big Bauden moved off. Sal could no longer see the woman in the blue dress; as he stood he found she had disappeared into the crowd along with the mustached man that carried the bastard sword.

Everything had happened so fast. The woman in the blue dress must have realized he'd been the one who'd clouted her on the ear, and she'd decided to do the same in return. Only, who had the man been? Most like, he was a bodyguard, a hired sword or some such, and based on the punch he'd given Sal, a damned capable one.

Sal shook his head like a wet dog to clear the ringing in his ears. By the time he had grounded himself, he realized the duke's carriage had long since passed. The tail of the retinue was departing from the bridge, moving up High Hill. The crowd slowly reverted to the usual goings-on of a congested market.

As he watched the last rider of the retinue cross beneath the High Town bridge tower façade, Sal realized he had missed his chance to see Duke Tadej and learn whether there was any truth to the rumors of his ill health.

As Sal considered his misfortune, he cursed himself for being such a fool. Rather than take full advantage of the distraction the duke's retinue had provided, Sal had been struck dumb by the display. He had stood idle and made himself an easy target for the woman in the blue dress. All the while he could have made some coin, and instead he'd taken a few licks.

Sal was rubbing his jaw, looking for another good place to pick some pockets, when he spotted a mummers show across the bridge. He turned, walked headlong into someone, and stumbled back. Sal was quick to regain his feet, but he quailed the instant he realized he'd crashed into a steel cap.

The man wasn't much taller than Sal, but the armor and coned helm made him seem a giant. His face was covered in small, pitted scars, no doubt the result of some pox in his youth.

"Oy," said the pox-scarred steel cap, leveling his poleaxe. "Watch where you're going, boy, or I've a mind to skewer you."

The other steel cap had a thick red tangle of a beard. He merely growled before the pair moved on, leaving Sal to regain his breath and slow his racing heart. When he'd stumbled into the steel cap, Sal had nearly dropped his day's takings to the paving stones. Luckily, the steel caps had not been the most observant of patrolmen.

He crossed the rest of the bridge vigilantly watching his surroundings. The mummers show was being performed with string marionettes. For the day's performance, the mummers had decided upon *The Sundering*, and they were nearly through the third act.

A puppet wearing robes of white walked across the small stage, his little wooden hands raised high.

"*I have seen what you did to our father, Sacrull. I charge you, Brother, release our mother, and resume your banishment in solitude.*"

The black-robed puppet laughed a dark, resonant laugh.

"*This realm does not belong to the Light. Nor does this realm belong to you, wandering son. This realm is mine. In darkness it began, and to darkness it has returned.*"

Sal moved through the captivated audience, hoping that they'd not already been picked through, as the play was so far along and the morning grown so late.

"*You murdered our father, I have seen his body scattered among the heavens!*" shouted the little Susej puppet in the little white robes. "*A covenant was forged. A place was made, and for your crimes, banishment. For these new crimes, I can see no fitting punishment.*"

"*And they say I am he who is blind,*" replied the miniature Sacrull. "*With your open eye you see all that I cannot, but I can see what you do not. I see within, and to the depths which one can reach. You tell me what you see, but I say to you it is wrong.*"

Sal searched the crowd for easy targets and possible competition, and out of the corner of his eye he spotted Bartley. Even had Sal not known his friend was picking, he'd have been able to spot Bartley for a thief a mile away. Bartley was far from the city's most talented snatcher; if not for the big jobs, and some help from Sal, Bartley would have likely starved on the street long ago. To his credit, Bartley was an excellent climber and was small enough to fit places that most others couldn't, which was why he got work when the big jobs came around.

Sal sighed, hoping against hope Bartley wasn't going to get himself caught. Gods knew it wouldn't be the first time.

The little black puppet waved his arms above his head and sounded a nonsensical chant. The crowd gasped as two grotesque puppets came onto the stage, clearly meant to represent the guardians of the Under Realm, the Beasts of Six. One of them was vaguely doglike, the other a lion. The beasts moved toward the white-robed Susej, pawing at the air and roaring fiercely.

But the little Susej did not budge. The puppet raised its hands and called fire from the sky. Another mummer appeared torch in hand and lit the grotesque beasts aflame, and the crowd burst into cheers as the puppets burned.

Sal slipped through the crowd like a fish in the river, hand sliding in and out of jerkin pockets, finger-knife cutting purses and purse strings without his victims feeling even the slightest touch. If there was one thing at which Sal was truly good, it was picking.

"It is too late," said the little Sacrull marionette. *"I have bound her. Forever will this world be burdened by the child which I have sown. Malevolence shall be her name, second daughter of Tiem."*

"That which was broken shall be mended."

The little black-robed Sacrull laughed. *"None can defy my rule. Father Order is dead, I have killed him."*

"I am all that is true. I am the Son that is Light!"

"A curse upon thee!" shouted the little Sacrull.

The Susej marionette wobbled, his little wooden arms waving above his head.

The black-robed Sacrull began to writhe upon the stage, gurgling and moaning.

Sal felt something like a stillness in the air, a palpable tension, when out of the corner of his eye he saw a commotion. As he focused, he realized Bartley was being held by the wrist by a big, balding man.

The man shouted, "Thief! Thief! Bastard thief!"

Sal saw heads turn in the direction of the commotion, but no one moved to help. That is, until two steel caps began pushing their way through the crowd. They were the same two steel caps Sal had run into earlier—the pox-scarred guard and his red-bearded companion.

Sal looked around frantically.

Suddenly the big, balding man let out a shrill cry, as Bartley slashed at him with his finger-knife. The man clapped his hand to his wrist, blood streaming between his fingers.

Bartley shoved his way through the crowd, trying to get away from the man who'd grabbed him. Unfortunately, the Yahdrish was headed straight for the two steel caps.

Sal pushed his way into position. When the steel caps came close, their attention intent on Bartley, Sal stuck a leg out and tripped the pox-scarred one.

The steel cap fell headlong into the crowd. A man shoved him. He collided with his red-bearded companion and they fell to the paving stones in a tangled heap of armored limbs and ungainly weaponry.

Sal ran to Bartley, and together they slipped through the crowd and back onto the bridge. They were headed for Low Town, which was a problem, as six armed steel caps waited beneath the arch of the Low Town bridge tower, while three crossbowmen waited above.

Sal and Bartley both knew they would never make it. If they tried to fight their way through, they were as good as dead.

"We have to jump!" Sal shouted to Bartley.

"Sacrull's balls, that'll kill us," Bartley said.

Sal shook his head. "We can make it, just try not to drown."

Without another word, Sal pushed his way to the edge of the bridge, stepped up onto the parapet, and jumped. He felt a rush of vertigo, and a flash of terror just before he struck the water's surface.

The contact was like hitting cobblestones, a shockwave that shuddered through his feet, up his legs, up his spine, and into his skull. His jaw snapped shut so hard he thought he'd shattered his teeth. He was dazed, yet he scrambled for the surface.

He needed air, but the Tamber had swept him into its rushing current. He tumbled and rolled beneath the water, too confounded to know which way was up.

He panicked. His ears pounded. His lungs burned as though at any moment they would burst.

He thrashed, limbs flailing for purchase, until his head broke the surface of the water and he gasped for breath. One quick suck of air before he twisted beneath the water once again. Another breath as fury sprayed around him, and he rolled, once, twice—crack!

Sharp, blinding pain, and blackness.

4

THE BELLS

Sal stepped as quietly as he could, his nerves on edge. He could hear them within the solar, indecipherable voices muffled by thick stone walls. They were the voices of prominent men. Men whose business was as secretive as it was significant. Scarvini, Novotny, Dvorak, Moretti, and Svoboda, the five families that made up the Commission. All together in one place, at one time.

Sal continued down the hall, picking up his pace as he passed the closed door of Uncle Stefano's solar.

A floorboard creaked underfoot. Sal held his breath but moved on, fleet of foot and shaking with fear.

He gripped the jar all the tighter and made for the stairway at the end of the hall. Up the steps and along another hallway, then out onto the terrace and he was finally able to breathe easy.

His sister stood at the edge of the terrace, hands on the stone parapet as she looked out over the city. Funny how much she'd begun to look like Mother.

Sal stepped up beside her. He looked down upon Dijvois, the city walls stretching as far as the horizon, all the buildings and roads laid out below him like a map. The black water of the Tamber, so peaceful from this distance. High Bridge, the Bridge of the Lady, and South Bridge, the Big Island and the Little Island. Knöldrus Cathedral, with its great rose window and colossal façade towers, the abbey's vast lawn and extensive orchard. His gaze moved south across the Singing Bridge to the clock tower, Town Square, and the great fountain of Uthrid Stormbreaker. He scanned over East Market, then back across the Tamber to South Market and farther west to the Gold Gate.

"Beautiful, isn't it?" Nicola asked.

"It's only the city."

"Only the city?" Nicola said, turning on him with narrowed eyes.

Sal shrugged, and his sister sighed, her look softening. Gods, how she was beginning to look like Mother.

"I suppose it's not the view from the Red Tower of the High Keep, but it's certainly something. You can see all of Low Town from here."

"What was it like, living in the castle?" Sal asked.

"In the High Keep?" Nicola said. "I suppose you wouldn't remember, would you? You were so young when we left. There were always strangers coming and going all hours of the day. And the other children. They were all about, bastards and stafflings and the sort. I had my friends. Funny, I don't remember their names now, but we used to play in the practice yard and the stables." Nicola smiled a big, wide smile. "Mother used to hate when we played in the stables. One time the stable master caught us, and Mother, she—"

"She still hasn't come out of bed," Sal said. "Not since those bells began to toll."

Nicola pursed her lips.

A season from her seventeenth year, Nicola had grown into a woman. By the way the men watched her at market, others had noticed this long before Sal. Nicola was long of limb, slender, and taller now than Mother, almost of a height with Uncle Stefano. Even the way she spoke now, like an elder speaking with a child.

Though Sal didn't mind so much. He preferred his sister's conde-scension to the outright indifference of his uncle.

"Do you think he's really dead?" Sal asked. "The prince, I mean."

"What a thing to say. Though he must be, that's what the bells were for. Five bells. It means a death in the ducal family. Why would you ask?"

Sal shrugged.

"There was an execution, I've heard," Nicola said. "The killer confessed and everything."

"I went, you know."

"You what?"

"To the execution," Sal said, "of that man they say killed the prince."

"Salvatori, why?"

Sal hesitated as he considered telling the truth. "I was only wondering, I guess."

"Wondering," Nicola said. "What's to wonder? That man murdered the prince, and he was executed for his crime. Why would you want to see such a thing?"

"Curious, I guess," Sal lied.

"You shouldn't have done that. You should never have gone."

"There was this man, he was shouting all the while. He shouted at me," Sal said.

"Shouted at you? Who, when?"

"During the execution. An old man. Shouted at most everyone he could."

"What was he shouting about?"

"Said the man, the killer, you know, said he was his son. Told everyone that his son was innocent. He shouted it, but nobody listened."

"You shouldn't have gone there," Nicola said.

"Uncle Stefano said it would be good for me."

"Ah, now I see."

"What do you mean?"

"He made you go?"

Sal shrugged and Nicola's look sharpened.

"Mother wouldn't have approved," Nicola said, her lips pursing.

Sal looked out over the city.

"Do you think he could have been?" Sal asked.

"Been what?"

"Innocent. Not the man shouting, but his son. The man they say murdered the prince. Do you think he really could have been innocent?"

Nicola frowned. "Is anyone innocent?"

"But it would be difficult to kill a prince, right?" Sal asked. "Just about impossible?"

It was Nicola's turn to shrug. "I've not tried."

Sal felt a smile form at the corner of his mouth.

A moment of silence fell, and Nicola joined him in looking out over the city.

"What's that?" Nicola asked, nodding at the jar Sal held.

"Honey," he said.

"Her throat, it's bothering her again?"

Sal nodded.

Nicola put on a smile. It was meant to comfort him, he knew, yet it did just the opposite.

"Has it always been this way?" Sal asked.

"She has always worried," Nicola said.

"She seems so sad," Sal said. "I wish she would get out of bed."

"We can wish all we want. It won't change the way things are."

"I could," Sal said, making fists on the stone parapet.

"You can't change the way things are, Salvatori. You'll learn that when you're older. The way things are, the way people are, it's out of your control. All you can do is better yourself."

Sal shook his head. "I won't accept that. She can get better. We just have to remind her—to tell her—" He could feel the tears coming on, welling in his eyes as a knot formed in his throat.

Nicola stepped close and wrapped him in her arms, hushing him in a soft, soothing voice.

"I will," Sal managed to croak before the tears came on in full. "I will save her."

5

NABU AKKAD

"No, nothing permanent, I hope. There was no water in his lungs."

The speaker sounded like a woman, but Sal didn't recognize the voice. He could hardly think through the pounding in his skull. His eyelids were too heavy to open.

"And his head?" said Bartley. "All that blood, he must have hit it hard. He isn't—well, he won't be—"

"Simple?" said the woman. "I should think not. I was able to stitch things up quite clean, and so far as I could tell there was no damage to the brain. That's what matters. We won't know until he comes to, and even then I fear he will have such a headache we may not glean much from him for some time."

"How long will it take?" Bartley asked.

"It's difficult to tell. He could be days in recovery, he could be weeks. Injuries to the head are trickier than other parts of the body."

"I meant, how long before he wakes?"

"Ah, well, this is equally difficult to predict, as everyone differs. You must understand, every injury damages the flesh, the mind, and the spirit, and while my art mends the corporeal, the mind and spirit are separate matters entirely. He will not be truly healed until his mind overcomes the trauma. Even then, damage to the spirit will linger. Despite all of that, I would predict he should not be long. My patients never are."

"Reckon I ought to stick around," Bartley said. "He may wonder at waking."

"I don't suppose you would want to tell me what possessed the pair of you to take a swim in the Tamber?"

Silence was the answer. Sal heard only the throbbing in his ears. He saw only the black backs of his eyelids, but he smelled the sweet tang of incense. This, more than anything, made him wonder where he was and how he'd gotten there.

"I thought not," said the woman. "It was worth the trying. Ah, but look, someone stirs."

Slowly, Sal opened his eyes. The soft, flickering candlelight took only moments to adjust to after he'd blinked a few times. A gently flashing white pearlescent light caught his attention. It was not a flame, more a glowing liquid that moved and swirled within a glass orb.

Bartley moved to stand over Sal. He breathed hard, with apparent anxiety, as water dripped from his black curls. "All right there, mate?" Bartley asked.

Sal put two fingers to his temple and began rubbing in a small circular motion. "Never better," Sal said, a wry smile playing across his lips.

Sal sat up, and the woman placed her palm against his forehead. She looked older than he'd imagined, her hair more white than blonde. She had slight wrinkles at the edges of her eyes. Yet for all of that, she was attractive.

The woman put her hand on the side of his head. "Is there pain here when I apply pressure?"

"No."

"And here?" She asked, shifting her hand slightly.

"No."

"Good, very good," she said. "And your head, is the ache insufferable?"

"Not so much that I can't hear myself think."

The woman nodded.

"Pardon," Sal said, "but who—"

"Oh, of course," said Bartley. "This is Alzbetta. Betta, this is Salvatori Lorenzo."

Alzbetta flashed him a wicked grin.

"A Talent?" Sal asked.

"A mender," Bartley corrected.

Alzbetta harrumphed. "Crude terms. I am an artist. A weaver, if you must. Though I am no ordinary weaver, no crone that blisters fingers at a loom. I am a weaver of flesh, of muscle, vein, and sinew, of bone, marrow, cartilage, and viscera."

Sal's attention was once again captured by the softly glowing orb of white light. Distracted, he merely asked, "How did we . . ."

Bartley seemed to know what he was asking. "Fisherman, off the Little Island, pulled us both out and took us to shore. I had to carry you all the way here by myself."

Alzbetta cleared her throat. "As I recall, the two of you arrived behind a pair of cart horses, a beautiful chestnut mare and a flea-bitten gray. Though I dare say that driver looked a tad shady."

"As I recall, no one asked you, woman," said Bartley.

Alzbetta cleared her throat once more, and her eyes narrowed.

"M'lady," Bartley corrected.

"And the steel caps?" Sal said. "Did they see us getting out of the river, were we followed?"

"None came downriver," Bartley said. "Most like they thought we'd drowned. Even still, we'd do best not to be seen for a time."

"Mayhap you'd like to tell me why the two of you jumped into the river to begin with?" Alzbetta said, with another of her wicked smiles.

Sal could feel himself start to blush, but he swallowed his timidity and did his best to be charming. "Ah, well, you know how it is under the scorching autumn sun," he said, the words dripping with sarcasm. "The cool water looked right for a swim."

Alzbetta's smile turned from seductive to genuine. "I see. And you were swimming with the city watchmen?"

"More like *away* from the city watchmen," Sal said. "We leaped from the Bridge of the Lady."

Bartley coughed and nudged Sal's shoulder, but Alzbetta only smiled all the more.

"That would explain quite a lot. Is there any particular reason you chose to jump from the Lady?"

"I put a leg in the path of a steel cap," Sal said with an easy shrug, his attention again captured by the softly glowing orb of white light. The thing was small, but Sal couldn't tear his eyes away. "Pardon, My Lady, but what is that?"

Her gaze followed to where he pointed. "Ah," said Alzbetta knowingly. "A little device one of my associates cooked up. He gave it to me as a sample, in hopes that I would come back to him for more. A flasher, or so he named it. Told me that little orb held the power of a star. I imagine it must be some variant of snap powder, possibly a flash oil. He claims I need only break the glass and light shall burst forth as though the Lord that is Light himself appeared in our midst. For the life of me, I can't think of a good use for the thing, though it is pretty, in an eerie fashion."

"Captivating," Sal said with a nod.

"Like it, do you?" said Alzbetta.

"It's beautiful," Sal said. "Haven't been able to keep my eyes off of it since I woke."

Alzbetta picked up the orb she'd called a flasher. It was no bigger than a chicken's egg.

Sal accepted the flasher for a closer examination. The orb was lightweight and smooth to the touch. The light within glowed pearlescent white, slowly swirling like thick liquid.

"Would you be willing to sell this?" Sal asked, looking up from the orb.

Alzbetta arched an eyebrow. "I don't know if that would be responsible. I'm not even certain what this orb does. I've only some unsubstantiated claims, made by a madman—a friend, mind you, but a madman all the same."

"I know my share of madmen," Sal said, flashing the mender a reassuring smile. "If it's repercussions you fear, I assure you there shall be none."

"It is not repercussions from you, but my conscience, that concern me."

Sal shrugged. "I'm sure it's nothing a few krom and a good night's sleep won't cure."

Alzbetta frowned. "I couldn't."

"Oh, but you could."

"No, I cannot," Alzbetta said firmly, holding out a hand for the flasher.

"I think we'd best be off," Sal said, handing back the orb and getting to his feet. "What do we owe you for your services?"

Alzbetta placed the orb back on the shelf. "Your friend has already paid."

Bartley gave him a sheepish grin, and Sal shook his head, thinking of their talk about loan sharks just that morning.

"I fear he has only begun to pay," Sal said seriously, eyeing his Yahdrish friend.

Bartley's cheeks turned the color of cherry blossoms, but he didn't bother with a retort.

Sal took a shaky step. His knee buckled and he stumbled into Bartley, shoving him just so.

Bartley stumbled into a rack containing glass vials of various sizes. Two vials fell, one of which Bartley managed to catch; the other shattered on the floorboards, filling the room with a sharp vinegar scent.

As Alzbetta rushed to Bartley's aid, Sal swiftly pocketed the pearlescent flasher before joining in to help.

"I apologize, My Lady. I fear I felt a spell of dizziness," Sal said. "Please, take some coin to cover the costs. What was that worth?"

"It was only distilled vinegar," Alzbetta said. "There is no harm done. Are you feeling all right now?"

"Much better," Sal said, giving her a reassuring smile. "Still, I think we'd best be off before anything else is broken."

Alzbetta smiled warmly. "So long as you are feeling well, there is truly no harm done."

Sal and Bartley left Alzbetta's home together, Sal covering his pocket somewhat awkwardly with his wet cloak, which he'd bundled beneath his arm.

The sky was clear, and although the sun was directly overhead, the salt air was brisk with the chill of autumn. Bartley was quiet. More than like, he was worried about the coin he owed. They'd both lost their day's taking when they'd jumped—a good thirty krom in coin and jewels, now scattered at the bottom of the Tamber. Bartley had used the coin in his boot to pay Alzbetta. It was the last of the recent loan—a loan Bartley would no doubt struggle to repay now that he'd lost his takings from the bridge.

When they'd reached the Hog Snout, Bartley offered a cap, but Sal made up something about his head hurting, and they parted ways beneath the wooden sign with the crudely painted likeness of a boar. In truth, the memory of falling from his window after the last time he'd smoked a cap with Bartley was still fresh in his mind, and with the injury he'd sustained in the river, Sal had no desire to repeat the incident.

———

When Sal made it home, he found the door locked, Nicola must not have been back yet, likely out enjoying End, as Sal should have been. Still, nothing about the celebration sounded half so good to him as his bed. He was forced to scale the wall and pry open his bedroom window to get inside. Without hesitation, he went directly for the straw-stuffed mattress. Lying beneath his blanket felt as good as the warm embrace of a lover. His eyelids were heavy, and he let them close.

No sooner had he closed his eyes than they began to itch. He lay there, doing all he could to remain still, breathing deep, pushing away thoughts of moving.

Yet something seemed to tug at him.

Sal opened his eyes. He could hear something, like a call of distress, an urging, though he knew the sound was only in his mind.

The room was silent.

Still, he felt a tug, and without thinking, opened the drawer to his bedside table and removed the locket. As his fingers touched the tarnished gold, a surge of cold energy flowed into him. Thick as two silver krom stacked together, and only slightly larger around, the small gold locket felt right in his hand—as though without it he'd been missing a part of himself. It was a strange feeling, and he wasn't sure he was comfortable with it.

He ran a finger across the smooth gold surface and over the rune engraved upon the locket's face. Sal had never seen the mark elsewhere, three vertical lines closely placed to signify a cohesive symbol, the leftmost stripe blood red.

He slipped his fingernail between the two halves of the locket and attempted to pry it open, to no avail. It seemed the locket was sealed, though Sal could not see how.

To get his mind off the locket he stood and walked to his window, looking out on the bustling market. He watched peddlers move from person to person hawking their wares, as vendors cried out the contents of their carts and flapped their arms for attention. The market-goers walked like cattle in a run, pushing and scrambling for a place to spend their coin.

Sal should have been out there, practicing his soft touch, picking until his pockets were so full he could hardly move. But even for all the gold in Dijvois, he couldn't convince himself it was worth leaving his bedroom.

He glanced at the Godstone, standing tall at the center of South Market. About the foot of the stone were small white petals— hundreds, maybe tens of hundreds. It had become a tradition on the day of End to scatter the petals of the hadrisk flower about the Godstone. The hadrisk bloomed in the late autumn and lasted until the first snows fell. It symbolized the good and long-lasting health of the duke upon his return. Sal had heard it said the hadrisk itself was full of healing properties, though he'd never tested this himself.

Downstairs, the door screeched open. Someone entered.

Sal slipped the locket into the pocket of his jerkin and felt his insides go cold. He headed to the stairs and heard his sister laugh.

Sal relaxed and considered walking back to his bed and lying down, when he heard another laugh, deep and carefree. There was a man in the house.

Sal rushed down the stairs, taking them two at a time until he found himself on the ground floor, face to face with his sister.

For half a heartbeat Nicola seemed startled, but she quickly regained her composure. "What are you doing here?" said Nicola.

"I live here," Sal said. "What, might I ask, is he doing here?"

Nicola darted a nervous glance at her gentleman companion. They were holding hands, and she had been leading him toward the stairs. "But why aren't you out celebrating?" Nicola asked, letting go of the man's hand.

"I could ask the same of you," Sal said defiantly, putting his hands on his hips the way their mother always had.

The man stepped forward. He was a good head and a half taller than Sal, but Sal didn't back up. He stood his ground, his features set in an expression of defiance.

"Oliver Flint," the man said, extending a hand.

Not of the merchant class, but the gentry, the son of some landed noble, no doubt. Sal looked the man over once again, in case he'd missed something. Oliver's clothing was fair and richly made, yet slightly threadbare and out of fashion. His hair was meant to be styled, but seemed to have grown too long. On top of it all, the man had an oily smile that made Sal feel greasy just for looking.

"Cute," said Sal, making no move to accept the nobleman's gesture, "but I was speaking with my sister. You have my leave to go."

"Cute?" asked Oliver Flint.

Slowly, Sal turned back to the man. "Yes, you are quite cute. Like a kitten in a rainstorm, or a muddy little street urchin. Cute enough at a distance, but I'd not touch it."

"Excuse me?" said Oliver, a look of pure incredulity on his noble visage.

"Yes, by all means, you are excused. As I said, you have my leave to go."

"Salvatori!" said Nicola. "That will do. Apologize to Oliver and leave us be."

Sal ignored his sister and addressed the nobleman. "Sweetest, what are you still doing in my home? You were asked to leave."

"I do believe your sister asked *you* to leave, boy."

"Do you think I'll stand by and let you lay my sister? If so you'd best be prepared to pay the bride price and take her to wife."

Nicola gasped, but Oliver Flint only smirked.

"Salvatori, get out of my home this moment," Nicola said, "or I swear on the gods, I will never speak to you again."

Sal had been in enough fights to know when it was time to admit defeat and run. He huffed loudly and headed for the door.

Nicola took the noble's hand, and as they went up the stairs, Sal felt a pain like a punch to the gut. He didn't know what irked him more, the thought of his sister lying with that oily toff, or the fact that he'd lost the fight.

Once out in the street, he couldn't help but think of that line from "Piddle on the Diddler":

And if the diddler diddles your sis, go on and give that diddler a kiss.

In truth, Sal would have preferred to give the toff a kick in the teeth. However, Nicola was his older sister, and as it was she who'd kept a roof over his head, he had little to no say in whom and how she chose. He only wished she had better taste in men.

Sal had walked without thinking. The din of his headache still throbbed, and he had hardly realized where his feet were leading him. He found himself standing before a pawnshop on Penny Row, one of the few streets in Dijvois that wasn't bustling with the celebration of End. He tapped the pocket of his jerkin and felt the reassuring lump of the locket. Touching the opposite pocket, he felt the small glass orb the mender had called a flasher. Sal pushed through the door of the pawnshop.

The shop smelled of mildew and the sweet spices of incense. Cobwebs clung to every corner and sconce, while dust collected about the baseboards. The rugs were Miniian spun, but stained and heavily trafficked.

The man leaning behind the counter was preposterously fat. His skin was the color of tanned leather, and his braided black mustache glistened with oil. He wore a brightly colored orange turban and an absurdly small red vest over white robes. Upon his thick brown fingers he wore rings of gold and silver, set with precious gems that sparkled in the candlelight. With a look of curiosity in his black eyes, the whale of a man rested on one elbow and drummed his fingers on the countertop.

"Nabu, how is it I can always find you in this shop, even on a day like this?"

Chins quivering, Nabu Akkad flashed a benevolent smile. "I am the blood of Akandi and Panalu. Why should I go out and pay homage to this duke of yours?"

Sal shrugged. "End seems less about homage and more an excuse to get drunk and dance in the streets one last time before the winter snows."

"Ah, this is the way of it, yes? Winter snows, bah! If I'd known such a fell thing as snow could fall from the very sky, I never would have left home. This is what comes of a wife, I tell you. Light a fire under my feet, she did. Yap, yap, until I agreed to cross the sea. Show you the burns, I could, and this ear, deaf I am from the yapping. And what to show for it? Winter snows!"

"I know little of Shiikal, but are not the summer sandstorms the equal to our winter snows?"

"No man ever froze to death waist deep in the sand," Nabu said, his fleshy brow wrinkling. "Ah, but you are not my wife. She has not been so young and handsome in many years. And what of you, young Salvatori? You have found a new fence, yes? Why else would you have been avoiding my shop?"

"Avoiding? No, Nabu, you have me all wrong."

"Dear Uncle Stefano, he has asked of you, as well. I wonder myself, why a man should needs ask after his own kin, in a place such as this, no less. Then it comes to me that I am not the only person young Salvatori has neglected. So, I ask this again. You have found a new fence, yes?"

"I told you, you have it all wrong. I've been busy. Luca had us scouting a full fortnight before the last job."

"Luca? This is not the Luca Vrana?"

Sal gave only the slightest of nods.

"No, surely you have more sense than this?"

Sal shrugged. "He had work. Work that pays well enough to keep me off the rooftops for half a year at the least."

"Pays well? You were paid generously for this job of his, yes?"

"Well, no," Sal said. "But only—"

"You would be better served to stick to the rooftops. At least then there is only a chance you will fall and break your neck, but Luca Vrana . . ." Nabu shook his head. "This man, I have heard him called a butcher, and yet what meat is he serving, do you think?"

"Look, it wasn't Luca's fault no one got paid. The job was botched, plain and simple."

"A botched job? This was the High Keep?"

Sal's breath caught. "How?"

Nabu let out a dry chuckle. "I have ears to hear, eyes to see, and enough sense in my head to put one and two together."

"Are people talking?"

Nabu's head bobbed side to side.

"And what are they saying?" Sal said, his voice more frantic than he'd meant it to sound. "Has anyone mentioned my name?"

"No names, only that there was a job, a big one. Five person job, they say."

"Seven," Sal corrected.

Nabu fixed him with a pointed look. "As I said, a big job, and it went sidewise, yes? Though not for the reasons one would expect. I heard tell of city's watchmen in the High Keep. One might wonder at such a thing. Why steel caps and not the duke's own guards? Unless my sources were misinformed? Still, not much of a heist, officially nothing was reported stolen. Though there is rumor of a letter. By whom the letter was written and to whom the letter was sent, I do not know."

Sal shook his head. He was unsettled by the amount of information Nabu had about the job at the High Keep.

"Now, don't try and pretend you picked this up on the street," Sal said, doing all he could to keep the panic from his voice.

"I have made no such pretending, and do not say this to be so."

"This source of yours, they were on the job, I suspect? How else would you know so much?"

"Ah, but there is more to this, no?" said Nabu, fixing Sal with a knowing look.

Sal's hand slid over his jerkin pocket. He reached inside, fingertips brushing against smooth gold. As he wrapped his fingers around the locket, icy veins of energy coursed through his entire body. It felt as though a hand had reached inside him and tugged at the frayed edges of his soul.

"I see by the way you make silence that this is the truth of things," Nabu said, his head bobbing.

"I don't put much stock in rumors," Sal said.

"And what of murders?" said Nabu.

The question tore Sal's thoughts away from the locket. "That would depend on your source," Sal said, hesitantly.

"Let us say the source is a most reliable person."

"Who was killed?"

"A Talent," Nabu said. "I believe you knew him. One of the ward-smiths."

Even before Nabu said the name, Sal knew by the sinking feeling in his gut just who it was that had been killed.

"Pavalo," Sal whispered.

"Ah, so you have heard this already?"

Sal shook his head. "Had a feeling, is all."

"He worked on this job with Luca Vrana, no?"

Sal gritted his teeth but nodded all the same. "It was Pavalo Picarri, then? He ratted us out to the steel caps?"

"If I knew this thing, you would be the first to be knowing," Nabu said, as he made a show of frowning. "This Pavalo, he is not the only casualty, I am hearing."

"No?" Sal said, his pulse quickening. "Who?"

"But you know already, I am thinking. This friend of yours, Antonio Russo. He was killed on the job, I have in my hearing."

"At last it seems your source has steered you wrong. I heard just this morning that Anton is breathing, but has yet to wake."

"Ah, but this is the way of things. A cruel world we are living in. I tell you, be wary of this Luca Vrana. He is a dangerous man."

Sal smiled. "Don't you worry, Nabu. I'm well aware."

"Do not worry? As well ask a crone not to nag. Old men worry, my boy, it comes with the aging. What of you, then, young Salvatori? Surely you have not come to my shop only to take advice from an old fool. Perhaps you have something to show me?"

Sal squeezed the locket tighter. He felt a sudden urge to flee. He should never have set foot in Nabu's shop, not now that there was a chance that Anton could live. Still, he wanted to know something—anything—about the locket, and if anyone would know something, it was Nabu.

Sal forced himself to withdraw his hand from his pocket, the locket clutched in a white-knuckled grip as though his body itself resisted. He placed his hand on the countertop and slowly opened his fist. Something inside him tore as each finger lost contact with the gold.

Nabu's thick black eyebrows rose as he leaned in for a closer look. Hesitantly he reached for the object, then jumped back as if stung. "I want nothing to do with this!" Nabu said, spewing a stream of foreign curses. He flicked a wrist and backhanded the locket off the countertop.

Sal caught the locket out of the air before it went clattering to the stone floor. "Lady's sake, you sun-addled Shiikali, what's gotten into you?"

"Be gone from here, and take that accursed thing with you!"

"Take it easy, Nabu," Sal said, handling the locket gently as he inspected it for damage. "I don't understand."

"Understand this: I want naught to do with this thing. Destroy it, throw it into the sea, or bury it where it will not be found."

"If this is some new bargaining tactic, I must admit you have me at a loss. But listen, I'm not trying to sell it, it isn't even mine to sell. I only want—"

"I care not what you do with the thing. So long as you are rid of it. Now be gone with it, yes, I'll not have it in my shop. Bring this thing here again, and you shall not be welcome."

Sal forced a laugh. "Surely this is some sort of jape."

Lips pursed, Nabu merely pointed to the door with a thick, ringed finger.

6

THE FLASHER

S al left Nabu's pawnshop shaking slightly, though it had little to do with the chill of the afternoon air. Nabu's reaction had worried him more than he'd let on. He couldn't help but wonder what it was about the locket that had caused Nabu to act so strangely. After all, Nabu had never once turned away Sal's business, no matter how hot the merchandise in question. It was one of the things Sal loved best about Nabu Akkad, and one of the reasons Sal had never used another fence. Besides, he hadn't even gotten the chance to show Nabu the flasher he'd nicked off that Talent. If anyone would appreciate the novelty of the flasher, it was Nabu. Though after the way the fence had reacted to the locket, Sal wasn't so sure.

But why had Nabu acted that way?

Sal closed his hand around the locket. Rivulets of energy pulsated up his arm. There was no denying that the locket held power, but the nature of this power was entirely unclear.

For the second time that day he'd been kicked out of somewhere he'd always considered safe, a place he'd thought his own. First his sister, then Nabu; it was as though he were alone in a city of thousands. Sal's pace quickened. He felt a sudden desire to be far away from Nabu's shop.

He slipped through the crowd before ducking into another alley. His hackles rose with the feeling of being watched. He dropped to one knee, reached for the pigsticker in his boot, and pivoted before rising.

There was pain as something clasped a handful of his hair and wrenched his head back—and there was the sharp edge of a dagger at his throat.

"Pull that poker, and I slit your fucking throat." Sal recognized the voice, gruff and cold, entirely devoid of sympathy.

"I'd rather you didn't. I much prefer my throat the way it is." Sal moved his hand away from his boot, but Dellan did not relinquish his grip. "Mind letting me up? I fear if you pull my hair much harder, I'll end up with a monk's tonsure."

Dellan snorted derisively and shoved Sal awkwardly so that he landed ass first on the cobblestones.

Sal looked up at the tattooed Vordin, dressed head to toe in black wool and boiled leather, a wicked grin displaying filed teeth. His piercing blue eyes lit with an intensity that made Sal want to shake in his boots.

Instead, Sal got to his feet and stood before Dellan, defiantly meeting his stare.

It didn't matter that Dellan was a killer; Sal knew plenty of killers. Dellan was something else entirely. He didn't merely kill, he lived to kill. Even worse, Dellan was the sort of man who took pleasure in causing pain.

"You lost?" Dellan asked.

Sal shrugged. "What's it to you?"

Dellan pulled a folded piece of linen from his pocket. He unfolded the square of cloth to reveal a black smear of ash.

"Tracer," Sal said, his senses going on high alert.

A tracer was something easily whipped up by a minor Talent. All it took was a piece of the person someone was looking for, be it a hair or a toenail shaving, and the Talent could make a device that would guide the hunter to their quarry.

Dellan smirked and threw the linen square to the cobblestones. He barked out a little laugh as he sized up Sal. "If I went to work on you with my knives, boy, that pigsticker of yours would be good as spit."

Sal readied himself to draw the knife from his boot. What Dellan said was true. If he pulled his pigsticker he was a dead man, but that was doubly true if Dellan attacked while he was still unarmed.

"What are you doing with a tracer? Someone want me dead?"

The tattooed Vordin barked another laugh.

"Luca?" Sal asked.

"Gods, boy, you frightened?"

Sal was shaking, but tried his best not to let it show.

"Why should Luca want you dead? Something you want to tell?" Dellan asked, sniffing loudly. "What is that I smell, rat?"

"What are you doing here, then? Why did you have that tracer?"

"Luca," Dellan said.

Sal couldn't help but smile.

"Something droll, boy?"

"No, no, nothing. It's only, well, are you Luca's errand boy these days? Surprising, really, considering your previous occupation. What happened? Don Moretti isn't upset with you, is he?"

Dellan drew his knives so fast Sal didn't even have time to flinch before he felt the prick of steel. He'd kept his feet planted but didn't know whether that was due to bravery or paralyzing fear.

"I could do you, you know? Right here." Dellan said, grinning to show off his filed teeth. "Tell you true, I'd rather take my time about it. Do things slow, the right way."

For once in his life, Sal had no smart remark. He stood still as a statue and prayed to the Lady that Dellan would decide not to cut him open there and then.

The Vordin slowly withdrew his knives from Sal's skin and sheathed them. "Luca is waiting for you at the Crown."

The Crown was an alehouse on High Hill, near the walls of the High Keep.

Sal nodded, not daring to speak lest Dellan change his mind and decide he'd rather just kill Sal after all.

Without warning, Dellan turned and walked out of the alley.

Sal waited long enough to be sure that Dellan was gone before making his way through the alley. It was only after the excitement had passed that Sal began to recall how much his head still hurt. There was no pain on the outside, but inside, his head throbbed. Alzbetta had said it would take time for the spirit to catch up to the flesh, which Sal took to mean he was going to have headaches for some time. Still, he'd do well not to keep Luca waiting. The man was irascible at the best of times, and if people were being killed, the last thing Sal wanted was to upset Luca Vrana.

Sal passed a pair of black-hooded acolytes. They belonged to the Order of the Flame, a sub-sect of the Vespian Order. Made up entirely of women, the Order of the Flame was charged with, among other things, maintaining the streetlamps throughout the city. The hooded acolytes always traveled in pairs, each holding a pole-candle the length of a man, which they used for lighting the streetlamps every evenfall.

Sal watched the acolytes for a moment before slipping back into the crowd and pushing his way north. The quickest way to High Hill was to cross the Oleander on the Singing Bridge, cut through the cathedral district, and pass over the Tamber on the High Bridge.

Sal had always hated crossing into High Town. As if things weren't bad enough on his side of the river, the people in High Town tended to eye him as though he were something less than they. Even worse, more steel caps patrolled the streets, and so far as Sal was concerned, the fewer steel caps the better. The cream atop the cake was that crossing into High Town merely salted old wounds. It wasn't so bad as when he was younger, as time had dulled most of the pain, but some memories were still fresh enough to sting.

Altogether, the walk took him a good half hour, not because any steel caps stopped him but because the streets were filled with the masked revelers of End—most of them loud, unruly, and so drunk they could hardly stand. As he crossed the High Bridge stuffed in the crowd like a Fitzen's feast roast, Sal was confident that by morning's light some unfortunate souls would have stumbled over the parapet due to either drunkenness or a chance shove.

Even jostled among the crowds, sullen and sore as he was, once he'd crossed over the Tamber Sal couldn't help but notice the subtle beauty of High Town, from the clean paving stones of the streets to the strongly mortared brick of the buildings, from the brightly burning, freshly polished lanterns of the streetlamps to the shuttered glass windows of the homes. The drastic dichotomy between High Town and Low Town never failed to move him—in what direction, he didn't know. Yet it was not only the infrastructure of High Town but the people of the district that contrasted with Low Town.

Dijvois was a melting pot of the latest fashions, influenced by Vinigre to the west, Skjörund to the east, and Kirkundy to the north. The men of late had begun slashing the sleeves of their doublets. The women cut the necklines of their gowns ever lower, and no longer lined their winter garments in furs such as vair and miniver but preferred sable and marten as the cold months approached.

The Crown was a reasonably posh establishment, high-class enough that a working stiff like Sal was looked over twice by every patron he passed. He was scrutinized the same way a steel cap might scrutinize a begging street urchin.

Luca had a table in the back in his usual spot, a cushioned booth laden with pillows where the dock thug could recline and see everything happening around him. There was a jug of beer and a bottle of wine on a table filled with half-eaten plates of food. Luca was never a man to deny himself simple pleasures.

"Salvatori, come, sit. Have you eaten?" Luca motioned for one of the serving girls. "My friend will take a cup and a plate. I'm certain he has a knife, but a fork will serve nicely."

When the serving girl returned with the cup and plate Sal cut a thigh from the capon and Luca himself poured Sal a cup of the wine. The capon was crisp and greasy, and the wine fruity with an overly sweet finish.

Luca plucked a few grapes, plopping them into his mouth one at a time, while Sal ate his fill. When Sal had washed down his last bite of capon with a second cup of wine, Luca began to speak.

"Tell me, kid. That last job, has anyone spoken more of it since that night?"

"Not much," Sal said with a shrug. "Someone mentioned how it was strange the steel caps showed when they did."

Luca frowned. "Oh, and that's all they're saying?"

"I heard a rumor," Sal said, "about that ward-smith, Pavalo Picarri."

"Know something about Pavalo, do you?" Luca asked.

Sal thought it best to tread carefully. There was a dark look in Luca's eyes. He'd been jovial thus far, but Sal knew as well as anyone how quickly things could change in a conversation with Luca. His temperament was much like the weather; it could alter drastically with the slightest shift of the breeze.

"I don't know anything. Just heard from the rumor mill that— that Pavalo had been done."

"Funny, I heard the same rumor."

"Funny how?" Sal blurted before thinking.

"Funny because I go looking for a rat, and next day a man involved in our operation drops dead." Luca smirked. "Might be it's only coincidence. Whatever it is, it is rather droll."

Sal's head was pounding harder than ever. He reached for the jug of wine and poured himself another cup.

"Anyone behaving oddly?" Luca asked. "Anybody thrown around any extra coin since the last job?"

"That the reason you summoned me?" It must have been the wine that had given him the courage, but once the words were out, they couldn't be put back in. "I don't know anything about the rat. If there was a rat at all, he wasn't one of us that were at the High Keep. I can guarantee that much."

To Sal's surprise, Luca smiled. "That's what I like about you, Salvatori, you're not afraid to speak your mind. You'd be surprised at the men who hold their tongues when speaking to me."

Sal doubted he would be too surprised.

"Look, Luca, I just wondered what you wanted me for. You know, the tracer and all. It put me on guard."

"You've got balls, kid, and I was impressed with the way you handled yourself on the High Keep job. You kept your head. If it weren't for that Yahdrish pup, you might have finished the job. Still, so far as the scouting went, you were everything Antonio promised. I want you for the next job."

Sal realized that as Luca spoke, he wasn't asking, but telling. It was as though he had already assumed Sal's compliance. Still, Sal had no intention of accepting the job offer. Nabu was right. He had been mad to take the job with Luca Vrana the first time, and it was a mistake he would not be repeating.

"Heard anything about Anton?" Sal asked.

"I didn't call you all the way up here to talk about Antonio Russo, I called you to hear about a job," said Luca with a touch of irritation. "The job's simple, and it pays well. It's nothing you haven't done for me before, only there are a few specifics I want you to watch for. The estate is large but heavily guarded. I need to know a point of entry or any weaknesses in the guard rotation. Most importantly the daughter. I need to know her comings and goings. Memorize her schedule. I want to know her every habit. That is of the utmost importance to our employer. Every tick of the girl's every day should be recorded. She will have a man with her, an armed guard. A big bloody Bauden bastard. He too is quite important to our plans. I need to know if there are ever times she is without him."

"Right. Well, listen, Luca, I don't know that I'm right for——"

"I want you to start tonight, evenfall."

"Tonight? I——"

Luca slid a folded piece of parchment across the table. "You can go now. Here's information on the man and where to find his estate. I know you'll do well, as always."

Sal was losing ground quickly. He needed to put a stop to it there and then. "Luca, listen, I can't pick up any work just now."

"You have other work?" Luca asked, sitting up straight, his nose twitching. "With who?"

"No, nobody, I just—well, I can't start tonight."

"What, you've not dipped your wick yet? Light's name, kid, you've had all day."

"It's not that. I only—I really shouldn't."

"Look, I need it done tonight, and you're the man I need for the job. Don't let me down." It seemed Luca had his mind set; he wasn't going to take no for an answer.

"Who's the mark?" Sal asked, relenting at least that much.

"Fourth Seat of the High Council, Lord Hugo Bastian," said Luca proudly.

The High Council! Sal wanted to shout. He should have expected no less of Luca Vrana. First the High Keep, now Lord Hugo. Whatever else they said of Luca, the man was ambitious. "What sort of job are we talking here?"

"Scouting. If there's anything else, I'll see you're told."

"He do something, this Lord Hugo?" Sal asked.

"Seems he's been stepping on some toes of late—connected toes, mind you. Making trouble for some of the trader vessels that bring in Commission supply. Worse, he hasn't stopped there. As of last night, he's proposed a ducal edict restricting all imports, along with higher tariffs, namely on goods coming out of Shiikal and anywhere else out of Naidia."

"I imagine that pissed off the Commission," Sal said.

"You can see why this needs to be done, right? I need a good man on it, someone I can trust."

Sal knew better than to turn Luca down a third time. Unless he wanted find himself lying facedown in the bay, he'd best take the job. "I could, mayhap, start on the morrow—"

"Tonight," Luca said.

"Uh, right," Sal said as he stood, shoulders hunched, head down. "Sure thing. I'm on it."

Luca stabbed the parchment with two fingers, once, twice.

Sal picked up the folded piece of parchment and tucked it into his jerkin pocket beside the flasher, and Luca dismissed him with a hand. Just as he had when he'd entered the Crown, Sal felt the eyes of everyone watching as he passed.

Sal unfolded the parchment and read the directions. As he was already on High Hill, it didn't take him long to get where he was going. He simply scaled a stone wall, using the gaps in the mortar for handholds, and made his way along the rooftops. On a crowded night such as End, the roofs were far faster than the streets.

The rooftops in High Town weren't as close together as they were in Low Town. This made them more difficult to navigate than elsewhere in the city. Still, there was no shortage of strong, reliable walls in High Town which Sal could use to bridge the gaps in the rooftops.

Far worse than the distance between rooftops, and deadlier by half, were the clay-shingled roofs, something never found in Low Town due to their cost. Clay shingles had become quite popular about High Town, not only because they were fashionable of late but also because they were deadly to thieves doing second-story work. Sal had made the mistake of trying to cross a clay-shingled roof only once, and ever since had been wary of the things.

From what Sal knew of Lord Hugo Bastian's home, the estate somewhat mirrored the master of the house: a gaudy mansion, as decadent as it was bloated.

Sal watched from a rooftop, near enough to the Bastian estate that he could see anyone who came and went. Seated next to a chimney in the false-light before dawn there was no chance of him being spotted.

Two guards stood at the front gate, two more pairs at the front and back doors, and another one at the east entrance. Sal assumed there were more men-at-arms inside, so he doubled his count for safe measure. Fourteen men. Lord Hugo's security payroll must have been as atrociously swollen as his home.

There was only a little light coming through the windows of the estate. Silhouettes of patrolling guards passed by the glass every so often, but otherwise there was little happening within. If Lord Hugo was home, perhaps the man was sleeping.

However, much of the gentry preferred to enjoy the festivities of End with lavish parties at their estates. As Bastian did not seem to be entertaining, it only stood to reason that the lord was out. Mayhap he'd been invited to the party at the High Keep. Sal had always wondered what that would be like. Someday he meant to attend and see for himself.

Sal leaned back against the roof and nestled tight to the brick chimney. As he waited, his mind wandered back to the locket. He slipped a hand into his jerkin pocket and clasped the small gold piece. Currents of electric energy snaked up his arm and circulated through his body.

Holding the locket by his thumb and forefinger, Sal scrutinized it, wondering what it was about the thing that had terrified Nabu so much. The locket contained a power of some sort. How that power was unleashed was something Sal would need to figure out for himself.

As far as jewelry went, the locket was rather plain. Gold, yes, but old gold, a tarnished, lusterless yellow, unadorned with gems or other precious metals. There was a marking on the face. The unfamiliar rune, three vertical slashes parallel to one another.

He lay on his back, examining the locket for a full turn before a carriage arrived at the black iron gate of the estate grounds. The armed guards let the carriage through. As the small yet ornate two-horse affair rolled down the drive, light flickered behind the windows of the mansion.

The guards at the front door drew to attention when the carriage came to a stop. A short, fat man rushed excitedly from the front door, while simultaneously a tall, muscular Bauden stepped from the carriage. The Bauden sported a thick mustache and was undoubtedly a man-at-arms. He wore a bastard sword strapped to his back, and a stiletto as long as a man's forearm sheathed at his hip. Oddly enough, something about him rang of familiarity.

The fat, balding man was a head shorter than the man-at-arms and easily twenty years his senior. He was finely dressed, a good eighty gold krom in his sable cloak and ermine-cuffed gloves alone. There was no telling what the entire outfit had set the little man back, but Sal could imagine it cost a pretty penny or two. Judging by his age and dress, Sal surmised the short man was Lord Hugo Bastian.

Behind the man-at-arms, a woman exited the carriage. By then the dumpy Lord Hugo had waddled his way to the carriage and raised a hand to help the woman down. Lord Hugo embraced the woman, and she affectionately reciprocated.

The woman was beautiful, and somehow strangely familiar. It was then Sal realized why he had recognized the big Bauden wearing the bastard sword. He was the same man that had knocked Sal down on the Bridge of the Lady and threatened to chop off his hand. The woman was the one wearing the blue dress and the sapphire earrings. She was the woman that had slapped him twice on the ear.

The realization made Sal sick to his stomach. He wanted to be off the roof. He wanted to be done watching. He was exhausted, his head hurt, his body ached, and now nausea was setting in. Luca couldn't say Sal hadn't done all he could that night. He wasn't going to risk getting any closer to the estate at that hour. It was too conspicuous. He'd made first contact, and that was all that could be expected of him.

Sal made his way to the edge of the roof on his hands and knees, crawling like a badly deformed crab. He lay on his stomach and slowly lowered himself over the side until he was hanging by his fingertips. Sal let go and dropped to the next level of the rooftop. He repeated the process until he was again hanging by his fingertips. This time when he let go, he dropped to the cobblestones of the alley.

The landing sent a shockwave through his legs, and although he bent his knees to absorb most of the impact, the shock traveled up his legs and into his back.

He winced in pain. The drop had been farther than he'd expected. He closed his eyes to center himself and scrounge together whatever reserves of energy he had left. When he opened his eyes, he saw two men standing at the mouth of the alley.

Not merely men, but a pair of steel caps.

"You there!" said one of the steel caps.

The other lowered his poleaxe until the steel spike was level with Sal's chest.

"What is your business here?" said the first steel cap, as the other began moving forward.

Sal's head was spinning. Panic made it impossible to think of a course of action. He was like a boar with one leg caught in a snare.

"Your business, boy. What do you think you're doing here?"

The other steel cap closed slowly, though he kept his poleaxe leveled as though he meant to run Sal through.

"I, uh, listen, I'm only trying to find his lordship's place of residence."

The one who'd spoken yelled something, then caught up with his partner and together they closed the distance to Sal. The speaker looked him up and down, frowning as though he didn't like what he saw.

"And what business might you have with his lordship?"

Before Sal could answer, a trio of steel caps rounded the corner and spilled into the alley at a run. They slowed, presumably when they saw their comrades had the situation under control.

Where there had been two, Sal now faced five steel caps. One of the newcomers stepped ahead of the other four. He was neither tall nor thickly muscled, yet he carried himself with the swagger that comes with authority. His coarse black tangle of a beard did little to hide the burn scarring on the left half of his face.

The scarred steel cap wore a gold band about his right bicep, signifying his rank of lieutenant within the City Watch.

"Got a name?" the lieutenant asked.

Sal said the first name that came to mind. "Oliver Flint."

The lieutenant cocked an eyebrow, then turned and spoke in a whisper to the other steel caps. When he turned back, there was a smile on his ugly burned face.

"You look a bit young. Or do you claim to be the son?"

Sal cursed inwardly. It was just his luck the Flint family were known gentry.

"His nephew," Sal said.

"Oliver Flint, nephew to *the* Oliver Flint," the lieutenant said doubtfully.

"You know, Lieutenant, the kid might be telling the truth," said one of the steel caps. "I've had dealings with the Flint family in the past. The kid has the look."

"The kid has the look of the royal family," said the lieutenant. "Would you claim he is the long-lost heir of our duke? Should we give him the ducal treatment?"

"I was only trying to help, sir."

"You'll be more help with your mouth shut and your sword arm at the ready. Should I for some unholy reason need your input at any point I'll not hesitate to ask for it." The lieutenant turned back to Sal. "And what of you? What are you doing prowling the High Hill at this hour?"

"Beg pardon, but there was no prowling from me, sir."

"Aye, well, I say you were prowling. So don't bother with correcting me, just answer the fucking question. Where were you going and why?"

"I was on my way to his lordship's estate. Only I got a bit turned around."

"Turned around, you say? So turned around that you found yourself skulking on rooftops instead of the city streets?"

"By the gods, no."

"No? You look the part, young and lean, ripe for second-story work. If you weren't out here prowling for open windows, what is it you're doing on the Hill?"

"As I tried to tell you, sir. I was on my way to his lordship's—"

"Aye, off to his lordship's as you said, yet you've neglected to tell me why. To what ends would his lordship summon you at this hour?"

"I don't know the reason for his summons. I'll grant, it is a strange request, but I would never dare question his lordship. I serve and obey."

The lieutenant's eyes narrowed, his lips pursed.

"Who might this lord of yours be?"

"Lord Hugo," Sal said, again blurting the first name that came to mind.

"Lord Hugo Bastian?"

Sal nodded, feigning hesitancy. "Unless there is another Lord Hugo in the city."

The lieutenant's features softened. "Right, then, I must say this story of yours sounds quite credible. You're free to go."

Sal was more than a little confounded. His story had been shaky at best, his performance even less impressive, and yet it seemed the ruse had worked. The lieutenant was going to let him go.

The lieutenant turned to his four comrades. "Young Oliver Flint is free to go. Although seeing as he was lost, what do you say we escort this citizen to his lordship's estate?" The lieutenant turned back to Sal, a wicked smile twisting his features. "After all, Lord Hugo's estate is right around the corner."

The other steel caps took the lieutenant's meaning and snapped into action. Two of them circled behind Sal to block his escape, while the other two grabbed him by either arm.

"Right this way," the lieutenant said, taking the lead.

As the Bastian estate was just around the corner, they reached the black iron gate long before Sal was ready. He had a hazy sketch of a plan in mind, but the more thought he gave it, the more he realized his likelihood of survival was not high.

Two armed men stood guard outside the gate. They wore iron half-helms with nasal guards and chain mail coifs beneath. They were garbed in chain mail hauberks, lobstered gauntlets, steel greaves, and iron-shod boots. Over their chain mail they wore the livery of Lord Hugo Bastian, tabards bearing a black bull on a field of forest green. Each guard was armed with polearms, and a short sword at the hip.

Except for the shield slung over the back of the guard on the left, the two were nearly impossible for Sal to tell apart, beneath the helms and the challenging grimaces they sported as Sal and his escort of steel caps approached.

When the lieutenant was but an arm's reach from the gate, the guards crossed their polearms to block his path.

"Open the gate," said the lieutenant imperiously. "I have business with your lord."

The guards didn't budge. Instead, they looked at the lieutenant as though he were a bug to be squashed underfoot.

Since the initiation of the City Watch by King Bethelwold the Great, household guards throughout the city had seemed to cultivate a mutual enmity with the steel caps. The City Watch had the authority of the magistrate to back them, and the magistrate's authority derived directly from the duke. The knowledge that the City Watch held a sort of unchecked authority seemed to make household guards cagey and obstinate around the steel caps. So, rather than work together, household guards and steel caps often fell into petty arguments and minor squabbles.

Sal hoped he might witness something of that nature at present. Mayhap it would offer him an opportunity for escape, or at the least more time to hatch a proper plan.

"What business do you have with his lordship?" asked the guard on the left.

For a heartbeat it seemed the lieutenant might not deign to answer, but to Sal's disappointment the steel cap relented.

The lieutenant motioned to Sal. "I found this one skulking through an alley. Says he has business with his lordship. My boys and I thought we'd come along to make certain he got to where he was going safe and sound."

"Mighty kind of you, that was," said the guard on the left. "Only, nobody said nothing to us about no nighttime visitors. So you and your boys can escort him elsewhere, or go bugger yourselves with them poleaxes, either will do fine."

This seemed to upset the lieutenant. His amiability of moments before seemed to vanish in an instant.

"Listen here, you sod-sucking fops. I won't be put off by a couple of hired hands. You see this?" the lieutenant said, pounding his chest where the magistrate's seal was sewn onto his surcoat. "I have the authority to arrest the pair of you. You'll be tried on a count of obstruction, but only after you've spent a fortnight in the under-cells."

The four other steel caps readied themselves should a fight break out. The two in the rear stepped up and leveled their poleaxes; the two holding Sal released him and reached for their swords.

Tension was building in the air, so thick it was palpable.

The guards stood their ground, seemingly unintimidated by the steel caps' posturing.

The lieutenant turned to his men, and Sal knew the time was almost upon him—he would have one chance. He put a hand in his jerkin pocket.

"Easy, boys, there is no need for a fight here."

As the lieutenant spoke, Sal pulled the small glass orb out of his pocket. He held the flasher tight, wound his arm back, aimed, released, and closed his eyes.

"There's no reason we should need to—" The lieutenant was cut short.

Sal had aimed the flasher at the chest of the lieutenant, right at the axe-and-moon sigil. He'd expected to hear a crack, or snap, or some sort of explosion, yet all he heard was a soft thump of glass on cloth, then the *tink, tink, tink* of the orb bouncing on cobblestones.

The lieutenant let out a curse, and Sal opened his eyes. The lieutenant looked furious, the guards confused.

Sal braced himself for an axe blow, but no such blow came. He glanced at the ground and saw that the orb was rolling in his direction. Without giving it another thought, he leaped at the orb and closed his eyes. He felt as much as heard the crunch of glass underfoot.

Pained shouts sounded all around him. Even through closed eyes, Sal saw the flash of light. He felt slightly dazed and more than a little nauseated, but there was no time to dally.

Sal opened his eyes. Nearly all the others had dropped to their hands and knees or writhed on the ground. Only the lieutenant remained upright.

The lieutenant's eyes were unfocused. He looked unsteady, wobbling as he tried to keep his feet.

Sal took a step back, fearing the lieutenant would attack, but he looked closer to spewing sick than giving chase.

Without another moment of hesitation, Sal ran and didn't look back until he reached the Bridge of the Lady.

II

THE READING

*For it is what we hold sacred that unites us. Let life provide the answer,
for life is the first and final of the sacred truths.*
—Bethelwold the Great

Cut their fucking throats and be done with it.
—Vallachenka Smirnichezk

7

RECRUITED

INTERLUDE, FOUR MONTHS EARLIER

"What is this place?" Sal said.

"My safe house," Anton said. "Comes in handy when I need a place to lay low."

"Safe house," Sal scoffed. "Smells like a stable. There's not even a window, for Lady's sake."

"Thinks he's a big man now he runs his own crew, does he?" Anton said. "Whatever happened to that scrawny kid from the Shoe? I seem to recall he moaned less."

"Like you said, I have a crew now."

"Yeah, right, your own crew," Anton said derisively. "Three strong now, isn't it?"

"We're a growing enterprise. These are early times."

"And what is it you call yourselves now? The Shadow Guild, is it?"

Sal shrugged to hide the twinge of embarrassment. "Bartley's idea."

"Bartholomew Shoaly," Anton said, nodding knowingly. "A big mouth on that one. Don't know what you see in him."

"They all ask me the same of you," Sal said with a smirk.

Anton smiled in return. Despite his sharp, angular features, the smile was warm, almost brotherly. "And you tell them what, that you see greatness?"

"A great disappointment is more like. You've always claimed to be going places, and look at you," Sal said, flicking Anton's chin. "You're still squatting here in Dijvois just like the rest of us. No farther up the ladder than the day we met."

Anton snapped a hand around Sal's wrist and twisted his arm.

Sal laughed and tried to fight out of the grip, but Anton was far too strong. The bigger man twisted until Sal dropped to his knees and called out for mercy, laughing all the while.

Anton smiled, held out a hand, and helped Sal to his feet.

"Look, kid," Anton said, once Sal had gotten up. "There's a job, a big one, and I've been asked to recruit the players."

"I see. And who've you got so far?"

"The usual, Vallachenka, Odie, Dellan—"

Sal made a noise of disgust.

"You've got a problem with Dellan?"

"Seems to me he's the one with the problem. Those eyes follow me everywhere I go. Looks at me like he's a wolf and I'm his bloody quarry."

"Well, nothing I can do there, he was requested."

"Requested?" Sal said. "Thought you said this was your job. Who's really running this thing?"

"Luca Vrana."

"Vrana? Another one?"

"Sure, Luca's a bit off." Anton winked. "But he's an earner, and a well-connected one at that."

"You're sure this is a good idea, after what happened the last time, you know, with Fab—"

"Think I'd ever bloody forget about that?" Anton snapped, a look of something like regret in his eyes.

"But you think we can trust Luca?" Sal asked nervously, not wanting to press too far.

"As far as I'd trust a daggermouth."

"Far enough to earn a krom?"

"Precisely," Anton said. "Old Luca's a dangerous one, but I'll let him fill my plate before I cut him loose."

"And Luca, it was him asked for me by name?"

"Sure was," said Anton, "but don't let that go filling your head. Only reason Luca knows who you are is because of me."

"And what of my crew?"

"The Shadow Guild," Anton said, hunching his shoulders and wiggling his fingers. "So far as I'm concerned, Vincenzo is welcome on any job."

Sal swallowed. He knew it would come to this, it often did. "Vinny, right, and what about Bartley?"

Anton sighed. "Like I said, this is a big job. We're going to need a tight crew."

"Bartley is in my crew."

"This isn't your crew, kid. This is Luca's crew, and Luca doesn't allow for mistakes. Trust me on that. You remember Fabian?"

Sal arched an eyebrow. He would never forget Fabian.

"Listen," Anton said, "I want you on this one. There's a bonus in it for you too, fifty krom."

"Fifty—" Sal shook his head. "No, it's all or none. You want me, you're getting Vinny and Bartley too."

"Did you not hear what I said?"

"I heard you," Sal said, somewhat petulantly, "fifty krom, but I thought you said this was a big job? I'll take my chances with a cut from the share. My crew will want twenty-five points of the whole."

Anton shook his head, his smile cocky, his eyes narrowed. "You weren't listening. The fifty gold is a bonus, just for you. We can discuss point-shares once you learn what the job is, but I don't see any reason your crew can't walk away with fifteen of the whole."

"Twenty," Sal said.

"Light's name, you haggle like a Yahdrish fishwife. I said we'll talk point-shares later."

"This bonus," Sal said. "Fifty krom, on top of the point-share? That's a healthy chunk of coin, for a bonus. What's it really for?"

"Call it a side job. I have a backer, needs something nabbed.

Thing is, I want to keep this one on a need-to-know. You see? Only want to cut the shares as low as needs be."

"Right, then. Well, before we discuss this any further, I want to be certain we are clear. You get me, you get my whole crew."

"Bloody hell," Anton cursed. "There's that Yahdrish fishwife showing her ugly face again. Bartholomew Shoaly is rubbing off on you, I swear it. That's just what they do."

"Well?"

"Fine, the whole crew. The whole fucking Shadow Guild. But if that Yahdrish bungles this one, it's your head Luca's gonna take, mark my words."

"Trust me. You won't regret it," Sal said. "Now about that job?"

Anton arched an eyebrow and smirked. "You're certain you want to know?"

Sal shrugged. "I suppose it doesn't really matter. My crew can handle anything."

"Is that so? The Shadow Guild, right?"

Sal nodded. "It's why you'll be cutting us twenty-five points off the whole."

"Will we, now?"

"That you will," Sal said confidently. "But tell me, then, where is this job you're so keen to have us on?"

Anton cleared his throat and bounced his eyebrows. Then he spoke three words that lit up Sal's ears like braziers.

"The High Keep."

8

RED SMILE

Sal woke with a pounding headache. He'd slept on the floor among the rushes, using his cloak as a makeshift pillow.

Bartley still slept, snoring facedown on his straw-stuffed mattress.

Sal stretched and looked out the window. The sun was up, and the day was bright. Despite the pleasantness of the weather, Sal felt as though there were gray clouds overhead. His encounter with the City Watch the night before had his stomach twisted in knots. Panic had made a fool of him.

He only hoped he never saw the burn-scarred face of that steel cap lieutenant again.

Bartley stirred awake with a snort, followed by a sharp inhalation. He stretched, smacked his lips, and looked quizzically at Sal.

"Been up long?" Bartley asked.

"A turn or two."

"Smoked a cap yet?"

Sal shook his head.

"Get that pipe out, and might be we can do a bit of burning," said Bartley with a coy smile.

Sal retrieved the ebony box that Bartley used to store his pipe and skeev. He ran his fingers over the carved relief of the Dahuaneze goddess, thinking of the Lady White. When he extended the box to Bartley, his friend waved him off.

"You're getting this for free. So I'll let you do the loading."

Sal sighed, opened the box, and began to crumble the skeev into the pipe.

Once they'd smoked a full cap, Sal was no longer worried about the City Watch. He smiled. There was only one thing on his mind: the daughter of Lord Hugo, the woman with the sapphire earrings, Sal's new mark—Lilliana Bastian.

"What's on your mind?" Bartley asked, smirking stupidly.

"New job," Sal said.

"What's this?" Bartley said, ears perking up like a hound with the scent of his quarry.

Sal shook his head. "Nothing you want any part in."

"And what gives you the right to determine that?"

"Because this job is for Luca Vrana."

Bartley's eyes went wide.

"Didn't have much choice in the matter," Sal said with a shrug.

"And what, you're not going to bring me and Vinny in on the score?"

"What?" Sal asked, baffled by Bartley's wounded tone.

"Oh, I see. So you did ask Vinny, just thought you'd leave me out of it?"

"Bartley, take a breath, mate."

"You take a breath, mate," Bartley said. "And when you've done, go and bugger yourself. So much for the bloody Shadow Guild."

"You go too far," Sal said, standing. "Now look, I didn't ask Vinny to join this one either. Did you not hear what I said? The bloody job's with Luca Vrana. You don't want any part in that, I can guarantee it."

"I've some payments coming up. Loans I took out and coin I spent on your behalf, mind you. I need the scratch."

"Right. Well, we could all go for a bit of extra coin. Especially when you consider Luca has yet to pay us for the last job. Still, seems to me you must have forgotten what happened at the High Keep."

"Look at it this way," Bartley said. "My coin purse is so thin, were it my stomach, you'd see my ribs through my bloody shirt. Besides, I like my thumbs; hows about you help me keep them?"

"I'll not recommend you to Luca. Not after last time."

Bartley glared. "I don't need you to set up another meeting, that's been handled. Luca has seen me work. If he wants me on this job, there won't be a damn thing you can do about it."

"So you *haven't* forgotten about the High Keep job?" Sal said. "I guess you're right. He'll probably come calling. It was quite the impression you made on Luca, what with missing your mark and then getting shot and all."

Bartley spat, his arms crossed.

"The answer is no, mate," Sal said. "Besides, with Luca looking for a rat, you want to stay as far from this one as you can."

"And what is that supposed to mean?" Bartley snapped. "You suggesting I'm the bloody rat?"

"Whoa, Bart, I never—look, take it easy. All I'm saying is that if Luca is looking for a rat, he's not safe for any of us to be around. Lady's sake, you heard about Pavalo?"

"Pavalo Picarri, the ward-smith?"

"Aye, Luca's ward-smith."

"What of him?"

"Dead," Sal said. "Murdered the night before End."

"Murdered?"

"Nabu seemed to think it so."

"And you think Luca?" Bartley asked.

"He's a likely suspect. Didn't give much away when I asked him about it, but Luca has always been a difficult read."

"You think he will still try and do us? I mean, if Luca already took care of Pavalo, might be he was the rat, right?"

"Honestly, at this point"—Sal shrugged—"live or die, this is the last job I do for Luca Vrana."

"Whatever you say," Bartley grumbled. He took a deep breath, lifted his arms above his head, and yawned. "Listen, Vinny wants us to meet him downstairs, half an hour after sunup."

"Sun was up a full hour before we smoked that cap," Sal said with a grin.

Bartley scrambled to his feet.

"What's the matter?" Sal asked.

"We're late."

"Nothing to fret over. I mean, it's only Vinny, yeah?"

"Not today it's not."

"Oh, is someone with him?"

"You'll see when we get down there," Bartley said cryptically, opening the bedroom door and stepping out.

As Sal followed Bartley out of the room and moved toward the stairs, he picked up the scent of fresh meadowsweet. Before long the winter snows would be there, and the smell of fresh flowers in the rushes would be a distant memory.

The taproom was just short of empty. Those who broke their fast at the Hog Snout tended to do it early. Vinny was seated, alone except for the buxom barmaid who stood beside his table.

"Morning, Bessy," Bartley said, rather sheepishly.

The barmaid coyly stretched, in a way that showed off her ample cleavage. She yawned, then ran a hand through her long red curls before she spoke. "I suppose it is a nice morning. The sun is shining, the birds are singing, and there is a healthy crop of handsome young men just come strolling through my premises."

Bartley blushed a shade as red as Bessy's curls.

"If only Bartley ever left," Sal said, winking at the blushing Yahdrish.

"I never minded," said Bessy. "Wouldn't mind seeing him around more neither."

"Is that so?" said Sal, taking a seat across from Vinny. "Well, I suppose that makes one of us. As for me, I'd rather see food that his Yahdrish mug. I'll take a cup of the house ale, three eggs any way I can get them, a blood sausage, and some of those potatoes fried in oil. If you have some of that leftover gravy to smother on top of it all like last time, I'd much appreciate it."

"Ain't nothing I can't handle," said Bessy with a wink. "Just so happens I have some gravy left over from last night. And how about you, sweetie?"

Bartley blushed a deeper shade of red. "The same for me, if there's enough gravy to go round."

"Shouldn't be a problem," Bessy said, leaning close to Bartley and making a suggestive gesture with her hand. "Even if we run short, I've never had a problem whipping up a bit of gravy."

Vinny sputtered, spraying beer back into his clay mug, but Bessy went on as though she'd not noticed. "Mayhap we're low on eggs, but seeing how the boy can always fetch me more eggs, that don't qualify as much of a concern. You gents relax, and you'll be supping before you know it."

"Is that why you wanted to get down here so fast?" Sal asked Bartley as the barmaid walked out of earshot.

"That wench?" Vinny said. "Sacrull's hell, Bartley. You should have been concerned about making me wait. Although I reckon the thought of kindling a tinderbox without paying first has your blood in a boil. This'll be a first for you, will it not?"

"Wasn't in a hurry over some wench," Bartley said, brow wrinkling. "I'm here for the job."

"But of course the only thing a Yahdrish considers before a woman's snatch is his own coin purse," Vinny said, chuckling.

"Job?" Sal asked, turning to Bartley. "What job is that?"

"It's not one of mine. This is work Vinny pulled in. Seems at least one of our gang is loyal to the Shadow Guild."

"Right, I get it," said Sal. "Laying it on a bit thick, aren't we?"

"I only wonder why you would choose to hide work from your friends," Bartley said. "Makes a man wonder what else you might be hiding, is all."

"I'm not hiding anything, mate, and I'm not leaving you out of anything that would be good for you. Look, I have no intention of abandoning you."

"Bugger off. You keep talking to me like I'm your foundling and you'll see what happens."

Sal smiled. "So what's this job, Vinny?"

"Anton's job," Vinny said. "I'm only hiring out."

"Anton?" Sal asked, his hand moving to the pocket of his jerkin were the locket was nestled. He felt something in the pit of his stomach when he heard the name. But why should he feel guilty? He wasn't the one who'd felled Anton like a tree. Sal grabbed hold of the locket, his hand still on the outside of his jerkin, yet even through the wool fabric he could feel the power of the thing. Why hadn't he gone to see Anton? The question begged asking, but Sal wasn't sure he wanted to know the answer. "He's awake?"

"Only that, awake. He's been out of bed, but little else. He sent a runner out my way just last night."

"Have you seen him?" Sal asked. "How's he look?" Even as Sal asked the question, he wished he hadn't. The last he'd seen Anton, the man had one foot in the grave.

Vinny shook his head as he averted his gaze.

"What sort of job are we talking?" Sal asked, wanting to change the subject quickly.

"The sort that needs some extra muscle," said Vinny.

"Muscle?" Sal chuckled in an attempt to lighten the mood. "Surely you could do better than Bartley and me if you're looking for some size."

"Don't need size so much as numbers," Vinny said. "Seeing how Anton spent the better part of the week lying on his back with a mender stitching him back together, he's fallen behind on his collections. The shape he's in, he doesn't want anyone seeing him and getting the wrong idea. So he wants me to make his pickups for him. I figured I'd bring the two of you along, and it should help with some of the pigeons that might have had thoughts of holding out otherwise."

"Anton has a sizeable route, but I can't imagine there's much coin to be made split three ways. Not after Don Moretti, Luca, and Anton have all taken their cuts," Sal said.

"Don Moretti will get his cut," Vinny said. "But Luca Vrana is no don. I figure we split his usual payment three ways and that ought to make it worth the squeeze."

"And cut Luca out of the coin?" blurted Bartley. "Are you mad?"

Vinny took a swig of ale, then set his mug on the table, a confident smirk fixed on his face.

The Moretti family was arguably the third most powerful within the Commission. With control of everything south of Beggar's Lane, Don Moretti collected a protection tax for every business, racket, hustle, heist, and second-story job. Be they thief or shopkeeper, if they operated south of Beggar's Lane and west of Captillo Road, they paid their tax to Moretti. As boss of the Moretti family, Don Moretti collected from the Shoe, the Lowers, South Dock, the Wharf, Urchin Town, the Stretch, the Cauldron, and the Narrows.

"Look, Vinny, you know the Code. Anton runs with Luca's crew, and they are both made men under Don Moretti," Sal said. "You can't just cut a made man out of the coin. It doesn't work like that."

"I'm no made man," Vinny said, "and neither are you, Salvatori. The only code we need follow is the code we make for ourselves."

Sal shook his head. "I'm telling you, Luca will get his cut, one way or another. Best way to handle this is to pay the man upfront. You do that, and I don't see how the pay is there for a three-man job."

"Light's name," Vinny cursed, "I'm inclined to think you don't want the work. Come across a purse full of krom you just gonna leave it lying there on the side of the road?"

"Might be Salvatori is just flush for work," said Bartley.

"What's that supposed to mean?" asked Vinny.

Before Sal could explain, Bessy showed up with a tray. She plopped two clay mugs of frothing ale on the table, followed by two plates of steaming hot food. Sal's mouth watered at the sight of golden-brown potato slices and char-blackened sausage all smothered in a thick brown gravy.

"Anything else I can get you boys?" asked Bessy.

"Another ale for me," said Vinny, raising his mug.

"Fine, thank you," said Sal, starting in on the eggs.

The eggs were poached, the yolks orange and runny. Sal skewered a bit of everything on the plate with his fork, gave it all a dip in the gravy, and stuffed his mouth to the point of bursting.

"What's this about being flush for work?" asked Vinny.

"Only that Salvatori is taking jobs for himself and not bothering to share his windfalls with his friends."

Vinny shot Sal a questioning look.

"That's not the half of it," said Sal, more defensively than he'd intended. "I'm doing some scouting for Luca. You know I would have refused if I hadn't feared a red smile in return. Lady's sake, you heard about Pavalo?"

"That mad ward-smith?" Vinny asked. "What's he done now?"

"Died," Bartley said through a mouthful of food.

"Murdered, way Nabu tells it," Sal said.

"Pavalo Picarri, murdered," said Vinny. "What for? Unless—" Vinny's eyes widened. "You don't think—the rat? But that would mean—"

"Luca," Sal said.

"Right," said Vinny. "If Luca thought Pavalo was the rat he would have done it himself. But do you really think it was Luca?"

Sal shrugged. "Difficult to tell. He didn't exactly cop to doing it."

"And you're going to do another job for the man?" Vinny asked. "Sacrull's hell, I wouldn't go near Luca for the next fortnight no matter what you paid me, you know how he is. If he's found one rat, chances are he's going to go looking for another."

"As I said, this is one obligation I'd rather shrug."

"You could give the job to someone that needs the coin," Bartley said sullenly.

Sal only shook his head.

"Well, some of us won't complain of the work."

"I believe even your breakfast has taken the point, Bartley," said Vinny in a consoling tone.

Bartley opened his mouth to retort, but Sal beat him to the punch.

"No, Vinny," Sal said. "He's right. I've turned my back on the crew. When have I ever put my neck out there and vouched for either of you? When have I ever put work your way?" Vinny smiled, but Bartley seemed nonplussed. "Though I suppose there were all those jobs in the past, but what's that matter? This is the here and now, and when, in the here and now, have I ever extended an invitation to one of Luca's jobs?" Sal paused for dramatic effect. "Oh, that's right, the bloody High Keep. And we all saw how that one turned out."

Vinny reached across the table and squeezed Bartley's shoulder playfully, but the little Yahdrish shook him off and stood. Bartley headed for the door, mumbling something about meeting with Anton, leaving half a plate of food untouched.

Vinny looked to Sal for an explanation, but Sal could only shake his head.

"Listen, I know you said you're not interested in working the collections route," Vinny said, "but you should come along anyhow. Anton sent word he wants to speak with you."

Sal's hand went back to his jerkin pocket where the locket hid. Anton's client was probably hounding him already. Sal was only surprised Anton had not done the same to him, but supposed he'd been a touch preoccupied with simply living. Sal nodded. "I thought he might want to."

Vinny arched an eyebrow, but Sal didn't deign to explain. Instead, he shoveled down what was left of his breakfast and set a silver krom and two iron dingés on the tabletop.

———————

As Sal, Bartley, and Vinny trekked across Low Town, the weather turned for the worse. Black storm clouds blew in from the north. Thunder sounded the arrival of lightning, which was followed by rain. Bartley remained sullen, while Vinny was his usual quiet self.

Sal didn't mind the lack of conversation. He was still feeling the euphoric effects of the skeev, and there was something about the storm that felt right. Sal put a hand into his jerkin pocket and felt the electric energy of the locket course through him. He opened his mouth to the sky and drank the rainwater. It felt to him that the storm was as much within him as it was without. The walk to

Anton's was by no means a quick jaunt. By the end, Vinny and Bartley looked sodden and bedraggled, but Sal felt invigorated, his time in the rain cut too short.

Anton's place was a mere loft above a warehouse down Penny Row. The warehouse was one of the older buildings and had apparently not received regular maintenance. The paint had peeled. The rushes were stale, which made the place smell something like a stable, though there were no signs of horses. Three-quarters of the warehouse was stocked with burlap sacks of barley and wheat, stacked high as a grown man.

The rickety staircase had grayed with age, though color could be found in the black and orange-brown molds that grew on the handrail and steps. The stairs creaked and moaned, shifting this way and that as the trio climbed. The higher they went, the more the staircase moved.

Vinny led the way, pushing open a trapdoor overhead and pulling himself through. Next went Bartley, only rather than pull through, the Yahdrish stopped halfway between loft and staircase.

Vinny let out a curse, and Bartley stumbled back down. Sal clutched the railing as the staircase drifted ominously far from the wall.

"What is it?" Sal asked. "What's happened?"

Vinny continued to string together a litany of curses in the loft above, while Bartley retched over the side of the railing.

"What's happened?" Sal asked again.

Vinny had quieted, but Sal still heard movement in the loft above.

Bartley continued to be sick, the miserable look on his face making it clear he wasn't going to explain anytime soon.

Trying not to knock his friend off the staircase, Sal slid past Bartley and made for the trapdoor. He reached up and heaved himself into the loft. Though he'd been prepared for the worst, the sight still took him by surprise.

Anton lay faceup in a pool of blood, a deep red gash across his throat and a blank stare in his open, lifeless eyes.

9

SOMETHING FOR THE PAIN

A grimace was fixed upon Anton's lifeless face. His hair was matted and clumpy with patches of dark dried blood. Besides the gash across his throat there were multiple wounds to his naked torso that had bloomed red.

Vinny poked at one of Anton's hands.

"What in the Lady's name are you doing?" said Sal.

"Come here," said Vinny, bending down for a closer inspection. "Look at his arms."

Sal got as close to the fresh corpse as he dared and looked as instructed.

Jagged cuts latticed Anton's forearms and wrists. The hands were stiff with rigor mortis, making them look more like the claws of some storybook creature than hands belonging to a soft-touch artist. In life, Anton had been one of the best pickers in the city. Now his hands were black with dried blood and his palms covered in gashes, so many that the soft flesh looked like chewed meat.

"Ugly business," said Sal.

Bartley poked his head up into the loft. His face took on a sickly look, and he went back down out of view.

"You know what it means?" Vinny asked.

"Anton must have grabbed the blade when he was stabbed," Sal said. "From the look of it, they tried stabbing him half a hundred times."

"Right, but what does this tell you?" Vinny asked, as though he were asking a question to which he already knew the answer.

Sal shrugged.

"The attacker approached him head on," said Vinny. "Elsewise, Anton never would have been able to grab at the blade."

"Oh?" Sal said.

"Also," Vinny went on, "it tells us whoever went for Anton is an amateur. Couldn't find the ass end of a pigeon until it shat in his eye."

"What makes you say that?" Sal asked.

"Obvious, isn't it? A hired man wouldn't have made such a botch of the job. A true professional would have come at him from behind, cut his throat first, and saved himself the dirty work."

"I wouldn't say that was obvious."

"All right, call it observably apparent."

"No," said Sal. "I mean, I think you might be wrong."

"Like hell," said Vinny. "How else would you explain the cuts on his hands?"

Sal took a moment to gather his thoughts. "Look at this place."

Vinny looked around the loft. Stark walls and musty rafters. Old rushes and dust-laden furniture. The sconces were coated thickly with layers of candle wax, the ceiling black from smoke.

"A grim place, I'll grant, and Anton here don't do much to cheer it up, but what's your point?"

"No windows," Sal said. "No doors aside from the trapdoor, no other way in or out."

"Meaning the amateur walked right through the bloody front door," said Vinny. "But you still seem to be making my point. The man was a novice, why else do this here?"

"This is Penny Row," said Sal, "the warehouse district. Where better to kill a man? Not a soul around after evenfall to hear his cries for help. Besides, it could be he found another way in—"

"What are we still doing here?" said Bartley, poking his head into the loft. His face had taken on a greenish hue, and he seemed unsteady.

Sal's stomach had been feeling a bit queasy at the sight of all the blood. "I wouldn't mind going elsewhere," Sal said frowning down at the corpse of his old acquaintance, a twinge of sadness coming on.

Vinny looked as though he might protest, until he took another look at Anton and closed his mouth, swallowing whatever he was about to say.

"Should we summon the steel caps?" Bartley asked.

Sal and Vinny shared a look and simultaneously shook their heads.

Though the black clouds remained overhead, the storm had dwindled to a light misting. The walk back to the Hog Snout seemed all the shorter for the distracted state of Sal's mind.

When the trio pushed through the inn's door they were dripping wet. The warmth of the hearth burning in the taproom was as welcome as the smell of cooking food. Though it wasn't quite midday, and he'd broken his fast mere hours ago, Sal was hungry enough to eat a dead crow.

When he voiced this, Bartley eyed him and gave a sickly frown.

Although it was still morning, the taproom was already filling with the midday crowd. A singer with a lute had reached the final verses of "The Abbot and His Shoe" as Sal and the others found a place at one of the few empty tables.

> "A song sung as a lesson, a song sung to refrain.
> Yes, a cautionary tale,
> a song sung to refrain, toooo refrain!"

Bessy came to their table just as the singer called for song requests from his audience.

"Back already?" Bessy asked, not unkindly.

"Bartley here insisted on it," Sal said, patting his friend on the back.

The little Yahdrish looked like a cat confronted by a bear, but Bessy only smiled warmly. "Well then, what'll it be, gents?"

"A round of the house ale," said Vinny. "And have a second round ready. I've a feeling we have a thirst today."

"Anything to eat?"

Vinny waved her off, and Bartley made a face as though he might retch then and there.

"What are you serving?" Sal asked.

"Cooky whipped up a catch-o'-the-day stew. Let's see here, think he said it was potatoes, leeks, and northern pike. Got a duck on the spit, honey and clove, you know the way he does them. Or if you're in the mood, some salt beef has come in from Kirkundy, not half bad, that. I like mine with a glass of fresh milk."

"Stew sounds just fine to me, though if you could try and snag me a bite or two of that duck, I'd much appreciate it."

Bessy smiled and walked off with a nod.

Meanwhile the singer continued to go around the taproom taking requests for his next song.

" 'When Pigs Don Armor,' " called a woman.

" 'The Fool's Wit,' " suggested another.

" 'Doppel Doppel Day'!" someone shouted.

" 'Piddle on the Diddler,' " said a man at the table next to Sal's.

"Aye, 'Piddle on the Diddler,' " said another from across the room.

"Wouldn't be proper," the singer protested. "I play a lute, not the fiddle."

Despite his protest, others had taken up the call for "Piddle on the Diddler," and the singer relented.

He strummed his lute a few times to give the room a chance to quiet back down. Then he started in on the first verse.

> "A diddler will diddle, that's what diddlers do.
> That doesn't mean it should happen to you."

"Back in the loft," said Vinny, "you told me the killer found another way in. What did you mean?"

"No, say I, and no, say you.
Piddle on the diddler, for that's what we do."

"Right. Well, assuming Anton's killer wasn't soft in the head, I'm guessing he didn't approach Anton from the trapdoor with knives drawn."

Bessy returned with three clay mugs of ale and a steaming trencher of catch-o'-the-day stew.

"Careful," Bessy warned. "Food's hot."

"And if a diddler diddles your mum,
you've a right to feel it's wrong.
Piddle on the diddler, it's what he deserves.
Piddle on the diddler, we'll all take turns."

Bessy moved on to the next table, and Sal dug into the stew. It was hot, as she had warned, and burned his tongue on the first bite. Still, it was delicious. The broth was white, creamy and rich, the pike flakey and tender, the potatoes buttery and soft, the leeks sweet and savory. Sal relished every bite. He'd finished half the trencher before he looked up and realized Bartley and Vinny were staring at him, their ales untouched.

"Piddle on the diddler, do what's right.
The diddler won't put up a fight."

"Something wrong with your drinks?" Sal asked.

"Our drinks?" said Bartley. "Sacrull's balls, what's wrong with you? How can you eat after seeing that?"

"Might be I'm just hungry," Sal said, returning to the stew.

"A diddler often diddles his own;
it chafes the gods deep to the bone.

> Piddle on the diddler, the man is sick.
> Piddle on the diddler, it is no trick."

Sal found the singer to be louder than he was talented, filling the already noisy room with an unnecessary racket that made it difficult to hold a conversation.

Vinny cleared his throat and Sal looked up from his meal.

"Well?" Vinny said.

"Sorry, what now?" Sal asked through a mouthful of potato.

> "A diddler's riddle is done alone.
> He'll touch himself till he's full grown.
> Piddle on the diddler in the name of the gods,
> he'll diddle himself by all the odds."

"Bloody hell," snapped Vinny. "You going to spill it before evenfall? If Anton's killer didn't come through the trapdoor, how'd he get in?"

"Ah, nearly forgot what we were talking about," Sal said, and took a drink of his ale. "Unless this killer knows black magic, I believe it's safe to say he entered the loft through the trapdoor."

"Hold on," said Vinny. "That's not what you said a turn ago."

> "For when a diddler diddles a dame,
> to his house there falls great shame.
> Piddle on the diddler if you know what's good."

"No, what I told you at Anton's is that the killer hadn't entered the loft knives drawn. He didn't storm up the stairs and through the trapdoor stabbing at Anton like some amateur. Rather, when he went through the trapdoor, it was under a false pretense."

"What do you mean?" said Bartley. "The killer got there first and lay in wait?"

Sal shook his head. "I don't think he did. Guessing from where Anton was lying, he'd only just let the killer through the door."

By the look on Vinny's face, he seemed to have grasped what Sal was saying, but Bartley was not quite so sharp; the look on his face was one of puzzlement.

> "Piddle on the diddler, as right you should.
> A diddler tries to shrug the blame,
> but all who know will curse his name.
> Piddle on the diddler, for all do see
> the diddler's ways bring infamy."

"Why would Anton have let a killer into the loft?" Bartley asked.

> *"And if the diddler diddles your sis,*
> *well, go on now, give the diddler a kiss.*
> *Don't piddle on the diddler, give him a pass.*
> *Don't piddle on the diddler lest you keep the lass."*

"Well," said Sal, "he would if he thought the person to be a friend, yeah?"

Bartley nodded.

> *"Now, everyone knows there is no crime*
> *half so bad as a woman diddled in the blind.*
> *Though before you go piddle, consider you this:*
> *If not for that diddler, who'd diddle your sis?"*

"Makes sense," said Vinny. "If Anton had been expecting a friendly sit-down he wouldn't have been armed. The bastard could have walked up close enough to smell Anton's breath before he drew his knife. Still, who?"

Who was a good question, but Sal thought he had a pretty good idea.

> " 'Hypocrisy!' the diddler would scream,
> *for diddling is not all diddling seems.*
> *He'd point the finger; they'd fall to their knees.*
> *The diddler would smile, for the diddler'd be pleased."*

Sal looked at Vinny and arched an eyebrow, but Vinny only shrugged. He turned to Bartley. The little Yahdrish frowned and shook his head.

"You can't think of anyone that might have wanted Anton dead?" Sal asked. "How about anyone who might have wanted Pavalo Picarri dead?"

It seemed realization struck them both at once.

"Sacrull's balls," Bartley cursed.

The three sat and drank their ales in silence, pondering this latest observation and all the implications which inevitably followed.

> *"At long last the diddler would be*
> *vindicated and piddle free.*
> *He'd hold up his hands, and he'd make a big scene.*
> *Then out from his mouth would come the obscene.*
> *'Everyone's a diddler, you fools, don't you see?*
> *We all ought to piddle on you, not me.' "*

A few of the patrons about the taproom clapped and whooped.

"Again!" shouted a man from the other side of the room.

"I'll get Bessy. She ought to know we're ready for that second round," Bartley said as he stood.

"Order a bottle of something with a kick," Vinny said as Bartley turned. "Fire-wine, boyo. I find myself in need of something stronger than the house ale."

Bartley nodded, turned back around, and collided headfirst with another taproom patron.

The man cursed and struck out with a fist.

The punch took Bartley in the jaw, and the little Yahdrish dropped to the floor like an empty wineskin.

Sal and Vinny jumped to their feet, flinging curses at Bartley's attacker like crossbow quarrels.

The man stopped without raining any more blows upon Bartley. Instead, he backed up a step. His companion closed in, chest puffed, fists clenched tight.

Both men were bigger than Sal, closer to Vinny's height and build, if not bigger. It was just his luck that they should want a fight.

Sal looked at the second man's tightly clenched fist and noticed a black mark between thumb and forefinger. He studied the tattoo and saw it was a black cross, the symbol of the Moretti crime family. The two looking for a fight were made men.

Sal readied himself for physical confrontation. He planned to distract one of the men and try not to get bloodied too badly before Vinny could finish with one of them and make his way over to help with the other.

"The fuck you think you are?" said Vinny.

"Bugger yourself," said the Moretti man who'd hit Bartley.

Vinny made his move, and Sal quickly followed suit.

Made men or not, Bartley was one of Sal's own.

"Hold it right there!" shouted Bessy as she moved between Sal and Vinny and the instigators. "I'll not have any brawls in my taproom."

Vinny's blood was hot, and when in that state he didn't much care to be told to stop. "That Sacrull damned craven hit Bartley."

"I saw the whole thing from across the room," Bessy said, chin up, chest out. "I'll not have it. The four of you can call off whatever this is or expect service at my inn to come to an end. Danilo, Bruno, I suggest you make your way from my premises. Don Moretti would be most displeased to hear you were causing trouble in one of his protected establishments."

Without protest, the two men turned and made their way to the door.

Only then did Sal notice how quiet the place had gotten. It seemed all eyes had been fixed on the scene they'd been making.

"I suggest the two of you help that one to his feet," Bessy said, motioning to Bartley.

Bartley was conscious, yet even after they had lifted him, he stared into the distance as tears came to his eyes.

"I only—," Bartley sniffed, "I only wanted another round."

Bessy smiled gently. "You're a lot of fools, you are, picking a fight with a pair like Bruno and Danilo. They're made men, you know?"

"No one touches one of ours," Vinny said, still shaking with anger. "Don't care if they're made men or monks of the Light."

Bessy let out a little chuckle, then went back to the kitchen and returned moments later with three ales and a bottle of fire-wine.

"Ales are on the house," said Bessy with a wink. "Bottle is three silver. And, Bartley, if your injury should need looking after, stop by my room come evenfall. Might be I can do something for the pain."

Bartley seemed to come to, his eyes going wide as a stupid grin formed on his bruised face.

MOTHER

Interlude, Eight Years Earlier

Sal fidgeted with the twine that tied the cheesecloth over the jar, then tucked the jar under his arm and took a deep breath. He told himself it was only a door handle, wrought iron plated with bronze.

Sal told himself it was just a door handle, but he knew better.

He reached, hesitated, and felt his hand begin to shake. All he had to do was grab and turn, grab and turn. Sal lifted his hand again, reached, and grabbed hold. He felt cold sweat forming on his brow and in his armpits.

The handle turned of its own accord.

Sal was nearly tugged off his feet. He lurched forward and ran headlong into Uncle Stefano.

He backed up a step and froze, his heart pounding like thunder as Stefano stepped into the hall.

"I—I—Uncle—"

"She's not feeling well," said Uncle Stefano. "No reason for you to bother her now with your stammering, boy."

"But I—"

"Run along. She needs her sleep."

Sal kept his eyes averted from Uncle Stefano's glare. Instead, he focused on his uncle's silver ring: a crest with the five colors of the Commission families and the falcon of Stefano Lorenzo. Sal raised the jar from the crook of his arm. "But, Uncle—"

"Salvatori?" said Mother, from within the room.

Uncle Stefano's nose wrinkled, and lines formed at the corners of his eyes.

"Stefano, send him in," said Mother in a voice weak as watered wine. "I want to see my boy."

Uncle Stefano motioned with his head as he stepped out, and Sal entered the dimly lit room. The curtains were drawn. Her room no longer smelled of meadowsweet as it once had, but rather of the smoke from an oil lamp that burned on the bedside table.

Mother lay in the bed, propped up by pillows. The down covers were pulled nearly to her chin. She looked drawn. Her eyes were sunken, red-rimmed as though she'd been crying.

Sal edged to where her thin hand motioned him. He held up the jar so that she could see it.

The smile she gave him was as false as the smile he gave her in return.

"A bit of honey from my honey boy," Mother said.

Sal untied the twine and peeled back the cheesecloth covering. The golden honey smelled sweet, with a hint of clove and cinnamon.

"Light's name," Sal cursed. "I've forgotten the spoon. I'll come right back."

"Nonsense," said Mother, dipping a finger into the jar. "Why else should we have hands if not to feed ourselves? Go on, give it a try."

Sal did as instructed, scooping a gob of sticky honey with a finger. Mother smiled—actually smiled—then broke off a piece of the honeycomb and popped it into her mouth.

It was the first real smile she'd given him in a long time, and it made his stomach flutter as though he'd swallowed a thousand butterflies.

And quick as it had come, the smile vanished, along with the butterflies.

"Is there anything you need?" Sal asked.

"I have all I could ever hope to ask for," Mother lied.

"Is there something I can do?"

"You can tell me how you've been, and how your sister has been. She's not come to see me of late."

"Nicola is the same as ever. She did threaten to pack her things and leave just the other night. She and Uncle had another spat over the name."

"She won't take the name?"

" 'Over my dead body' were her exact words, I believe."

"And you? How have you been?"

Sal shrugged. "I might do best to follow if Nicola does leave."

Mother frowned. "Surely you don't mean that. Your uncle only wants what is best for you."

"Best for me, or best for him?" Sal asked. "Uncle has made it quite clear he'd rather I wasn't around. I'm never allowed a word. Whenever he—"

"Your uncle has been good to us, good to you."

"In a way," Sal said grudgingly.

"You have no reason to be ungrateful," Mother said, her tone bordering on scolding. "Now, come here. Give me a kiss before you go."

Sal edged closer and pecked Mother on the cheek.

She grabbed him and pulled him in for a weak hug. "I love you, Salvatori, more than you will ever know," Mother whispered. "Great things are in store for you, and nothing will change. Not now, not ever. You will be a great man someday."

Mother let go, and Sal straightened up.

"Would you that I were more like Uncle Stefano?" Sal asked.

"Your uncle has made something of himself," Mother said. "In his own right."

"I could be like Uncle Stefano," Sal said. "I could."

"Salvatori, my sweet honey boy, you will be so much more than your uncle. There is so much more to you that you don't know, but you will. You will be a great man someday."

"I will, Mother," Sal said, tears rolling down his cheeks. "I promise I will. You'll see."

Mother smiled. "I know you will, love. I know you will."

SOUTH BRIDGE

With the first sip, Sal recalled how aptly named fire-wine was. He'd known what to expect, but had forgotten just how badly the stuff burned. Fire-wine was a Skjörund drink, preferred in the icy north for its warming properties, and preferred by Sal's crew for the nostalgia it brought.

From what tales told of the stuff, fire-wine was the breath of dragons cooled with ocean ice and barreled by monks living high in the Ironfall Mountains. It tasted like peppered honey poured over coals, and it put hair on a man's chest thick enough to shame a bear. Or so the stories went.

Sal found it all to be complete and utter horseshit. In his opinion, fire-wine was the piss of sour old men cooled with the blood of the unworthy and barreled by cross-eyed crones. The taste was difficult to discern through the pain. So far as the chest hair was concerned, Sal had yet to unbutton his shirt to check.

The liquor felt like liquid fire as it rolled over his tongue and slid down his throat. Even after the burning had reached his stomach, the sensation had not left his mouth. As Sal coughed, fearing he might make sick, Bartley and Vinny laughed, the first sign of positive emotion either had shown since finding Anton.

"Sacrull's balls, Salvatori," Bartley said mockingly. "I knew you were a maiden, but I'd thought that was only with the girls."

Sal started to reply, but before he could get out the word *eunuch* he launched into a fit of coughing.

"It'll put hair on your chest," said Vinny, snatching the bottle from Sal and taking a swig.

"Foul," Sal managed to say between coughs. He took a swig of his ale, hoping to wash down the taste of the fire-wine, but the instant he did, he knew he'd made a terrible mistake. The line of fire from tongue to stomach reignited.

From the looks on his friends' faces, they had noticed his dilemma. Seemingly unable to contain their mirth any longer, Vinny and Bartley burst into new fits of laughter.

At that moment Sal hated them, but within half a turn he was laughing about it as well. The alcohol had helped, dampening his worry and revealing a sense of joy he'd thought lost.

For a good hour the trio drank, talking and laughing all the while. Vinny ordered them another three rounds of the house ale in quick succession, while Bartley and Vinny continued to pass the bottle of fire-wine until the thing was half gone and Bartley looked ready to make sick all over again.

After a short break for drink and food, the singer resumed strumming his lute and started singing "The Queen's Old Goose," a seemingly silly song about a queen and her pet goose. In truth the song was a social commentary, written about King Tadej the Younger, great-grandfather to the current Duke Tadej. King Tadej the Younger was said to have been an incompetent ruler and an incapable lover. It was rumored that his wife, Queen Jessabelle, ruled the kingdom in his stead, pulling his strings like some master puppeteer. The song told most of the history of King Tadej's reign, hinting at his follies through analogies. The greatest of his follies was the loss of his kingdom to the king of Nelgand. Altogether the song was a masterpiece, even when sung by a less-than-talented musician.

When the singer reached the verse about the loose goose being noosed by his own goose with his own noose for being loose with his goose, Sal laughed and sang "*'A noose,' they cried, 'a noose, a noose!'*"

along with the rest. It felt good to laugh, like he was somehow lighter, the stress of the morning passing easily as a cloud in the wind. As though he didn't have a single problem in the world. As though he'd not found an old acquaintance dead on the floor just that morning.

With that thought, the black clouds returned. Sal was no longer in the mood to laugh. No longer in the mood for bawdy songs and drinking. The full weight of realization had come down on him.

"This is fucked," Sal said.

Bartley looked up from his ale. Vinny arched an eyebrow.

"First Pavalo," Sal said, "now Anton. Who's next?"

Vinny shrugged. "Who said there need be more?"

"Anton's corpse did," Sal said.

"How so?" Bartley asked.

Sal glanced at Vinny, but he seemed not to understand either. Sal sighed. "One body would mean that person was the rat. Luca would be expected to kill the rat. But two bodies," Sal said, shaking his head. "Two bodies means Luca is cleaning house. Tying up all the loose ends on that botched job to make certain things don't come back on him."

Bartley looked like he might be sick.

"Could be happenstance," said Vinny.

Sal put a hand over his pocket where the locket hid. "They were both involved with the High Keep job. A job that went all wrong after we ran headlong into the City Watch. Now, I'm certain you both recall the way we left Luca. He was sure we had a rat in the crew."

"Could be one of them was the rat," Bartley said, "and the other was killed for something else."

That sounded unlikely to Sal. He was confident the deaths were related, and the commonality lay in the botched heist. Sal was certain of that. "It's Luca," he said. "It has to be."

Vinny frowned, and Bartley covered his mouth.

"How can we know?" Vinny asked.

"We wait for the next body to drop," Sal said. "If Luca is cleaning house, we'll know it soon enough."

"And if no one else turns up dead?" Bartley asked.

"Then we know they died for something else," said Sal. "That, or you can assume one of them was the rat, and go on living life. All the while hoping Luca doesn't decide to put a knife in your back."

"Seems to me we're overreacting some," Vinny said. "We still don't know anything."

"You don't think Luca would kill someone over what happened at the High Keep?" asked Bartley.

"I'd expect him to kill all of us, just in case one of us was a rat," said Vinny. "But fact of the matter is, we don't know why Pavalo and Anton are dead. Anton had a lot of enemies, and Luca wasn't one of them so far as I know."

"So what do we do in the meantime?" said Bartley.

"The best thing to do is to lie low," Sal said. "We sit tight and wait for the information to come to us. Wet work isn't just done. Maybe nobodies like Pavalo get done on the quick, but if someone is going to do a made man, they would need permission from somewhere up the ladder."

"And?" Bartley asked.

"And soon enough, word will make its way down," Sal said. "When it does, we'll know something."

"And if word doesn't come down?"

"Then we will know things were done outside the proper channels," Sal said, "and we will know we have something to worry about."

"And if Luca does us first?" Bartley asked.

"Then you won't have much more to worry over, yeah?" Sal said.

Bartley shifted uncomfortably in his seat and Vinny took a swig of the fire-wine. Bartley snagged the bottle from Vinny and took a pull.

"Listen," said Vinny, "we're not going to learn what happened until word starts to make the rounds. Or Salvatori can go speak to his uncle and find out if permission was given."

Sal shook his head emphatically, and stopped when it made him dizzy enough that he thought he might get sick. "Not my uncle. I want to stay clear of him for a tick. At least until talk of the High Keep job has died down some."

"Right. So I guess until then we'd do well to make the best of the situation," said Vinny.

When Vinny didn't offer an explanation, Bartley prompted him. "Meaning?"

"We have work," said Vinny. "I say we head out and collect."

"I think it would be a bad idea," Sal said. "Who do you think they will go after once they learn someone's been out collecting on a dead man's name?"

"No one will know. We go and make the collections, keep everything. How would anyone ever find out who it was?" said Vinny.

"Lady's sake, Vinny, you can't do it, because it isn't done," Sal said.

"Don't see why not," Bartley said. "Seems like a sound plan."

"Right, then. See there, majority rules," said Vinny.

Sal wanted to smash their heads together. Though if they cracked open, Sal expected he would find them empty of brains. He had to take a deep breath to settle his rising frustration.

"Look," Sal said, calmly as he could manage, "We've already been over this, it would be against the Code. You never collect on the name of a dead man unless you're claiming the stake, and you can only do that with the approval of the Commission."

"The Code?" said Vinny. "You keep bringing it up, but, Salvatori, you're not a made man, I'm not a made man, and Anton is bloody dead. We don't have to follow the Code. We're outside that life."

Sal swallowed the string of curses that came up. "You've never dealt with these guys, Vinny. If the crow-cages scare you, then the stories my uncle has told me will make you piss your underclothes. Don't try to collect without claiming a stake. Let me talk to my uncle for you, and he can get you with the right people. Do this thing the right way."

Vinny glared at Sal, a drunken belligerence showing in his eyes. He turned to the Yahdrish. "That makes you and me, Bartley. Two-way split on the night's profit, no tax. We'll get away clean and have a little coin in our pockets by false-light. No one out there knows Anton is dead."

"Aside from Anton's killer," said Sal. "It's a fool's errand. If you're found out, it'll mean death."

Vinny took a swig of the fire-wine, then looked pointedly at Bartley. "Let's go, before the storm starts up again."

Bartley fiddled with his clay mug.

Vinny motioned toward the door with his head, but Bartley looked down at the floor.

"Bartley?"

"I don't think it would be a good idea to break the Code," said Bartley.

Vinny slammed his fists on the table. He looked at them both with eyes like flint. Then he stood up, spat, and headed for the door.

Sal considered going after him but thought better of it. Vinny might be only half Norsic, but Sal suspected that was the half that came out when he drank.

Bartley reached for the fire-wine and took a long swig.

Watching Bartley sway in his seat made Sal realize just how drunk Vinny likely was. Collecting protection tax that deep in his cups was dangerous in its own right. Not to mention everything else wrong with Vinny's plan. For a second time Sal considered going after his friend, and again he remained in his chair as a thought occurred to him.

"What if it was the Commission that was responsible?" Sal said.

Bartley was rubbing at his eyes, a stupid smile plastered on his face. "A what?" he said, nearly polishing off the bottle with another long draw.

"The Commission. What if Anton did something wrong? What if he was killed because of something he did?"

"Anton, yeah, he's dead—dead as they get. Sacrull's balls, but I never thought he could have died. Not after that poleaxe."

Bartley went to take another drink of fire-wine, but Sal snatched the bottle from the Yahdrish's hand. He set the bottle on the floor and told Bartley it was time to head up to his room. Bartley, for his part, told Sal to shove a thick something up his wet somewhere. Sal was able to decipher the meaning of the slurred words without the accompanying hand gestures, though Bartley had provided them for clarity's sake.

When Bessy next passed, Bartley ordered them another round, only this time, instead of asking for the house ale he asked for kagish, a Shiikali wine known for its dry taste and cheap price.

When he'd finished his kagish, Sal's thoughts were swimming through a sea of molasses. He could only imagine how Bartley felt. When Bessy stopped by once more, she didn't ask what they wanted to drink, merely bent down and whispered something into Bartley's ear.

The curly-haired Yahdrish sat bolt upright and seemed to sober up in a heartbeat.

"We should head up," Bartley said once Bessy had walked away, a bead of drool running from the corner of his mouth into the patchy scruff on his chin.

"What'd she say to you?" Sal asked, though he thought he had a pretty good idea.

Without another word wasted, Bartley stood and began to hobble toward the staircase. Sal followed suit, hoping he didn't look nearly so drunk as his companion.

Once in the room, Bartley went for the drawer where he kept his ebony box. Sal began to salivate. As Bartley crumbled the golden-brown powder into the pipe, Sal used a bit of flint to light the hand-lamp. He handed Bartley the lamp, which the Yahdrish used to ignite the skeev, and soon the room was filled with white smoke that tasted acrid and burned his eyes.

Sal felt a rush of euphoria, not so intense as it had been in the past, but enough to settle his craving. He'd seen people who'd developed an addiction to skeev, heard of how they needed to do the drug or they'd find themselves in a bad way. They would develop the sweats, followed by the shakes, stomach cramps, and intense thirst. The effects usually lasted one to three days, depending on the degree of the skeever's addiction. A mender had told Sal that it was the vomiting that most often killed them.

Sal had never experienced any of the adverse effects of skeev aside from the need to continually up the dose to achieve the same high. However, looking at Bartley's sunken cheeks, red eyes, and yellowing teeth, Sal wondered if the drug wasn't taking a toll on his friend. Had Bartley ever experienced the sweats or the shakes? Until then Sal had never thought to ask.

Bartley was loading another bowl of skeev, crumbling the mushroom cap between his fingers. Only a portion of the golden-brown powder found its way into the pipe; the rest of what Bartley ground up in his drunken state fell to the floor, wasted. Despite this, the skeev had somewhat sobered him. It was one of the strange effects of the drug: the more one used, the more it seemed to counteract the effects of alcohol.

"Where do you buy your skeev?" Sal asked.

Bartley paused. "Looking to start buying for yourself?"

"I'm only curious. The stuff has been in Dijvois for years, and yet in the last couple of span, it's become far more prevalent. Might be worth investing some coin on the distribution end."

"A business opportunity?" Bartley asked.

"Could be someone is already making a big play on the market," Sal said with a shrug. "I'll have to ask my uncle if he's heard of any deals being made within the Commission."

"My guy's name is Ticker," said Bartley. "He might know something. He's been in the business awhile now."

"Right. Well, if you can put in a word for me, I'd much appreciate the gesture."

Bartley put the flame to the bowl of the pipe, drawing on the stem in short, sharp inhalations. When he exhaled, a cloud of white smoke rolled from his open mouth. He coughed and handed Sal the pipe and lamp.

"What about Luca?" Bartley said, as though continuing a conversation they'd been having.

"What of him?" Sal asked, confused by the question.

"You know, what if Luca was behind it."

"Lady's sake, Bartley, where were you the last few hours?" Sal said. "I thought it was decided. We don't know for certain, so we're going to wait and see what we hear."

"No, I mean what about your job?" Bartley said. "Aren't you supposed to be working a job for Luca?"

"Lady's tits," Sal cursed. He'd nearly forgotten about the scouting job.

"What'll you do?"

"Not much I can do but finish the job," Sal said, gritting his teeth.

"Right, then," said Bartley. "If there is nothing to be done about it, suppose we'd best do nothing. Now, are you going to smoke that, or do you mean to have your way with it?"

Sal touched the lamp flame to the pipe. As he inhaled, the powder flickered cherry red. His lungs burned, and he coughed violently as he exhaled in short, stuttered breaths. Then came the feeling, a sort of pressure behind his eyes, a rush of euphoria at the back of his skull. His world spun, but he hung on to the feeling, taking the ride for the pleasure of it. He passed the pipe back to Bartley and set the lamp on the bedside table. Bartley placed the pipe in the box and snuggled the box back into its proper place in the dresser drawer.

"I best be off, then," Bartley said. "You're welcome to stay here if you need a place to sleep, the bed ought to be free for the nonce."

"What's this, then? It's only midday, what's all this talk of beds?" said Sal. "And just where are you going? If you're going to join Vinny, know that's a fool's errand."

"If you don't want to use the bed, sleep on the floor. Midday or not, you look as though you are going to sleep," Bartley said. "As for my business, it's a man's business."

Suddenly it dawned on Sal where Bartley was headed.

"Bessy?" he asked.

Bartley couldn't help but crack a smile. "She has two hours before the dinner bell, and I mean to make the most of them both."

Sal took his cloak and one of Bartley's blankets and returned to his makeshift bed among the rushes. He curled up like a cat, and before he knew it, sleep took him.

H*elp me*, it said.

But Sal couldn't move, paralyzed as though he'd petrified. Dumb, yet not deaf. Bereft of feeling but not of sight.

Help me, it moaned.

Sal couldn't turn away, couldn't close his eyes. He tried to open his mouth, but found it shut tight. He was forced to stare into the sightless, cloudy blue eyes of the corpse.

Help me, pleaded the corpse, though the blood-crusted lips never moved, the pale, waxy face twisted in an eternal grimace.

There is nothing I can do, nothing I could have done, Sal thought.

You should have helped, replied the corpse. It held up bloody hands, the flesh torn to ribbons from palms to elbows. *Should have helped.*

What could I have done? You were dead. Dead before we found you.

The hands spasmed as they reached out. *Should have helped.*

The hands came closer, black and red, scarce looking like hands at all, but Sal couldn't move, couldn't look away. He was forced to watch, eyes wide, as the hands came closer, Anton's lifeless eyes staring into his.

Help me, said Anton's corpse. *It must be you.*

Cold, dead hands grabbed him by the throat, and though there was no pain, he could no longer breathe. As Sal panicked and tried to thrash for air, Anton looked into his eyes. Only, the face of the corpse no longer belonged to Anton. Somehow it had changed. The face now belonged to his mother.

Should have helped, it said.

Sal burst awake. With a surge of will, he forced his face away from the cloak that had nearly suffocated him. He rolled onto his back, gasping for air. Sheathed in sweat, he shivered as a chill ran through him.

He looked around, and though it was dark, he quickly realized he was still lying on the floor of Bartley's room. It had only been a dream. He wondered how long he'd slept. A few hours, at least, as the sun had set and the Lady White was in full bloom.

Sal used the blanket to wipe the sweat from his face and arms, brushed the dust and straw from his cloak and slipped it on. He sat on the bed and tried to relax. After he'd caught his breath, he decided to light a candle, and with the light found himself moving to the dresser drawer where Bartley kept his carved ebony box.

The feeling of being watched crept up the back of Sal's neck, but when he looked over his shoulder, there was nothing behind him but faint light and flickering shadows. Bartley must still have been in Bessy's rooms. Sal turned back to the drawer. The brass knobs of the drawer were cold to the touch, but it slid open quietly, if reluctantly.

Jade was set in the relief of the Dahuaneze goddess carved into the lid of Bartley's box. Sal brushed the back of a finger along the hem of the goddess's dress for luck, the same as if she were the Lady White, and lifted the ebony box from the drawer.

Sal had accepted the Lady White as his patron years ago. It had been shortly after the incident at the Moretti card game that Sal had decided to break all but his final tie to his uncle. He had put aside his uncle's god for a goddess of his own.

It was said she was the child of Tiem and Sacrull, wife and son of Solus. The Lady White was the result of lust, rape, and betrayal. Unwanted by her mother, she was cast from the world and made to find a new home. Unwilling to live with her father in the Under Realm, she chose the heavens. But Solus would not have her in his sky, the constant reminder of betrayal that she was, and so she avoided his eye, never showing her face in the sky of day. Instead she made night her home, providing light to those who, like her, had been cast out into the dark.

Sal placed the box on the straw-stuffed mattress and lifted the lid with a twinge of guilt. He thought he sensed something or someone. A presence of some kind. He whipped around. His eyes searched all about the small room, but again he saw naught but shadows dancing in time with the movement of the flame.

Inside the box were six golden-brown caps of skeev, a roll of wicking, a pipe, and a shard of flint. It took him mere moments to crumble half a cap into the pipe, light a handlamp, and fill the room with a cloud of thick white smoke.

Sal sat on the straw mattress and propped his back against the wall, a feeling of euphoria coursing through his entire body. When he closed his eyes, it was as though someone began talking to him, calling him, urging him to open his eyes.

There was no sound aside from the noise inside Sal's head, yet he heard the call nonetheless. Like the prod of a hot iron, the feeling made him stir.

His eyes shot open, and for the third time since waking in Bartley's room, Sal sensed a presence. He searched the room, unable to determine where the call had come from. He was alone, and yet he couldn't shake the feeling of being watched.

The call sounded again, so faint it was difficult to hear, and somehow too urgent to ignore. It was then Sal realized what was urging him. He reached into the pocket of his jerkin and slipped out the locket. It was warm to the touch, and it sent tendrils of energy surging through him. Sal stared at the tarnished gold, running a skeev-coated fingertip over the three vertical slashes.

The locket seemed to drink in the golden-brown residue of the skeev.

Sal pulled his finger back as though bitten, though he felt no pain, physical or otherwise. Instead, the current of energy flowing from the locket into the hand which held it seemed to increase tenfold. He felt stronger, faster, nigh on invincible.

There was a boom of thunder, and Sal felt the storm closing in. Only, when he looked out Bartley's window, he saw a clear night.

It was happening again. Sal moved away from the window, fearing he would be pulled through just as he had on the night he'd stolen the locket. He still didn't know whether the events that night had been real or imagined, but whatever the case he wasn't willing to risk it.

Sal looked at the locket. He thought about what Nabu had told him, and the recollection sent a shiver down his spine. This thing was dangerous, and Sal knew it. Nabu had said as much, hadn't he? No, he had said more.

"Destroy it," Nabu had said.

With one last look at the tarnished gold locket, Sal's mind was decided. He slipped his cloak on, jammed the locket back into the pocket of his jerkin, and headed out the door.

Once down the stairway, through the taproom, and outside the Hog Snout, Sal breathed deeply of the crisp night air. He made for South Bridge, weaving a route through alleys and side streets, past flophouses, warehouses, alehouses, skeev-houses, and whorehouses. He took the long way around to avoid the Magistrate's Compound, cutting through Docker's Avenue and up the Bayway, when he saw something that nearly caused him to trip over his own feet.

A gang of street urchins twenty strong lined either side of the Bayway ten paces ahead of Sal. The instant he stopped, they moved to block the street ahead, closing in like a pack of feral dogs.

When alone, or in small groups of two or three, street urchins often resorted to begging. They would position themselves on streets leading to and from marketplaces, or near the steps of Knöldrus Cathedral, grasping at skirt hems or shirt sleeves and pleading for iron dingés or scraps to soothe their aching bellies.

They were harmless.

But a gang of street urchins twenty strong was another matter entirely. They'd been known to prowl the streets of Low Town at night, setting ambushes in the quieter places and alleys, waiting for a lost noble or an alehouse drunkard to stumble past.

Sal reached for his boot and drew his pigsticker. Nine inches of cold steel flashed in the moonlight as Sal readied himself for an attack.

Twenty pairs of sunken eyes looked to the apparent leader, a pug-nosed, round-faced kid half a head taller than the next biggest, and nearly of a height with Sal.

Sal backed away slowly, his pigsticker held out before him, a silent threat but not one to go unheard.

Wordlessly the leader shook his head, and the gang dispersed, slinking back into the shadows, behind old fish crates and piles of rubbish and into the alcoves and alley mouths along the Bayway.

Sal slipped into the nearest alley, tucked away his knife, and climbed up a loosely mortared wall. The air was cooler, fresher upon the rooftop. The slight breeze chilled his slick skin beneath sweat-soaked cloth.

Moving through Low Town by rooftop was slower than walking the cobblestones, and although there were no clay-shingle roofs to contend with, the rooftops of Low Town presented dangers of their own. Many of the structures were old and had been left to deteriorate with time. Others were poorly built, with rafters too weak to support the weight of a man. Both the neglected and the poorly constructed had to be avoided. Some parts of Low Town, like the Kettle, the Lowers, the Narrows, and the Shoe, were simply impossible to navigate by rooftop, as many of the homes were wattle-and-daub shacks roofed with straw.

Despite the drawbacks, one obstacle the rooftops of the Bayway did not present was a gang of street urchins. Likely victims of the urchin gangs were most often found at ground level, as anyone walking the rooftops was likely a thief or a hired killer.

To Sal's relief, he reached South Bridge without incident.

In truth, South Bridge wasn't one, but two bridges, which connected Low Town and High Town via the Big Island. Sal walked out across the damp planks of the Low Town half, pleased to find the bridge empty. The bridge towers looked to be vacant, as there was no light shining through the arrow slits.

Sal approached the stone parapet. The bridge planks creaked underfoot. He was still uncertain whether he would follow through with his plan, uncertain whether he could.

Sal reached into the pocket of his jerkin and shivered at the contact between skin and metal. The smells and sounds of an approaching storm filled his mind. The locket was warm to the touch—strange how it seemed to change. When he took hold of the locket, it sent a jolt of energy into Sal's arm and throughout his body, an alien feeling but one Sal had come to enjoy.

He gripped the locket tightly in one hand and placed the other upon the rough stone of the parapet to support his now shaking legs. Reflected moonlight danced on the surface of the black water below. He looked down at the tarnished gold locket and noticed the tips of his fingers were still coated in the golden-brown skeev residue. His hand shook, and the energy of the locket continued to pulsate in him, the sounds of rolling thunder filling his mind.

Sal knew what he had to do. Since the day he'd walked into Nabu's shop and seen the fence's reaction to the locket, he'd known.

He had to be rid of the thing.

He pulled his arm back and focused on a spot way out in the black water of the Tamber.

Sal threw the locket, but before he let go, he felt a tug so jarring it ripped him from his feet with the force of a lightning bolt. For an instant his throat, stomach, and manhood seemed to occupy the same space. He tore through the air. An overwhelming sense of nausea and vertigo swept through him, and the next instant he went crashing into the cold black water.

The current of the Tamber swept Sal along with it like a leaf in a windstorm.

As he fought to keep his head above the surface, the cold water made his chest feel constricted so that he gasped for air and could not catch his breath. His limbs felt weak and sluggish. He was unable to fight the overwhelming power of the river's current.

He needed both hands if he was to keep himself above water. Yet he found he was unable or unwilling to let go of the locket still clutched tight in one fist.

His mind was numb, his head throbbing, and all the while the sound of rolling thunder and the pulsating energy of the locket consumed his thoughts.

It had happened again, as it had the night he'd fallen from his window. He'd been pulled an impossible distance by an unstoppable force. Only this time he was going to die, drowned like a wet rat.

He kicked, flailed, and trod water. It was all he could do to keep his head above the surface, and still it got into his mouth as he tried to breathe. He drank it unwillingly, sputtering and coughing with each forced gulp. The river was ice cold, and each breath was more difficult to draw than the last. If only he could swim out, but the current was too fast, the shore an impossible distance.

Then it hit him, an idea that struck like a bolt of lightning.

Sal focused on the shore and used all the power his mind retained to will himself toward it.

Lightning took hold of him, a sharp sense of vertigo and an organ-jarring jolt. Suddenly Sal was skidding across cobblestones on hands, elbows, and knees until finally he came to a stop. He sputtered and coughed, then doubled over trying to catch his breath.

After a moment Sal rolled onto his back, taking deep breaths and staring up at the starlit sky. He had survived, against all the odds, against the very laws of nature; he had managed to pull himself from the grip of certain death.

Sal got up on his hands and knees. The pain made him wince. He was covered in scrapes and bruises, his heart pounded against his chest, and his head felt ripe to bursting.

Then something took hold of him, a sort of madness, an idea that was felt more than it was thought. An idea he couldn't resist trying. He clutched the locket tight in his palm, the current of energy flowing, tendrils of electricity taking root as he centered his mind.

Sal focused on the roof of a nearby building and willed himself there, gripping the locket tight. The next instant, he rode the lightning. Vertigo returned as he lurched forward, rushed through the air, and landed feetfirst upon the rooftop.

BANISHED

B y morning the events of the night before felt like a dream. Sal had done magic—again.

It was not the sort of commonplace magic done by the local Talents. Sal had done magic told of only in stories. Now it seemed the locket was something far more spectacular than he could have imagined. He almost couldn't believe he'd intended to throw the thing into the river.

Sal rolled out of bed, groggy and sore. His body was throbbing, scraped and bruised from head to toe, but he forced himself to dress through the pain. His mind was full of questions, and there was one person he knew that might have answers.

The house was quiet. Sal guessed Nicola had already headed out for the day. He hoped her plans didn't involve Oliver Flint. Of all the men Nicola had brought home over the years, that one had rankled Sal more than most. However, she might have trouble seeing him if those steel caps from the other night had clapped Oliver in irons for resisting arrest outside the Bastian estate. So far as they knew, the man who'd thrown the flasher in his escape had been named Oliver Flint. Still, Sal didn't wish that on the man; even that oily toff didn't deserve such a fate as the under-cells, nor for that matter the crow-cages.

Sal checked the kettle hanging in the hearth and spooned out a bite of simmering pottage before he headed off into the morning storm and made for Penny Row.

As he walked, Sal kept a hand inside the pocket of his jerkin, clinging to the locket and drinking in the rain as the smooth gold pulsated faintly in his palm. Oddly enough, unlike the night before, the locket was cold to the touch. The rain felt good on his sore body. It seemed to dull the pain somehow, and made the walk seem all the shorter for it.

Just as Sal reached Penny Row he saw the door of Nabu's shop open, and to his dismay a pair of steel caps exited. They clinked with every step as their sword hilts rubbed their chain mail hauberks. For an instant, Sal worried that they were there for him, but he quickly convinced himself the notion was nonsense.

Still, the steel caps were headed in his direction. Panic took root, and Sal considered running, but that was pure madness, bound to get him killed. Sore as he was, he couldn't have outrun a lame child, much less two armed steel caps.

Instead, Sal knelt and bent down to hide his face, pretending to adjust his boot. When the steel caps had passed, Sal stood and headed for Nabu's shop, hoping he wouldn't come face to face with more steel caps inside.

The sweet smoke of burning incense couldn't mask the reek of mildew within the shop. Nabu had yet to clean the cobwebs that clung to every corner and sconce, or the dust that had collected on every surface in the shop. The Miniian rugs looked so tattered and threadbare they might have been older than Dijvois itself.

Nabu Akkad was alone in the shop. He leaned behind the counter, drumming the fingers of one hand on the countertop, the rings upon his fingers rapping the wood with a soft *click, click*. With his other hand, he stroked his braided black mustache.

"Ah, the face of welcome company," Nabu said, one eyebrow arched. "The gods are good, yes?"

"Good morrow, Nabu. Trouble with the City Watch?"

The fat man winced. He stroked his mustache with his right hand and tapped the counter with the ringed fingers of his left, *click-click, click-click.* "Trouble, oh yes. This City Watch is full of greedy thieves. More even than your Commission. Always with the collections, always I am paying and always they are wanting more."

"Collections?" Sal asked in surprise. "Why should you pay a tax to the steel caps? You pay your due to Don Svoboda, don't you?"

Nabu flashed a sad smile. "A man would not stay in business long if he did not pay his protection fees to his don. But when these City Watchmen come knocking on my door, I must pay, yes? Not even the power of the Don Svoboda can protect a man from the magister's hounds."

"How often does the Watch collect?"

"I am thinking once a fortnight, sometimes more, sometimes less. Though this is not the only reason for their visit this day."

Sal sensed a trap but couldn't keep his curiosity in check. "Why were those steel caps bothering you?"

Nabu examined his fingernails. "What else should a man with my talents for procurement be harassed for but the very nature of his business? These men came to me asking for information about a certain item. A stolen item."

Sal rolled his shoulders and yawned, feigning nonchalance, as cold sweat beaded in his armpits. "Something of value?"

"Jewelry," Nabu said, leering at Sal across the counter. "A locket. Old gold, and round, they said it was, with three vertical lines upon the face."

Sal went cold. His heart felt like to burst. It had grown hard to breathe and nigh on impossible to speak.

"These City Watchmen, they seemed most interested in this item. Said a man would be well rewarded if he were to come across such a thing."

Sal took a slow, labored breath. "What did you tell them?"

There was little warmth to be found in Nabu's stony expression. "That my shop operates under the king's laws of Nelsigh and the laws of their duke. There has been no one trying to sell stolen goods of late. Should any such attempt this thing, I shall alert the noble order of this City Watch posthaste."

The hammering of Sal's heart slowed. "I thank you for your discretion, Nabu."

"I trust there is no chance this thing will be bothering me any longer?" Nabu said, one thick eyebrow arched. "You did destroy it, yes? It is gone?"

Sal looked down at the dirt-stained Miniian rug. The weight of Nabu's eyes had grown too heavy to bear.

"You have not come here with such a thing. This I know. You would not make such a trespass."

"Nabu, I—"

"Know this, Salvatori Lorenzo: lie to me now, and you will never again be welcome within these doors."

"I need to know more," Sal said. "Why would the steel caps want it, and why do you fear—"

"Out!" shouted the fat man as he lost his temper.

It had happened again, just like the time Sal had shown Nabu the locket. Without explanation, Nabu had grown angry and fearful.

Sal backed up a step.

"Please, Nabu, what is—"

"Out!"

Sal turned and went for the door. He left the dingy shop with a stomach full of guilt and a head like to split with questions.

A BOLD REQUEST

INTERLUDE, EIGHT YEARS EARLIER

The dark stone walls of the hallway seemed to close in around him as he stood looking at the brass handle of the door. Without giving thought to caution, Sal put a hand on the door handle and turned. He barged in, bold as a king entering his sleeping chambers. Resplendent light shone through the bay windows like the very image of Solus himself, reflecting from the thousands of crystals on the golden chandelier that hung at the ceiling's center.

Sal stepped onto the elaborately patterned Miniian rug and froze.

Three men were in Uncle Stefano's solar.

The look Uncle Stefano fixed on Sal could have spoiled salt. It made him want to turn tail and run, as fast and far as his feet would take him. Still, he had no choice. He would do it for Mother. He swallowed, steeled his nerve, and approached his uncle's high-backed armchair.

A glance at the two men standing behind Uncle Stefano set his entire body to shaking: Benito and Hamish, a pair of thugs that were as ugly as they were mean. Hamish, a red-haired Kirkundan, looked the more formidable of the pair with his toned muscular build, but Sal knew that beneath the sagging fat and flesh, Benito Rici was the more dangerous of the two. Nearly twice the age of Hamish, Benito had been in his uncle's service as long as Sal could remember. Fat and balding and with a goiter to boot, Benito was nothing to look at, but in a scrap he was one of the best men in the city to have at your side.

"What do you want, boy?" Uncle Stefano asked, removing his reading lenses.

"I—I'm sorry, Uncle. I hadn't realized—"

"Did you barge in here only to stammer like a jackanapes? Out with it."

Benito and Hamish made low chuckling noises.

Sal clenched his hands into tight fists. It was now or never. "Uncle, I believe I'm ready."

Lines formed at the corners of his uncle's eyes as his frown deepened.

"I'm ready to earn my keep," Sal said, hoping the clarification might spark a different response.

"Oh?" said Uncle Stefano, arching an eyebrow.

The ugly brutes behind his uncle exchanged a look. Benito cleared his throat, and Hamish smiled a big, dumb smile.

"And how is it you propose to earn your keep, boy?"

"I can work for you."

"Work for me? Just what is it you think you would do for me?"

"I could earn."

Benito scoffed, while Hamish laughed aloud.

Uncle Stefano didn't laugh. He didn't even give Sal his usual frown. Instead, he stroked his chin. He sat that way for a moment, silent, thoughtful. But eventually the frown formed, and Uncle Stefano shook his head. "What would your mother say?"

"She would be proud," Sal said.

"Proud?" asked Stefano, then understanding seemed to come over him.

"Yes, proud," Sal said defiantly. "She would know that—that no matter what—what happens, she would know that I can earn my keep."

After an instant that seemed to stretch for a turn, Stefano gave a curt nod toward the door.

"I'll think on it. Now, I've business."

He could feel his legs shaking, but Sal kept his feet planted.

Stefano's eyes narrowed.

"You want me to take care of this?" asked Benito.

"I'll do it," said Hamish, stepping toward Sal.

Stefano held up a hand, his silver ring reflecting the light. Hamish stopped in his tracks.

"Take a seat, boy."

Sal stopped holding his breath, amazed he'd managed to defy his uncle and walk away unscathed. No, not walk away, join. He was going to join his uncle. He took a seat in the high-backed armchair beside Stefano. He sat up straight as an arrow, although it was all he could do not to collapse into the chair with a sigh.

Just then the door opened, and Greggings entered. Two bearded Yahdrish men followed in the servant's wake.

"May I present Master Achava Cherkas and his son, Adar."

"Please, be seated," said Uncle Stefano, gesturing toward the divan across from him and Sal.

The older man nodded, taking his long beard in hand as he sat. "Most kind of you, most kind."

With everyone seated, Greggings closed the door.

Uncle Stefano proffered a hand palm up, signaling for the Yahdrish to begin.

"My Lord," said the gray-bearded one, "this past fortnight has been one of difficulty for my family. My son has just had a son of his own. My daughter—an accident has left her—I tell you this so that you might understand the predicament in which I find myself. You see, I have paid my dues to your man, but these past weeks another has come calling, claiming rights of collection."

Stefano's jaw was clenched as the Yahdrish spoke.

"Who?" Stefano asked.

"Bruno Carbone," said the younger Yahdrish. "He has claimed right of collection under Alonzo Amato."

"Amato?" asked Stefano.

"He's one of Moretti's," said Benito. "Got a crew."

Stefano nodded. "Achava, you have my condolences for your hardships. You would ask of me a boon, for your loyalty. You have kept faith, and I shall keep faith with you. Consider the matter taken care of."

The gray-bearded Yahdrish practically jumped to his feet. His head lowered, he murmured praises to Stefano. His son, Adar, stood beside him, thanking Stefano as well.

Stefano nodded, and the men moved for the door, which was opened swiftly by Greggings. When the Yahdrish men had left, Uncle Stefano turned to Sal.

"Your thoughts?"

Sal's mind began to race. This was a test, but what did his uncle want to hear?

"I would send a pair of thugs, not unlike the ugly brutes behind us," Sal said, hardly believing his own audacity. "I'd have them speak with this Carbone fellow, let him know whose protection these Yahdrish are under. And if he and his don't back off, give him a taste of steel."

Stefano looked at Sal, emotionless, his face betraying nothing of his thoughts. Then he nodded. "You may leave."

Heart racing, wondering whether or not he'd done well, Sal stood and went for the door.

14

FITZEN

A chill in the air warned of the approaching season, as if the bustling streets of the city were not enough to remind him. Fitzen was upon them, the holiday of winter's welcome.

Fitzen wasn't all bad, Sal merely wasn't in a mood to celebrate. He'd been feeling down. The second incident with Nabu had been the catalyst for a series of questions that had eaten at his mind for weeks. The constant nightmares that plagued his sleep had kept him on edge as well. Always the same dream: Sal, alone in Anton's place, Anton's bloody corpse asking him for help, telling him he could have helped, he could have done something. Always it ended the same. The corpse would twist and writhe. It would change shape before his very eyes until it took on the image of his mother, her voice, her words, her blood.

Sal would wake in a sweat, gasping for breath, tears welling in his eyes. It was enough to make him wish he'd never found Anton. Enough to make him wish someone else had been saddled with the burden of that discovery, the burden of his guilt.

He'd had steady work with the side jobs he, Vinny, and Bartley had been able to find, along with the scouting job he was doing for

Luca—the job he could not seem to shake, from the employer he feared yet could not seem to escape.

It felt as though he'd spent a lifetime watching the Bastian family, memorizing every movement of their day. He'd spent weeks observing the house, learning the routines and habits of the guards and household servants, as well as weeks following the routines of both Lord Hugo and his daughter, who Sal had learned was named Lilliana.

The time spent watching the Bastian estate was like pulling his own fingernails. Cloudless hot days on the rooftop, and days of heavy rains and cold winds, Sal had braved them without complaint, thankful the snows had not come early. Not all days were torture. There were even some he looked forward to, the days he spent following Lilliana.

After nearly two months spent watching the Bastian estate, Sal had come to realize Lilliana Bastian was the most beautiful woman in Dijvois, if not all of Nelgand. She had black hair that fell just past her shoulders, eyes of lapis lazuli, and soft pink lips made for kissing. Her olive skin was not the milk-white flesh common to her class, but showed she'd spent time in the sun. Her sense of fashion was unique, elegant but simple, with a streak of fearlessness that bespoke a rebellious nature.

She lived the charmed life of the nobility, though it seemed much of her time was spent in Low Town. While she did spend a goodly amount of her time shopping, Sal had seen her take much of the clothing and food she purchased to street urchins in some of the nastier parts of the city, even giving some of them coin.

It was a futile, even foolish gesture, as Sal had seen firsthand the destructive nature of well-intentioned giving. Still, it was the thought that counted. Sal couldn't fault her for ignorance. Though he couldn't seem to fault her for anything.

When she smiled, Sal felt himself smile in turn; likewise when she laughed. She was his muse, his inspiration for going to work each day. He even found that after a time he'd grown jealously protective of Lilliana.

Still, he was a damned fool to harbor any hope of ever attaining her favor. Lord Hugo Bastian would make a match for his daughter with some other noble's get. Royalty, nobility, and gentry were all the same in this. Marriage was merely another currency, to be spent with the sole intent of advancement—political or social, it mattered not.

It was all enough to make Sal grateful he was a bastard. Common folk, at the least, had some say in a marriage. Among the commoners there was little concern for trade alliances and house pacts. Some women even spoke of marrying for love, though that was more a fancy of the times than a routine.

In any case, whether for love, money, land, or social advancement, Sal had no chance in Sacrull's hell of ever marrying a woman of Lilliana's standing. The most he could hope for was more time to watch her from a distance.

Thus far, Luca had not indicated when he planned to use the information Sal had gathered, nor when Sal would be done gathering information on the Bastian estate. He had often found himself bored with the work, and his attention had drifted to the locket. He'd strung the locket on a thin silver chain which he'd placed about his neck. Whenever his attention drifted, he found his hand inside the neckline of his shirt, clutching the locket, the faint pulse of energy flowing into him.

He knew for certain the locket was magic. He'd accessed the thing's power thrice, and although he'd only managed to activate the power once intentionally, Sal had been confident he'd be able to do it again.

But despite his best efforts, he had failed.

It seemed the secrets of the locket remained hidden. No matter how hard Sal had willed the thing, how he had poked at it, rubbed it, or cursed the locket to the deepest level of Sacrull's hell, the thing had refused to yield its power. Eventually Sal had grown vexed with the locket.

He wore it around his neck at all times, even while sleeping and bathing, and he had taken to examining it, running a finger over the etched rune and letting the energy pulsate through him, but he'd stopped trying to force the magic from it. He merely hoped that when the time came that he needed it, the locket would once again rise to the occasion.

Ever since he'd seen the steel caps at Nabu's, Sal had worried the locket could be what had gotten Anton killed. The news he'd gotten from Nabu regarding the locket had put him doubly on edge. He worried that not only the City Watch, but whoever had commissioned the theft might be out there looking for the locket.

In the end, it was all speculation. Sal still didn't know why Anton was killed. It could have been because of the locket, and it could have been because Luca was tying up loose ends. Might even be that Anton was the rat. Then again, it could all be one big coincidence. Mayhap Pavalo and Anton had been killed for entirely different reasons. There was a chance Sal had misread the whole situation. Thus far, he'd yet to hear any word of why either Anton or Pavalo had been killed. And it was the not knowing that frightened him most.

He did know the steel caps were looking for the locket. It was a fact that had taken some time for him to dissect, despite the obvious implications. Sal had stolen the locket from the High Keep the very night they had been ambushed by the City Watch. After he had seen steel caps at Nabu's shop, and heard Nabu confirm what they were after, it was clear to him that someone wanted the locket.

On the morning of Fitzen, Sal found himself skulking through the Shoe. He walked cautiously, still uncertain whether his life was in danger. He'd decided it was better to lean toward caution.

Vinny's place was on the north end of the Shoe, not far off Beggar's Lane. Sal had agreed to meet there a turn after dawn. Even in the Shoe, where most feared to travel unarmed, the feeling of joy and the energy of the masses was palpable. Fitzen was in the air.

The home belonged to Vinny's father. It was a single-story hovel built of old stone, crumbling mortar, and loosely laid thatch. Sal knocked and entered. The poorly fitting door grated on its hinges. Vinny sat at the table, cup in hand, a sour look on his face. There was the sound of snoring coming from the far side of the room. Vinny's father slept on the floor, huddled near the hearth.

"He all right?" Sal asked as he took the seat across from Vinny.

Vinny scowled, the look in his eyes darkening. "The sodden lush only just stumbled in an hour past."

"Truly?" said Sal, with the hint of a smile.

Vinny didn't smile back. His scowl deepened. "Seems he found the cache of coin I'd been saving. Decided he'd have himself a droll little evening of drinking and dicing. Twenty krom, for Light's sake, twenty bloody krom. The coward didn't even have the stones to look me in the eyes when he came stumbling in just before light's break. Walked in and curled up on the floor like a fucking dog."

Sal's smile slipped; the situation no longer seemed quite so funny. "What'll you do?"

Vinny took a swig. His cup looked to be filled with a heady dark beer. He shrugged and brushed a lock of long blond hair from his eyes. "Suppose I'll do nothing," Vinny said. "Scarce little else I could do, apart from kicking the old bastard until his insides are a jellied pulp."

Sal didn't know how to respond. If someone had stolen twenty krom from him, he might want to give them a thrashing. Not that Sal had ever given anyone a thrashing; fighting wasn't his forte. Vinny, on the other hand, didn't share Sal's distaste for violent solutions, and he was plenty big enough to give most anyone a thrashing.

Vinny's father was full-blood Norsic. He stood half a head taller than his son, but due to years spent at the bottom of a bottle, what brawn the man had once possessed had wasted away until only sagging fat and loose flesh remained.

"Let's be off," Vinny said as he slammed his cup on the table. "Another minute in this stinking hovel and my thoughts may turn to patricide."

The Hog Snout smelled of meadowsweet, which made Sal smile. The taproom was packed full. Bartley had saved them seats near the back, an empty clay mug on the table, another half-filled mug in his hand, and a stupid smile on his face. The Yahdrish slapped the tabletop when he spotted Sal and Vinny, swaying in his chair as he waved at them. He must have started celebrating early. It was only midmorning, yet heavy bags hung under his bloodshot eyes and his face was sunken and drawn. Either Bartley had gone without sleep, or smoking skeev day and night had begun to take a toll.

The room was filled with a cacophony of voices, the singer's loudest of all as he sang "The Queen's Old Goose."

> "For her goose was loose, as the court well knew.
> 'A noose,' they cried, 'a noose, a noose.' "

Bessy was at their table in no time. She put her hand suggestively on her hip as she asked what they'd like.

Vinny and Sal ordered house ales, and Bartley asked for a bottle of fire-wine, as he was wont to do. The thought of the scalding alcohol made Sal nauseous, his stomach turning over in disgust.

"Bessy," Sal said before the barmaid could leave, "who's the singer? The man seems to have taken a liking to your taproom."

Bessy turned and looked at the man strumming his lute.

> "For many a man had fouled her fowl,
> plowed her like farmland in need of a trowel.
> 'A noose,' they cried, 'a noose, a noose.' "

"He'll be around once a span, at the least," Bessy said. "Thought he might liven things up a tick. Don't seem like it on a day like this, but the Hog is hurting for business. I thought a singer might draw in some crowds on the slower days. It's not Fitzen every day, you know."

Vinny scowled. "Most like to drive business off with that wailing, he is."

"Might be he don't have the most handsome of voices," Bessy said with a frown, "but that face singing them bawdy songs is going to bring in a good crowd, and don't you doubt it."

Bartley and Bessy shared a look before the barmaid moved off.

"Oy, Bart," Sal said. "Are things as serious as that?"

Bartley turned a deep shade of red.

"Most oft it's the woman who grows unsatisfied earliest," said Vinny, the first sign of good humor he'd shown that morning.

"Trust you me," said Bartley. "No woman I ever pleasured had cause to complain."

"How could you know?" Vinny asked. "Not likely you ever *pleasured* any woman with that little worm you call a manhood."

"What would you know of it?" Bartley said. "Not as though I've ever seen either of you with a woman. Pair of maids, I'll reckon."

Vinny stood, but Sal headed him off.

"Easy now, mate, he was only having a bit of fun. No need to get good and mean."

"And he was having a bit of fun at the expense of my honor," said Bartley. "I won't be beaten bloody by a silk glove, no matter who the son of a bitch is."

Vinny stirred, but Sal put a hand firmly on his chest.

"Right, then," Sal said. "Might be best if we all sit back down."

Bartley took a big, messy swig of his ale and stood. "Not me. I want to be at the bottom of this. If a man's going to talk tough, he'll need to back it up. How is it we've never seen you with a woman, Vincenzo? What are you, some kind of a sodder?"

It seemed Sal had misjudged just how deep into his cups Bartley was, and in just how dark a mood Vinny had been.

With one smooth movement, Vinny brushed Sal's hand from his chest and went for Bartley.

The little Yahdrish stood his ground, putting his fists up as though he meant to deliver a few blows of his own, but in the end he never had the chance.

It took one punch from Vinny's big fist, and the fight was over. A straight shot to the nose. Bartley squealed, blood sprayed. His head whipped back, and his knees buckled to the floorboards.

Bartley clapped a hand over his bleeding nose, tears welling up in his eyes. "Sacrull's balls," Bartley moaned, blood streaming over his lips and dripping from his chin.

Vinny snapped to, as though breaking from a trance. He moved toward Bartley with a hand extended to help the Yahdrish to his feet. Their fight had attracted the attention of some of the tables around them, but the taproom was filled with enough commotion that many patrons didn't deem to notice.

The singer played on, his voice and lute carrying above the din.

"For queen she was, but whore she'd been,
a stain ne'er washed from the eyes of men.
'A noose,' they cried, 'a noose, a noose.
String up queen whore, and hang king goose.' "

Bessy bustled up to their table, a tray held at shoulder level. Two clay mugs and a bottle which, just to look at, made Sal's insides burn. Bessy placed the mugs of ale on the table and began to hand Bartley the fire-wine when she noticed the Yahdrish's nose. "Light's sake, what's happened here?" she asked, and kept hold of the bottle.

"A misunderstanding," Sal said.

Bessy set down the fire-wine, flashed Bartley a suspicious look, and moved on to another table.

Vinny sipped his ale tentatively, as Bartley glared, pinching his nose with thumb and forefinger to stem the flowing blood.

"For when the realm fell to disrepair,
what was to blame but her affair?
'A noose,' they cried, 'a noose, a noose.' "

"Right, then," Sal said. "Might we call it a day?"

"Day's only just begun," Bartley said in a nasal tone. "Like hell if I'm going to miss Fitzen over a nosebleed."

"Sorry about the nose," Vinny mumbled.

Bartley pointedly pretended not to hear. He drank his ale and turned his attention to the singer, who was now working his way through "When Pigs Don Armor."

Sal took a big swig of his ale, downing half the mug in one go. "And what did you have planned for the day?" Sal asked.

Vinny shrugged. "I for one am a touch short on coin. Can't afford much merriment, unless someone had a quick job in mind."

Bartley stirred, but kept to himself, still pretending to listen to the singer.

Sal cleared his throat. "I don't know that a job would be wise, not with the amount the pair of you have had to drink."

"This is only my second cup," Vinny said, bristling and holding his mug up for them to see.

Bartley took a drink, his nosebleed halted for the time being. "I've got a job in mind," Bartley said. "That is, if you maids think you can handle it."

Sal shook his head.

"Come now," said Vinny. "Let the Yahdrish speak. You've not even heard his proposition."

"It's not a proposition worth hearing," Sal said. "Besides, weren't you at his throat just a tick past? When did you start defending him?"

"It's nothing big, if that's what's got your underclothes in a bunch," Bartley said, slurring his words slightly. "Heard talk from a couple of pushers on Penny Row. They had a job lined up, but things fell through. Target is still there, though, ripe for the picking by the first hand that takes it. I've got Valla and Odie on board already."

"If Valla and the big man are in, I'm in," said Vinny.

Sal didn't know if it was the thought of no longer having a krom to his name, or a combination of alcohol and guilt that fueled Vinny's enthusiasm; either way, Sal found it disconcerting. As much as Sal liked the little Yahdrish, he never had, and never would, go on a job concocted by Bartley. He was too green, too cocksure, and too clumsy by half. Bartley would never have the head for planning heists. At best, he was a middling second-story man, which made it hard to believe the big man and Valla were on board. Odie wasn't exactly brimming with acumen, but he did possess a certain base instinct for survival. Valla was shrewd, cunning, and assertive. If Valla was in on the job, it was more than likely she'd been the one who'd planned everything. It wouldn't be the first time Bartley had taken credit for another's work.

"How about you tell us your plan," Sal said.

Bartley grabbed the empty mug and the bottle of fire-wine and began to talk. As Bartley explained his plan, Sal found it difficult to criticize without time to consider all the angles. For the moment, he was forced to take the Yahdrish at his word so far as the details went.

Deep in his cups as Bartley was, and enthusiastic as Vinny was, they didn't stick around the Hog Snout for long. After Bartley went up to his room to smoke a cap while Sal and Vinny each had another ale in the taproom, they paid their tabs and headed back out into the bustling streets of Dijvois.

Fitzen had put the city into a frenzy of celebration. Foot traffic was shoulder-to-shoulder. Had it not been for the half-Norsic in their trio, Sal and the little Yahdrish could have easily been swept up in the human current that pushed through the streets.

Beer flowed like a river, and the citizens of Dijvois willingly embraced the rapids, gullets opened wide. The monks of Knöldrus did their part, giving a cup of beer to any who called. All they asked was a prayer to Solus and a copper shill from those who could afford it. Still, their generosity was not purely altruistic, as it allowed the monks to clear out what was left in their cellars to make room for the new batch they would brew from the autumn grains, the last harvest of the year.

Nearly every shop in Dijvois, be it miller or jeweler, tanner or tailor, cobbler or carpenter, closed its doors for Fitzen. Only the alehouses, taverns, wine-sinks, and inns did business on the holiday of winter's welcome, and they were stuffed to bursting with patrons.

The City Watch remained on duty, even increasing their numbers, hiring any brute or dock thug looking for extra coin, slapping a poleaxe in their hand, a tabard on their chest, and a coned helm upon their thick skull. Rather comical, really. Sal could always tell a steel cap from a holiday recruit, so scantily armed and clad were they.

It was a tradition on Fitzen that the children ran about masked. Some wore simple black or white masks that covered their little cherubic faces from just above the mouth. Others sported peacock plumes or polished glass gems that reflected the light. Even more extravagant were the masks fashioned after exotic beasts. Sal saw wolves and lions, phoenixes and cockatrices, a dragon and even a chimera.

It reminded Sal of the job he and Bartley had done at the Rusted Anchor all those years back, the card game that had nearly gotten him killed. He and Bartley had worn masks just like those the children wore.

The masked children would scour the city begging for sweets. Many adults carried candies to give when asked, elsewise the children were free to cause mischief. Some adults simply carried sticks, or weapons of a more sinister nature. Rather than proffer sweets, they would simply chase off any children who came begging. Sal and his friends employed this latter strategy, as sweets cost coin, but the looks in the eyes of the children when Sal pulled his pigsticker were priceless.

The whores made good money during Fitzen. In the pillow-houses they hardly had time to get off their backs between customers, and in the streets they paced alley mouths with tight bodices, low-cut blouses, and hiked-up skirts, calling after men and women alike.

"A shill and I'm yours! A krom and you can have me twice," one whore called. "A silver and I'll take the lot of you at once, supposing you don't mind either end!"

Bartley often stopped to talk, until Sal or Vinny dragged him along.

One impudent young streetwalker approached the trio as they neared Beggar's Lane. Blonde, skinny, and bowlegged, she had sores on her hands and arms that told she was a blisser. She grabbed Bartley by the hood of his cloak and began to drag him toward a dilapidated building. He went willingly, haggling a price as they walked.

Sal grabbed Bartley by the arm and reminded him they were headed for a job.

Bartley scoffed. "I'll not need long."

"And what might Bessy say?"

"Bessy? I've not married the wench, if that's what you're thinking."

The whore gripped his hood tighter and pulled harder. Sal tightened his grip in return, while Bartley did his best to shrug Sal off.

"Let him go, bastard!" said the whore.

Sal looked to Vinny for help, but Vinny only laughed, letting the struggle unfold as it would.

"Trust me," Sal pleaded. "You don't want to do this, Bartley."

The Yahdrish let his body go limp as a wet fish, and Sal lost his grip.

Bartley and the woman shuffled toward the crumbling brick edifice. The warped and splintered door hung on loose, rusted hinges that screeched as Bartley and his whore pushed across the threshold.

They were brought to an abrupt halt as Vinny took hold of Bartley's arm. When Vinny pulled, both the Yahdrish and the whore were tugged along.

Sal watched admiringly as Vinny part carried, part dragged Bartley by the arm as though he were a small child, the skinny bowlegged whore hanging on as if her next hit of bliss depended on it. Which, in all likelihood, it did.

The whore was dragged along as they strolled down Beggar's Lane before she eventually dropped to the cobblestones on her hands and knees.

Worried the woman would be trampled in the press, Sal helped her to her feet and off the road, where he sat her down and propped her against a stone wall.

The rush of revelers pushed by like a mindless herd. Sal slipped between people like a fish in seaweed, dodging this way and that until he stood at Vinny's side.

Bartley looked disgruntled, but he seemed too tired and far too drunk to fight.

"Where is this place, again?" Vinny asked.

"North of East Market near the Kingsway," Bartley said.

Vinny sighed. "Best be on our way. With these crowds it's like to take half an hour just to cross the Lady."

After an hour, they approached the Low Town bridge tower. Like on the day of End, there were no fewer than three crossbowmen atop the catwalk, perched behind merlons, crossbows cocked and ready.

Six steel caps lined the passageway, three on either side. Sal avoided making eye contact. After his recent encounters with the City Watch, steel caps were the last people in Dijvois Sal wanted to see. He kept his head down and mussed his hair with a hand to shield even more of his face.

As the trio passed the limestone statue of the Lady White, his compulsion outweighed the pressure of Vinny's glare. Sal couldn't resist reaching out a hand and running it along the hem of the Lady's dress for luck. Not to do so seemed almost sacrilegious.

Vinny had not been far off in his assumption; crossing the Bridge of the Lady took nearly an hour. Although the waters of the Tamber were calm, the bridge that spanned its great width was a den of madness. Vendors lined the parapets on either side, creating a bottleneck that reduced traffic flow to a single file in each direction. The vendors shouted their wares, haggling and pushing, stopping passersby and holding up traffic as they attempted to make a sale.

Spun-sugar unicorn horns, slices of peppered beef skewered with onions and sweet peppers, legs of lamb, honeyed dates, and steaming pastries were shoved under Sal's nose. Other vendors placed necklaces of glass and jet, agate and garnet about his neck, torcs and bracelets of gold and silver about his wrists, telling him of their worth, their rarity, and the unbelievably low price for which he could have them. He was sprayed with perfumes and nearly choked by smoky, sweet-smelling incense.

When they eventually reached the High Town bridge tower, it was as though they had been through a scuffle. Still, Sal had managed to pick a few pockets during the crossing and had even made off with a gold torc.

Another six steel caps lined the bridge beneath the High Town tower, and Sal once again lowered his head as he passed the bored-looking guards leaning on their poleaxes.

Once off the Bridge of the Lady, it was a swift journey to the armory as they took the Kingsway, bypassing East Market by cutting through a few narrow alleys.

It seemed there was some truth to Bartley's telling. The big man and Valla waited a few buildings away from the armory so as not to draw attention to themselves,

although it was near impossible for Odie not to draw attention. The big man was larger than life, the sort of man that made the ancient stories of giants seem plausible. He stood head and shoulders above the crowd, his massive shaved scalp reflecting the sun like a beacon.

Valla was subtler, leaning against a brick wall as though she were a lazy cat lounging in the sunlight, but Sal knew better. When she moved, it was with such swift feline grace that if she ever wanted him dead, it would happen before he knew what had stuck him.

"About time," said Valla, sliding off the wall and approaching the trio. She looked them up and down with shrewd appraisal. Her eyes narrowed to slits, and she grabbed Bartley by his already rumpled shirt collar, pulled him close, and smelled his breath. Then, just as quickly, she shoved him away with a look of disgust.

Bartley stumbled back a step and plopped on his ass. A look of bemusement twisted his features.

"Drunk?" Odie asked, his sonorous voice rolling like thunder.

Valla made a noise deep in her throat and walked away muttering something about Anton and Sacrull damned Yahdrish.

No one tried to stop her, no one called out or tried to chase after her. Once Valla was in a mood it was best to give her space, a lot of space, for a goodly amount of time. Sal pitied the next drunken reveler that stumbled across Valla's path.

"Right, then," Sal said. "I suppose that settles that. Care for a trip to the East Market?"

Bartley got unsteadily to his feet. "The hell if I'll call it a day just because that bitch has lobsters in her craw."

Odie cocked an eyebrow, and Vinny shifted his weight from foot to foot, hands in his pockets, eyes on the cobblestones.

"East Market it is, then," Sal said, his spirits a tick higher knowing he'd no longer have to follow through with Bartley's job.

"Bugger that," Bartley said. "We're going on as planned. We don't need Valla."

"And how exactly are we supposed to do this without a cat's-paw?" Sal asked.

"Odie can handle it," Bartley said. "He'd have an even easier time of it than she would have."

"Right, sure, sure," Sal said, bobbing his head like an idiot. "Only, how in Sacrull's hell is Odie supposed to climb through a bloody window?"

Bartley licked his lips. "Vinny, then. He can handle it."

"And who will disable the wards?" Sal asked. "Anything more than a single-rune ward is too much for me, and this is the armory. Even the privy will be warded."

Vinny cleared his throat. "I really don't think I'm up for it. I came along thinking I was playing mule once the window ward was down. I'm not prepared to play the cat's-paw if it came to that."

"Then it's settled," Sal said. "East Market."

Bartley balled his fists, his eyes starting to water. He looked to be on the verge of a tantrum. Sal half expected him to be writhing on his belly pounding fists and feet on the cobblestones at any moment. Instead, Bartley turned and moved off in the opposite direction from Valla.

Sal called after him and received a hand gesture in return. Whatever trace amounts of sympathy Sal had left for the Yahdrish burned away with that gesture.

Sal didn't bother voicing the question, merely tipped his head in the direction of East Market. Odie shrugged, and Vinny nodded. Then the newly forged trio made their way back into the press of the crowd on the Kingsway.

In comparison to South Market and Town Square, East Market was like another world entirely. Though the taste of salt air carried throughout the city, there were few other similarities between the two marketplaces. Book sellers, sweet shops, charcuteries, bakers, tailors, and furniture makers at East Market all sold their wares at exorbitant prices, partly because the gentry, nobility, and affluent merchants would pay them not to have to cross the Tamber to go to market, and partly because the rents in East Market were so high proprietors were forced to make adjustments to compensate. Still, it was not so costly as the Agora—but then again, nothing was. In the Agora there were boutiques, delicatessens, florists selling sweet-smelling flowers, galleries displaying oil-painted canvases, and diminutive shops selling peculiar treasures from the Far East.

Sal, Vinny, and Odie seated themselves on stools next to a wine vendor's cart. They each ordered a cup and watched the dancing. A five-member band was playing a jaunty jig, and townsfolk danced in the market's center square.

> "Though before you go piddle, consider you this:
> If not for that diddler, who'd diddle your sis?"

Sal pulled a handful of coins from his pocket and laid them out on the makeshift bar top. Two iron dingés, a copper shim, and a gold krom—his take from the Bridge of the Lady, and not a bad take it was. He swept the coins into his palm and handed them to Vinny along with the thin gold torc he'd nabbed.

"It's not much," Sal said. "But seeing as Bartley's little job fell through, this ought to get you through the day."

Without a hint of reluctance, Vinny accepted and thanked Sal earnestly.

The trio sat quietly, watching the crowd as they drank their wine —a wine so red it was nearly purple, with notes of cherry and plum and a surprisingly peppery finish. Sal liked it enough to have a second cup.

"This sweet wine is . . .," the big man said, gesturing as though he would grab the words he sought from thin air, "is missing . . ."

"Fire," said Vinny, nodding.

"You bloody Norsic oafs and your fire-wine," Sal said. "I'll never understand what it is you like so much about that piss-water."

The big man took on a serious expression. "Not only Norsic, but Vordin and Adilaie. By the gods, all of Skjörund drinks fire-wine, it flows through our very veins. Even that little Yahdrish drinks the stuff."

"Yes, well, no one ever claimed Bartley was right in the head."

"I'll second that," said Vinny, raising his cup. "Bartley isn't much of a measure to go by in one's life."

"My friend," Odie said, turning to the vendor, "I've done with this maiden's grape. Do you have fire-wine?"

The vendor scowled but produced a bottle and filled Vinny's and Odie's cups. He offered Sal a pour, but he waved the man off.

"Believe I've had my fill," Sal said.

As Sal paid the vendor for the wine, something caught his eye. Standing at a clothier's cart, not two vendors away, Lilliana Bastian held up a blue scarf. Sal found himself on his feet before he'd even thought to stand.

Vinny flashed him a questioning look.

Sal downed what was left in his cup and gathered up his courage. "I've got something needs doing," Sal said, and headed for the clothier's cart.

15

LILLIANA

It could have been the mood of Fitzen, a madness in the air. It could have been the wine and the ale he'd had, inspiring an act of drunken courage as loutish as it was fearless. It could have been the pent-up lust, the aching desire built up from watching a woman for weeks without the chance to act. Whatever it was, something propelled Sal toward Lilliana.

He was doing his best to look sober, focusing on even, steady strides, when he bulled headfirst into someone. Someone big, solid, and unmoving.

When Sal regained his balance, he realized just who it was that had stepped into his path.

A large Bauden man, with a thick black mustache, a stiletto sheathed at his hip, and a bastard sword slung on his back—Damor Nev, bodyguard to Lilliana Bastian—blocked Sal's path.

Somehow, in the haze of alcohol, Sal had forgotten about Damor Nev. Now, with the man standing before him, Sal's jaw began to throb, a phantom ache from the punch the bodyguard had given him on the Bridge of the Lady.

"Pardon me, sir," Sal said coolly, despite the weakness he felt in his knees. "Wasn't looking where I was going."

"Back off, and look them eyes elsewhere," said the bodyguard.

The alcohol coursing through his veins gave Sal enough liquid courage that he decided to sidestep the man-at-arms and address Lilliana directly. "That one there is the one you want," Sal said, trying to convey more confidence than he felt. "True indigo will bring out your eyes."

"I told you to back off," said Damor Nev, putting a hand on his stiletto. "Back off or I'll put this in your belly, I will."

Lilliana laid a consoling hand on the bodyguard's arm. "You look familiar," she said to Sal. "What do you know of scarves?"

"Little and less," Sal said. "But I know something of weaving, and even more of dyeing, and that scarf you're holding is true indigo."

The cart vendor, a little man with big ears and a mouth of widely spaced yellow teeth, perked up at this. "That is the truth, yes, genuine indigo."

"Go on," said Lilliana, her perfect lips forming a smile. "Why should that matter to me?"

"Here in Dijvois," Sal said, "woad is far more common because it's cheaply acquired in Pargeche—or any province of Nelgand, for that matter. True indigo is only found in the East. It has always been difficult to acquire in Pargeche, but due to recent trade tariffs set in motion by the High Council, the price of indigo has nearly tripled."

"The Naidia tariffs?"

"Why, yes, that would be them," Sal said. "The High Council has imposed yet another tariff, which has upset the balance of things—or should I say, kept the power in the hands of those who have the coin."

"Oh, and you know it was the High Council?" Lilliana asked with a knowing smirk. "But why not the duke, if you are going to blame someone? Or me, for that matter. You're certain it was not me?"

Sal smiled. "Oh, My Lady, I could never fault you, but I do blame the duke. Of course, Duke Tadej merely had his High Council place the tariffs due to pressure from the merchant guilds."

"The merchant guilds? You assume this is the reason? Would

not the Dijvois merchant guilds profit from cheaper indigo?" Lilliana asked playfully. "Would they not have petitioned against such tariffs? Whereas I would have nothing to lose."

The Shiikali scarf merchant seemed to have little to say where trade tariffs were concerned. He looked to Sal, mouth open.

Lilliana's eyes were stunning, in the literal sense. When their gazes locked, Sal felt his body shut down. His thoughts seemed jumbled, his tongue thick and heavy as though it did not fit in his mouth. Sal swallowed. "The merchant guilds would benefit where indigo is concerned, but much of the indigo in Nelgand is shipped here by the Naidia Trading Company. What little indigo the Nelsigh merchant guilds handle pales in comparison to their trade in woad. If indigo were cheaper, how would the Nelsigh merchant guilds unload their stocks of cheaply acquired woad dye?"

"And how is it you know so much about trade?" said Lilliana, running the wool scarf through her fingers.

"It's not trade I know. As I said, I know something of dyeing, and a bit about wool, for that matter."

Something flashed in Lilliana's eyes—curiosity, or mischief perhaps. "And tell me, should I buy a scarf because it is a pretty color? This day is Fitzen, the day of winter's welcome. Not long and the snows will be upon us. Should I not want for something warm as well as beautiful?"

The little merchant opened his mouth, but Lilliana held up a hand, palm out. "Dear sir, I would like to hear what this man has to say about the subject."

The merchant's brow wrinkled, but he closed his mouth and made an obsequious little bow.

"The character of the object is equally important as the look. Though I think you will find that scarf there is as well suited to the winter snows as it is to your alluring eyes."

Damor Nev scowled.

"How do you know the weave is good?" Lilliana asked.

"Do you see the cross weave?" Sal asked. "That pattern comes from a special loom found only in the East. That pattern is the marking of a spider loom. They're the best looms in the known world, and can create such things as a weaver could only dream of if they were using a traditional spinner's loom."

Lilliana nodded. "I'll take this one," she told the merchant.

The little man smiled an ugly smile, rubbing his wrinkled hands together. "A wise choice. This is one of my finest pieces indeed. As you have heard, it is of the highest quality, and of course commands a considerable price."

"How considerable?" asked Lilliana.

"But My Lady, certainly a woman of your, uh, social standing would not balk at a figure if it was indeed fair, yes?"

"How much?" Lilliana said, her tone flat.

"I would need sufficient krom, yes, fifty silvers is fair. Forty if you are paying in the gold."

Lilliana gave a false laugh and tossed the scarf at the little Shiikali. "Thank you for your time," she said to the merchant.

"Forty krom," the merchant said, "Thirty-five if this is in the gold."

Lilliana did not deign to respond. She turned and walked away from the cart.

The vendor pursued, thrusting the scarf before her. "Thirty silvers, I could not go any lower."

Lilliana gave the man a scornful look. "I'll not pay nobility tax in my own city."

"Dear lady, please, twenty-five in silvers, I could not possibly sell it for a dingé less than this, else I lose money in the sale."

"I'd give seven if I believed it was worth five, but I will pay five if it will get you gone."

"Five? By the gods, this does not cover the cost of dyeing alone. I can go no lower than twenty in silver."

"Nine gold krom," Lilliana said.

"Oh, but lady, surely if you can do nine, you can do fifteen."

"I'd not pay him more than five and an iron," Sal said, fixing the little merchant with a knowing look.

The man stammered, knowing good and well that Sal had the right of it.

"Ten," Lilliana said.

"Dear lady, my wife shall rage when I tell her how cheaply I have sold this, yes. But a man must feed his children. Five hungry mouths with little hands tugging at the sleeves of my shirt for want of food to fill their empty bellies. Ten it is, yes, ten krom gold, but know I have made little in profit this day, very little. It is for the sake of your beauty and the need of my children that I am willing to do this thing."

Lilliana smiled at the man and slipped him an extra krom. "For your children."

The man bowed, muttering words of thanks as Lilliana took her scarf and began to walk away.

"Thank you for your help," Lilliana said to Sal. "Enjoy your Fitzen. Come, Damor."

"My Lady, might I accompany you?" Sal quickly asked.

"I believe Damor is all the company I can handle at present. Good day."

Sal stepped forward, but Damor Nev moved into his path.

"The lady said good day, now bugger off."

Sal dodged the bodyguard and slipped past. "Is it not fate that we should meet again?" Sal called after Lilliana.

Sal winced as the breath was driven from his lungs. Damor Nev wrapped him in a tight hug and lifted him into the air.

Sal kicked and writhed, but Damor's grip was like a vise, crushing his chest and ribs.

"Hold a moment, Damor," Lilliana called out. "I've changed my mind."

The bodyguard set Sal down on his feet as easily as a grown man would a child.

"Fate," said Lilliana. "A most auspicious choice of words. Come, I believe I'll let you escort me after all."

Sal followed as Lilliana weaved through the crowd, Damor a step behind him.

"You must tell me," Lilliana said, "how is it you know so much of looms and dyes?"

Sal shrugged. "My elder sister prenticed to a clothier for some years before going off on her own. I apprenticed to my sister, and in turn picked up a thing or two about the trade. I also know some-thing of herb lore, if you're interested."

"Herb lore?" she asked skeptically.

"My sister uses herbs to press into the weave, gives the clothing a sweet smell. Lavender is her favorite, but I prefer meadowsweet myself."

"You're not what I expected," Lilliana said, smirking.

"Is that good or bad?"

She laughed. "This way. Just a bit farther now."

Damor followed a few paces behind, his mustache twitching in irritation.

They seemed to be headed for a tattered, faded green tent, patched with an assortment of colors, so many patches that it looked mottled. The tent was tucked into a dark corner of the square, one of the only deserted spots in the entire market.

"What's this, now?" Sal asked.

"Fate," said Lilliana, a slight smile playing on her lips—her soft, full lips that begged to be kissed.

"My Lady," said Damor Nev, a hint of concern creeping into his tone, "is this wise?"

Lilliana fixed Damor with a deadpan stare, her mouth pressed into a thin line.

The bodyguard cleared his throat. "Yes, right you are, My Lady."

She fixed her gaze on Sal. "Before we enter, there's one thing I'd like to clear up," Lilliana said. "You mentioned we've met before, and you do look familiar, as though I know you from somewhere. And yet I fear we don't move in the same social circles. It only now occurs to me to ask. How do I know you?"

"I—you slapped me on the ear once—no, twice—just before your big friend Damor here nearly broke my jaw."

Lilliana's eyes widened as realization struck home.

"The Bridge of the Lady," she gasped.

"You!" said Damor Nev, reaching for the bastard sword slung across his back.

"Damor, no," Lilliana said, gripping the Bauden man by the wrist before he could fully unsheathe his blade. "Not here, not now."

Sal's knees had gone weak. His heart was in his throat, his palms sweating.

"My Lady, this street scum deserves no less."

"Be that as it may, I am beginning to enjoy his company, and I fear that if you took his head he might become less than companionable."

Damor Nev scowled, lips curling back to show clenched teeth.

"Most grateful, My Lady," Sal said.

"Lilliana Bastian," she said. "And this is Damor Nev."

"Salvatori Lorenzo," Sal said.

"Well then, Salvatori Lorenzo, shall we tempt fate?"

Sal shrugged, trying to seem as though he'd not nearly loosed his bowels a moment before.

Lilliana gestured to the tent. "After you, good sir."

Sal pushed past the tent flap, heavy fabric that provided more resistance than he'd expected. Lilliana entered just behind.

The air was acrid with smoke. Before them was a table of cedar, a seven-pointed star carved into the top. Seated behind the table was an old woman, her thin hair so white it was nearly translucent, her brown, wrinkled skin like dried leather. She fixed Sal with milky white eyes devoid of pupil and iris. The look sent a shiver down his spine. Her eyes seemed to see nothing, and yet somehow they seemed to see everything.

The old woman put her nose in the air, sniffing like a hound. She stretched out a quivering hand. "I can smell the storm. It clings to you, boy," she said, fixing blind eyes on Sal, blind white eyes that seemed to see both into and through him.

"We've come seeking a telling," Lilliana said. "Will you gift us your sight?"

The old woman was a seer, though it seemed an odd title for a woman who was blind in both eyes.

"For the gift of far-sight one must first surrender their eyes," said the old woman, her eerie gaze still fixed on Sal as though she knew his thoughts. "This is the way it has always been, boy. I am no blind old beggar woman. No, I can see you upon all seven planes, upon all of the paths which your spirit would wander. Many paths I see within you."

Sal reached for the locket that hung about his neck. The pulsating energy circulated through his body.

"You will give us a reading, then?" Lilliana asked.

The old woman frowned. "I see the thing you wear upon your neck. I see it clearly for what it is, and I smell the storm within. It leaves a sour taste in my mouth. Unhand it or leave my presence."

Lilliana flashed Sal a questioning look, but he shook his head, deciding not to explain, and let go of the locket.

The woman closed her blind eyes and lifted her nose once more, sniffing at the air with long, slow inhalations. "And too, I smell the dead that haunt you. They come to you, call to you, do they not?"

The words sent a chill coursing through his blood. "They ask for help, but I can't help them," Sal said, ignoring the stare he felt from Lilliana.

"Seek not the knowledge of the dead," said the old woman. "The dead have no answers for the living, they have naught but regrets."

"I don't ask for answers," said Sal, "merely peace while I sleep."

"Peace will come," the woman said. "Yet it must be earned. Gifts are not freely given, nor lessons freely learned. Help is given to those who seek, and knowledge to those who listen. Heroes are not merely born, they are forged in the fires of life."

Sal sighed. That was all well and good, but what in Sacrull's hell was it supposed to mean?

Lilliana shook her head, a look of bafflement in her eyes. "Sorry, what are we talking about here?"

"You ask for peace, and peace will come. I have seen you in my dreams, and your dreams. I have seen your dead men, and I have seen what you will become. It will be your choice, to accept the call or to turn from the Light. No matter your choosing, peace will come."

"Right. Well, this has all been quite informative," Sal said. "But I think we'll be leaving now."

"I'd like a reading," said Lilliana. "From your deck."

The old woman turned her blind white eyes on the young noble-woman and flashed a crooked smile revealing yellowed teeth. She put her hand above a deck of painted wooden cards. As her hand hovered above the cards, she closed her eyes and a faint rush of energy emanated from the space between her wrinkled hand and the wooden cards.

The teller shook her head.

"What is it?" asked Lilliana. "Is there a problem?"

"No problem," the crone said, "but the deck has spoken. I cannot give you a telling."

When she opened her eyes, they were locked on Sal.

The chill returned.

"What do you mean?" Lilliana asked. "Why not? I can pay, and I have asked for a telling."

"It is not a question of coin. In matters of fate, I am merely witness. I do not control the deck any more than I control the future."

Lilliana opened her mouth and closed it. She looked to Sal, her big blue eyes imploring him to assist.

"Is there anything we can do?" Sal said. "She would like the reading. I can pay a considerable amount." She had said it was not an issue of coin, but when folk said that, Sal found, they usually meant they wanted more.

The old woman sneered, a less than appealing sight to behold. "I'd expect daft remarks to come from an empty-headed high-born. I have said this is no question of coin. Though should you desire, you may give me as much coin as pleases your empty head. But if you want to help, you may take a seat and close your mouth."

Sal sat.

"But," Lilliana said, "you only just told me you could not read my fortune—"

"Yours, no"—she turned her blind gaze on Sal—"but *his*."

"No," Sal said, standing and shaking his head.

"Whether you stay or go, the cards will be read. You cannot stop the passage of time by leaving. Would you hear what the cards have to tell?"

Sal sat, nervous and slightly queasy, but Lilliana was enthusiastic as she sat in the chair next to him. There was something about her joy that soothed the sick, ominous feeling in his belly.

The teller closed her eyes and drew the first card. The painted wooden card showed a young man dressed in motley, a dog running at his heels. "The fool, face up," said the reader. "New beginnings, blind loyalty, and limitless potential."

She slid the first card to one point of the septagram and turned the next card. It faced upside down, and showed an old man seated beneath an archway, with ten gold coins falling from the sky. "Ten of Pentacles. You have suffered loss, an inheritance"—she paused —"a kingdom."

Sal sat upright. He didn't understand what she meant. He had never been rich. Certainly he had never been in possession of a kingdom. For a moment he wondered whether the whole thing might be a sham.

The reader slid the second card to one of the seven points of the star and drew another. Her eyes were closed, her face growing grim as she revealed the third card.

Sal was bemused. He didn't know what direction the card faced. He had never seen a solid black card before, and had no idea what it meant.

"Death," said the teller, sliding the card to the bottom point of the star.

Without another word of explanation, she reached for the next card.

"Hold on," Sal said. "What do you mean, 'Death'?"

The teller gave no notice that she had heard, her clouded eyes fixed on a point behind Sal.

Sal looked to Lilliana to say something, but she was engrossed by the cards. Her hands were shaking as she watched with bated breath.

A vague statement, *Death.* Whose death? Pavalo Picarri's death, Anton's death? Or was she speaking of Sal's death?

The fourth card showed a golden chalice, silver coins spilling over its rim.

"The cup and coin, face up," said the teller.

Again she slid the card to an open point of the septagram and drew another. The fifth card showed a tower struck by lightning, and the sixth a man cowering beneath a shadow. Lilliana gave a sharp intake of breath as the reader placed each of the cards on its point.

Sal knew the reader would draw two more cards, but he had no desire for the old woman to continue. Sal was no teller, but he knew things were looking worse than bad.

The crone drew. The seventh card showed an elderly man standing near a pool of water, and in the pool the man saw his reflection. "The wise man," said the old woman as she laid the seventh card on the final point of the star and thus completed the circle.

For the eighth time the reader reached for her deck, drawing yet one more wooden card. It faced right side up and did nothing to calm Sal's nerves.

"The throne," said the teller, as she placed the final card at the star's center.

III

THE HERO

There are no heroes. Only those who act, and those who fail to act.
—Stefano Lorenzo

16

DINNER

S al knocked on the door frame. The door was open, allowing for a full view of his sister's room.

"You shouldn't be here," Nicola said, looking up.

"I wanted to talk," Sal said.

"Isn't that what we'll be doing at dinner?"

"I wanted to talk with you."

"We need to get ready. You know how Uncle is about punctuality."

"Bugger Uncle," Sal said.

Nicola smiled. "What's on your mind?"

"Is it true?" Sal said. "Is she really going to get out of bed?"

"Come in," Nicola said, sitting up on the bed and patting the spot beside her.

Sal sat. "Well, is it true? Is she going to come down?"

Nicola pursed her lips, then put a hand over her mouth as she thought. "I don't want you getting your hopes up," she finally said.

"What's wrong with her?" Sal asked. "You know, really wrong with her?"

Nicola unfolded her arms and put a hand on Sal's back. "We should go down. Uncle will be waiting."

"Uncle," Sal said under his breath. "He hates me, you know?"

"He doesn't hate you, Salvatori, it's just his way. He can seem cold, but——"

"How can you say that? You see the way he looks at me. No matter what I do, no matter who I try to be, he only looks at me with scorn. And you, you could spit in his face, and he would praise you for it."

"Now, there's an idea," Nicola said, smirking. "I had considered his tea, but his face would send a clear message."

"Mother brought up the name."

Nicola scoffed. "I'd not use that name were it truly mine."

"He did it as a favor, to Mother," Sal said. "She's been asking for years now."

"He can keep it. I don't want it. I may be stuck here so long as Mother needs looking after, but I'll not be branded by that name. Mother should know that."

"She would rather see you married, I think," Sal said.

"Any man who would take a wife for her name over her merit is no man I would ever call husband. Now off with you, Salvatori. Uncle will be in a right mood if we are any later."

———

G reggings stood outside the dining hall, a stern look on his face as Sal and Nicola neared.

"Don't look at us so, lest those wrinkles become permanent," said Nicola.

"It is not my wrinkled face that should concern you, My Lady."

"I'm no lady, Greggings," Nicola said, brushing past the manservant.

"As you say, My Lady," Greggings replied. "Still, you ought not keep them."

"Them?" Sal asked. "So she——"

Greggings nodded, and Sal felt his stomach flutter.

The doors opened with a creak that echoed in the vastness of the hall. Uncle Stefano sat at the head of the walnut table, a sour look on his face. Beside him, looking pale, and yet far better than she had in weeks, was Mother.

She smiled as Sal and Nicola entered and took their seats.

"Did you mean to keep us waiting?" said Uncle Stefano.

"Please, Stefano, there's no need," Mother said.

"The mule that wanders astray and is not kicked is still a wandering ass, is it not?" said Uncle Stefano. "Should we spare the boot, ignore the mule, and hope it corrects of its own accord?"

"That which was made by the Lord that is Light is perfect of its own accord," Mother said.

"We did mean to keep you," said Nicola, to Sal's utter horror. "Where else to find pleasure in such a place as this but to watch you stew to a boil while your supper chills?"

With bated breath, Sal remained perfectly still, not daring to look his uncle in the eyes.

Stefano made a noise in his throat, something between a scoff and a snarl. He took a long drink from his wine glass and waved for Greggings to send in the footman.

Toliver entered bearing a gold platter. A boy of an age with Sal, he had a mop of sandy blonde hair that he kept tied back. Toliver had been serving as the footman in his uncle's house going on a year, and Sal suspected he didn't have much longer. His uncle never kept them around for more than two years—his little charity cases, he called them.

At any rate, it seemed a cruel practice to Sal.

Toliver passed behind them, and before each he set a plate holding a half quail with a cranberry garnish, and what appeared to be a bowl of chopped vegetable soup in a beef broth.

As they ate the conversation was sparse. Mother's presence brought to the table a whole new element of tension that had been absent for weeks. Sal spoke little to anyone, focusing on his food and keeping his head down.

"So, Brother, Salvatori tells me you are close to a decision."

Sal froze and his heart jumped into his throat.

"Does he, now?"

Sal kept his eyes on his plate, but he could feel his uncle's stare burning into the top of his head.

"And has he told you what that decision is?" Uncle Stefano asked.

"It seems to me there are only two options," said Nicola.

Sal winced. First Mother, then his sister. Perhaps Uncle Stefano would do nothing to her, but Nicola was pushing Sal's luck.

Sal looked toward his mother, hoping to catch her glance, to somehow signal for her to change the subject.

"Well, boy, out with it," said Uncle Stefano. "What is it you've been telling Mommy?"

Sal clenched a fist beneath the table.

Mother pursed her lips.

"You've no right to talk to him that way," said Nicola.

"He sits at my table, beneath my roof," Stefano said, dangerously quiet. "He eats my food, drinks my wine, and fills my chamber pots. What more right could a man have? And when you're done cowering behind the skirts of the women, boy, you can come to my solar. You'll have your answer there."

"Stefano," Mother said, "he only wants to please you, you can't—"

"You dare tell *me, my* business, woman? The boy knows the Code. Don't you, boy?"

Sal nodded, barely able to hold back the tears he could feel coming on. He wanted to speak, wanted to defend himself, but he could feel a knot forming in his throat.

And just like that, his uncle gave him the look, the look that told him his moment had passed. The look that sent his whole world crashing down around him.

"Very well," said Uncle Stefano as he stood. "You'll have my answer, boy, that you will."

Sal watched his uncle leave, helpless to stop him. A feeling of dread came over him, as he realized what his uncle's answer would be. But as the doors to the dining hall closed, his uncle no longer in view, it was not the answer that came to mind, but the question.

May I join you?

17

THE TRUTH

"What is this?" Sal said, standing. "That black card. What is that supposed to mean to me? Of whose death do you speak?"

Sal and Lilliana were in the teller's tent. The eight wooden cards were aligned on the table, seven atop the points of the star and the eighth at its center.

"Are there so many deaths in your life that you would ask such a question?" said the old woman, her blind white eyes fixed on his.

"Do you speak of my death?" Sal asked.

The teller didn't smile. It seemed all humor had passed from her demeanor; there was a grim expression on her wrinkled face. "There are many paths, and the future is ever changing."

"Whose death?"

"The cards do not say."

"But you're a seer, yeah? You can read the Sacrull damned things. Tell me what it means!"

The teller merely stared at him.

Lilliana was looking scared.

Just then, Damor Nev poked his head into the tent. "Everything all right, My Lady?"

"Yes, fine, Damor. I believe we are about to depart. Wait for us without, won't you."

"Aye, My Lady. As you say."

The teller did not seem pleased with the interruption. She didn't seem pleased with much of anything. She looked tired, as though she had aged with the telling. She held her wrinkled hands cradled before her. They looked weak and withered.

"What does the throne mean?" Sal said, trying a new angle. He pointed at the card in the center of the seven-pointed star. "The throne, what throne is it? What is it supposed to mean?"

The old woman tilted her head. "A throne is a thing of power, a seat of kings. A throne can mean many things—authority, sovereignty, and ascension among them—but in the end, we must derive our own meaning."

"Derive our own meaning? If we cannot change the future, what good to derive a meaning if it should not come to pass?"

"The future is ever changing," said the crone. "Every decision opens a plethora of possibility, each path taken is a new set of possibilities opened."

"Will you speak only in riddles?" Sal said, his frustration getting the better of him. He was standing.

The teller had a dark look in her white eyes, her crooked old jaw set in a grimace.

Lilliana looked as though she might run at any moment.

"Come, My Lady," Sal said. "It seems there is little more to gain from lingering."

Lilliana stood, taking Sal's proffered hand.

"Good day," she said with a nod to the teller, and placed three gold krom on the tabletop.

"You needn't have done that," Sal said as they moved for the tent flap, just loud enough he was certain the teller could hear. "The woman's a fraud." Sal held the flap for Lilliana and followed behind.

Once they were outside the tent, Damor Nev eyed Sal threateningly and again asked Lilliana if everything was all right. She assured him that it was, but told him she was tired and would like him to have the carriage pulled around so that she could go home.

Sal took that to mean she no longer wanted to be in his presence, and he understood. He didn't much want to be around himself either. Especially after that reading. The lightning tower, the black card, the man cowering beneath a shadow—what good meanings could be derived from those omens? To Sal's untrained eyes it had all looked bad, and it felt even worse once he'd left the tent. It seemed as though death walked in his wake, a cold, ominous presence, always standing somewhere just out of sight.

At the edge of the market square, Sal saw Lilliana Bastian's carriage.

"Good day, Salvatori Lorenzo."

"Right, yeah, you as well, My Lady."

Damor Nev grunted, one hand on his stiletto.

Sal watched her step into the carriage before going to look for his friends. When he returned to the wine cart, Sal found Vinny and the big man had already gone. East Market was too crowded to spot anyone. It seemed even a man of Odie's prodigious stature could hide in such a crowd. Sal quickly gave up his search.

The warm, glowing effects of the alcohol in his system had turned to the groggy and disgruntling type, accompanied by a dry mouth and a throbbing in his head. Physically drained and feeling down after his encounter with the seer, Sal wanted to get home and into his bed more than anything in the world.

With the midday traffic reaching its peak, Sal reasoned the High Bridge was his fastest route home. If he tried the Bridge of the Lady or South Bridge, he would find himself hard pressed to fight the traffic flow.

Sal cut across the Kingsway and through a few alleys, and made his way into the press of the High Bridge. The bridge was only wide enough to allow four men abreast, and made for a slow crossing over the Tamber. From the High Bridge it was through the cathedral district, along the abbey wall and past the abandoned tower he and Bartley had used as a hideout in their younger years. From

Knöldrus Road he went to the Street of Steel, then down the Singing Bridge and onto Penny Row.

The moment he stepped off the High Bridge, Sal felt eyes upon him. It seemed as though he was being watched, but whenever he turned around or glanced over his shoulder, there was no one to be seen. Sal followed Penny Row for a few paces before cutting into an apparently deserted alley.

He had taken four steps into the alley when he heard a sound that stopped him cold.

It was the sound of a man squealing in pain. Once, twice, three times he heard the noise, followed by grunting and a muffled crying.

Sal wanted to run, but he couldn't move. He was frozen like a bloodless coward. He took a sharp breath, shook his head, and snapped from the daze. He steeled himself and took one step, then another, until he was once again walking, then running toward the sounds of the crying man.

Rounding a corner, Sal saw two men kicking something on the ground, a white pile—a large bundle—no, a man, curled up on the ground, a fat whale of a man in white robes.

The man on the ground cried out once more, and Sal realized he knew him. Nabu Akkad.

Sal rushed the closer of the two men assaulting Nabu and shoved the attacker.

The man stumbled back, and the other turned to face Sal.

He was an ugly brute of a man with a jutting jaw and a tangled mess of hair. He didn't carry any visible weapons, but his knuckles looked to be red and raw from throwing punches.

"Leave him be," Sal said, thinking to reach for his pigsticker.

But before he could grab for the knife in his boot, the man rushed him.

Sal reached for his neckline and grabbed hold of the locket. He felt the flowing tendrils of energy and he unleashed it, willing forth all the power of the locket's magic.

Only, nothing happened.

There was a sharp crack of pain on the side of his head, and white lights burst behind his eyes. Before he could get a grip on the situation, he took another blow to the other side of his head. His knees went weak, and he dropped to the cobblestones.

The air was driven from him as a booted foot collided with his ribs. He heaved for air, gasping and sputtering, tears welling in his eyes as he curled up to shield himself from the blows. He took a breath, a wet, shuddering thing, and braced himself for another kick, but it didn't come.

There was shouting and the sound of scuffling. A new voice had joined the fray.

Sal could hardly think through the pounding in his head, but he had enough presence of mind to scramble to his hands and knees. When he looked up, he saw the attackers fleeing. A man with sword drawn stood over Nabu.

Sal clambered to his feet, a bit wobbly at first, but he soon got his footing and made his way over to Nabu and the armed man. His mind hazy, his vision partly obstructed by the blood streaming down his brow, Sal had difficulty deciphering the identity of the man holding the sword.

He was tall, broad-shouldered, and clean-cut. When Sal saw the mustache, a name came to mind, but it made no sense.

Dizzily, he reached for his pigsticker.

"No need for that," rumbled the voice of Damor Nev. "They've gone."

The voice fit the man, but the man did not fit the place. What was Damor Nev doing there? Where had he come from?

"Damor Nev?" Sal asked, blinking and wiping at the cut above his eye with a sleeve.

"Aye," replied the bodyguard.

"Salvatori Lorenzo?" said Nabu. "Young Salvatori, this is you, yes?"

"Here, Nabu, and still living."

Nabu had managed to roll onto his stomach, but lacked the strength to press himself up to his hands and knees.

"A hand, if a hand you can spare," Nabu said.

Sal and Damor each grabbed hold of Nabu beneath an armpit and helped him to his feet. His right eye was black and swollen, a dark bruise had started on the side of his jaw, and his lips were cut and bleeding, but otherwise he was visibly no worse for the wear.

"All right there, Nabu?" asked Sal.

The fat man coughed and smiled weakly. "Sacrull damned debtor. The dock scum owes me seventy krom. That one walked past my shop. Asked him for my coin, yes, but he tells me he will not pay. When I go after the man, this friend of his helps him to attack blameless Nabu with fists and boots."

"You are unscathed, are you not?" Sal said. "I know of a mender who would aid us if you are in need."

Nabu scoffed. "I am a bull, my boy, a bull. I need no such magickers in my affairs. Ah, but who would this be?" the fence asked, turning to face Damor. "It would seem I am in debt to you, good sir."

Damor Nev dipped his chin in acknowledgment.

"The brute with the bastard sword is Damor Nev. As to what he is doing here I haven't the foggiest," Sal said, fixing the bodyguard with narrowed eyes. "Unless he was following me."

Sal had never expected Damor Nev could blush. Yet blush he did, and a frightening sight it was to behold.

Nabu looked from Sal to the bodyguard and back to Sal.

"You were following me, then?" Sal asked.

Damor cleared his throat.

"A most fortuitous occurrence it was that such an imposing figure would take to following you, I am thinking," said Nabu.

"Why would you follow me?"

"Her ladyship. I would not allow such as yourself contact with her ladyship without knowing more about you. I followed you to learn what sort of man you were."

"And why then did you bother helping?"

Damor Nev sheathed his sword and ran a finger along his coal-black mustache.

"Reasons matter little in such an event," said Nabu, his jovial demeanor getting the better of Sal's irritation. "I for one am most grateful to you, Master Nev. Should you ever be in need, know that I am indebted to you, good sir."

Damor Nev gave Nabu the slightest of bows. "I must depart. Under other circumstances, it would have been a pleasure to make your acquaintance, sir."

"The very words from my lips, Master Nev, the very words," said Nabu. "A most pleasant Fitzen to you."

"Indeed, and yourself, Master Akkad," said Damor Nev, and looking more than a touch awkward, turned to address Sal. "Lorenzo."

Sal grunted.

At that, the man-at-arms strolled back out of the alley the same way he'd entered.

"Salvatori, my boy, this was a most fortuitous happening indeed. There is no telling what might have become of poor Nabu had I been left to deal with those thugs alone."

"It was nothing. I could never have stood by and watched those men beat you to a puddle."

"Nothing? No, nothing this thing was not. You have saved my life this day, and I owe you as much a debt as this Master Nev. Should ever you need of anything, my boy, you say the very word and Nabu Akkad shall make it so."

The sketch of an idea formed in Sal's mind, but rather than voice his thoughts, Sal said, "Let's get you home, Nabu. Are you certain you don't need a mender?"

Even had Nabu been well, the walk to his shop on Penny Row would have taken a significant amount of time. As it was, with Nabu less than sound, the short distance took them nearly half an hour to cover.

They were greeted by the familiar stagnant smell of mildew, cobwebs from ceiling to baseboards, Miniian rugs so threadbare they were more dirt than carpet.

Nabu closed his eyes and inhaled deeply through his wide nostrils. "Good to be home, yes."

Sal looked about at the figures and oddities. A walking cane, the handle replaced with a raven's talon clutching a glass orb; an ancient suit of armor; a glazed vase from the Far East; a tapestry depicting the early conquest of Pargeche; and a layer of dust that had settled over everything.

Sal's hand wandered to his collar and grasped the locket beneath his shirt.

"Your uncle, you have gone to see him?"

Sal nodded, hardly hearing the words. His mind was on the locket, on what had happened in the alley. The way it had failed him in his time of need.

"Do not take offense at the direct nature of my speaking, but I wish now to be alone so that I might rest for a time."

"Right, of course, it's only—that debt you said you owed me. I thought I might collect early."

"Very much early, no? I made this promise with little expectation that I would be forced to act upon my words at so soon a time, but keep promises does Nabu Akkad. Tell me, what is this thing you would have of me? You are only to name it, and I will do all to make it possible."

Sal reached into his shirt collar and pulled on the delicate silver chain until he held the tarnished gold locket in his palm. The locket sent tendrils of energy pulsing through him. He could feel the power of the storm within, like snakes of lightning slithering beneath his skin.

Nabu flinched.

"I want you to tell me what this is, and why you fear it so," Sal said.

For a heartbeat, Sal thought the Shiikali would start into a torrent of curses, but instead, Nabu closed his eyes and stroked his mustache. The oiled braid glistened. When Nabu opened his eyes, there was something in them that Sal had never seen before.

The look frightened him more than Sal cared to admit, and he tucked the locket back out of sight. He took a deep breath, steeled himself, and again asked Nabu to explain what he knew of the locket.

Nabu sighed, as though what Sal asked weighed on him physically.

"To understand why it is I fear this thing, there is much you must know of history."

"I know history, Nabu."

The fat Shiikali scoffed. "Knowing something of this city hardly counts as history. Tell me, my boy, what do you know of the time of empires?"

"Little and less," Sal admitted.

"This does not surprise me. The young are ever ignorant of all that comes before them. A foolish oversight, yes."

"I am interested to learn. That's why I came to you. If you eased my ignorance, I would be grateful."

"This time was much a different age from our own. It was a time when empires warred and conquered and expanded across the earth. Empires so vast as to make the kingdoms of this day seem but pitiful things. Our kingdoms of Nelgand and Naidia, once ruled by one empire, yes. Prophets and priests walked the very ground, these men who spoke with the gods. A time of wars unending, for men, for their prophets, and for the gods. This was a time for heroes."

"Myths," said Sal. "You asked if I knew history. Not ancient fables of gods and heroes."

"Ancient myth, yes, rooted in truth. But if you would not hear this thing, I would rather be to bed."

"No, I apologize. Please continue."

"There is so much to know, and yet so little you are already knowing. This thing could take past the sun's rising with the little you know of history. Should we not continue another time?"

"Please, Nabu. I do know of the First Empire, but I'm eager to know more."

The fat man sighed. "Very well. Let us see, then—what is it you know of the Sahyasa?"

Sal wrinkled his brow. He had never heard of such a thing.

"The Nelsigh have stories of the Sahyasa, yes? Of this I am most certain."

Sal shook his head.

"Your people tell stories of the Sahyasa, servants to the Dark, I know this thing."

Servants of the Dark was a term he knew. "The Beasts of Six?" Sal asked.

"Yes, six, this is a good number to start from—"

"Should we sit down?" Sal asked.

Nabu tucked his chin, jowls wobbling, eyes narrowing. "You'll not be staying so long as this. Not with that thing about your neck. Now, where was I?"

"Six," Sal said helpfully, smiling despite, or like as not because of, Nabu's blunt speech.

"Six, yes, six Sahyasa, six beings of darkness fell, chosen to guard the realms below. Six summoned by the Shattered One when this god sought dominion over the world of men a second time. Seven was the number to answer this call. Seven heroes chosen by the Light to come to the aid of mankind and make battle with that which sought to usurp the Light's domain."

Sal did his best to understand, to process the information and make connections between Nabu's disparate threads of thought, but he couldn't.

"Six and seven, right, and what does this have to do with the locket?"

"Your impatience is as vast as your ignorance. Perhaps I will be taking a seat if this telling must happen at such a pace."

Nabu led Sal behind the counter and into the back room. Among the piles of unidentifiable objects were a table, three chairs, and a cooking hearth. There was a staircase which led to an upper-level loft that apparently contained Nabu's sleeping quarters.

"Place that kettle in the hearth," Nabu said, slumping into a chair twice the size of the other two.

Sal did as the man asked, lifting the kettle and hanging the handle upon the hook.

"The Shattered One, yes, Sacrull as you would say. 'Three of six,' this is a saying among you Nelsigh?"

"Sure, three of six," Sal said with a shrug. "I always thought it was a dicing term. What does it have to do with the Beasts of Six?"

"Have you never wondered why the tales of those Vespian monks only name three of his Sahyasa? Only three, not six?"

Sal shook his head slowly. "Karull," Sal said, "the arbiter, and Nithrull, eater of flesh. I don't recall the third."

"The flayer of souls, Berull," said Nabu. "But Beasts of Six, not three. When the Darkness returned, his beasts snapping at his heels, they were seven in all. The holiest of numbers this, and a most unholy mockery it was. The Light does not retreat before the Dark, and seven were chosen in the answering. Seven in the stead of one. They were led by Kellandravast, the one known to the Nelsigh as Kellenvadra the Fifth, forger of the final path."

"Kellenvadra? I've heard that name before, but Nabu, doesn't the Vespian Order claim Susej defeated Sacrull? It's known as the Sundering. Susej banished Sacrull, opened the paths and healed the shattered world, stitching it back together with the roots of the World Tree."

Nabu nodded, chins jiggling. "This is the truth of it, yet legends tell this sundering was thousands upon thousands of years before the time of empires. Though I do not doubt these Vespian monks find the stories of that time an inconvenience to their narrative."

"And how is it you know so much of this time of empires?"

"Why, the very nature of my trade. It is a poor fence who does not know his history. Such a man is liable to be taken advantage of. Also, I am the blood of Akandi and Panalu. I do not come from this land of the Nelsigh where your knowledge of the past has been shaped and pruned by men with brown robes and shaved heads, wanting to convey their own set of truths. These Vespian monks would seek to abolish all knowledge of this second coming of the Shattered One. It contradicts much of their teachings, but the holy orders of my nation can do no such thing, for the events of the second coming took place in the holy deserts of Shiikal."

"What events?"

"The final battle of Light and Dark, the last stand of the Seven, and the chaining of the Shattered One."

"I've not heard this tale."

"And this should surprise me, yes? No, this order of Vespians has done well in this. Few of your people know of these things which I speak, but I assure you, mere ignorance of a thing does not make it false."

"And what of this last stand? What happened?"

"Is it not apparent, this thing? We do not stand in darkness this day."

"So, the Seven defeated Sacrull and his Beasts of Six?"

Nabu nodded. "It is told the Sahyasa returned to this realm upon the paths of Susej, paths warped and corrupted and festering with evil until only the most fell could walk them. These Sahyasa forged paths of their own, paths to lead astray wandering sheep, charms to lure, and traps to snare. These six paved the way for his coming, this shattered lord of theirs, with corruption and fear, fire and plague. Still, the Seven stood in the path of the Sahyasa. The heroes chosen of the Light were victorious, they defeated the Sahyasa and chained the Shattered One. The details of this have been obscured by time, yet certain things are rumored. Things such as bindings, ancient magics used to mate the essence of a thing's power to an object which can serve as a vessel, sealed inside by a rune."

An uneasy feeling formed inside Sal's belly. He didn't like where Nabu's explanation was leading.

"There have been tales through time," Nabu continued, "tales from all over the known world, of these objects. Artifacts that contain a certain power, magics long dead to this world. Rumor of these objects tells of a rune. I know of one, written of in the text of Kellenvadra herself, that speaks of the rune which you have shown me. The very mark of the Shattered One. Three vertical lines. A simple thing, these three lines, unmistakable, yes."

Suddenly the pieces fell into place.

"I see by your looking that you understand this thing. Now that you are knowing, surely you see why this must be done, why you must be rid of this thing?"

Sal put a hand to his collar. He could feel the warmth of the locket through the fabric of his shirt, the rivulets of energy streaming into him. When Sal spoke, the words came out slowly, as though each word were being dragged past his teeth.

"How can you be certain?"

"Certainty is what you are wanting, yes, but I cannot give you this. I can only say that I believe it is so. Tell me, when you touch that pendant, do you not feel the power within? Anything out of the usual?"

Sal squirmed like a man come face to face with the Royal Inquisition.

"I see," said Nabu. "Any odd happenings?"

"Odd happenings? What do you mean?"

"I would that you told me. You know what I mean when I ask, I am thinking. Do not forget, this is not the first you have shown me of this thing, and I have touched it, yes, with my very hand." Nabu held up a plump hand, each sausage finger with a ring of silver or gold bedecked with jewels.

"Right," Sal said, his mind spinning with all the information. It was almost too much to take in. "I'll do it."

"Are you certain, my boy? I would do this thing. You are only to be asking it of me."

"No," Sal said, fist clenched. "I'll destroy it myself."

18

THE RUSTED ANCHOR

The anchor was a head taller than Sal, a massive hunk of orange iron, the surface pocked by years of weathering. It stood upon three curved hooks, a ring the size of a man's head atop the stock. It was rumored to be a remnant of the First Empire, but Sal had heard other rumors that the design was not nearly so old as that. Still, the thing was old and big, so big Sal had trouble imagining how it had come to rest this far inland.

The Rusted Anchor alehouse was named for the great anchor just outside its doors. Located near the toe of the Shoe district, the Rusted Anchor wasn't well known to anyone with any sense of dignity. The Rusted Anchor was a hole, filled with dice loaders and card sharps. The beer was flat, the shiplap walls moldy and peeling, and the rushes so old they crackled underfoot. Within the Rusted Anchor, the smell of the salt sea was replaced with that of stale smoke and sweating men.

As Sal passed a man making sick by the door, a young working girl locked eyes with him but didn't pursue when Sal shook his head. He stepped into the taproom and looked to the back. Valla sat at her usual table, sipping a mug and watching him with her sharp eyes.

The Rusted Anchor was an independent joint, much like the

Hog Snout. It wasn't owned by anyone connected, but just like everyone else, connected or not, the Rusted Anchor paid dues to the Commission. Valla made the collections, paying up the ladder to Don Moretti for the privilege. She was a good earner, and likely would have been dubbed a made man years ago, had she not lacked one crucial part of the anatomy.

Sal nodded and took a seat across from Valla.

"Shouldn't you be out scouting for Luca?" Valla asked. "Or have you only been claiming to work?"

Sal smiled. "Scouting encompasses a broad field. I like to look at all the angles before I commit to any specific strategies."

"What are you drinking?" she asked.

"Not today," Sal said. "This is purely business. I want a clear head."

"Business?" Valla said, arching an eyebrow and moving a hand slowly across the tabletop. She wet her lips and looked deep into his eyes. "This the sort of business you had in mind?"

Sal's pulse quickened.

"Is that what you think about when you see me?" Valla said, her voice almost a purr. "Hmm? You see me like some whore?"

"Whoa, Valla, I—"

"You want me to suck your cock, Salvatori? Is that why you're here?"

"No, come on, Val, don't be that way."

"And what way should I be? I see the way you look at me. Same way they all look at me. Difference is you aren't man enough to come out and say it."

"Slow down," Sal said. "I told you, I'm here about business."

"How many times you think I've heard that one?" Valla said, sneering.

"Anton," Sal said. "I'm here about Anton, then."

"Not going to suck him off neither. Especially not now."

"Funny," Sal said. "Did something happen? You seem a tad touchy today."

Valla pursed her lips. Then slowly a snarl formed. "Fucking

Dirge, that goddamn whoreson. I swear I'll cut off his cock the next time that pimp opens his mouth."

Sal understood. "The big pimp, over by the door?"

"If he weren't paying up the ladder, I'd have done it already. He won't always be in favor, though. Just you wait. I'll be made soon enough. Word came down from Alonzo Amato saying he would sponsor me."

"Truly? Valla, that's some good news."

"Ask me. It's a long time coming. If I had a cock swinging between my legs, I'd have been a made man years ago."

"Still, Alonzo Amato as sponsor, that's nothing to scoff at."

"Yeah, well, saying ain't doing. Word's come down, but word is all I have thus far."

Sal shrugged. "Well, listen, you hear word of anything else that's come down from the Commission of late?"

"Such as?"

"Such as word on Anton. Who approved the hit, and who might have carried it out."

Valla's eyes began to well, her bottom lip trembling slightly. Anton and Valla had been in the same crew for years, nearly as long as Sal had worked under Anton. Back before Anton and Fabian even. Valla shook her head. "The big man and I have been looking into it. Seems to me whoever did Anton did it outside Commission sanction. Still, it could be someone is just playing their cards close to the chest."

Sal shook his head. "That worries me."

"Look," Valla said. "In this business, people die all the time. Everyone knows that coming in. Anton as well as anyone."

"And you're willing to accept that?"

Valla shrugged in a most feline way.

Sal shook his head. "Well, I don't."

"And?" Valla asked, arching an eyebrow.

"I want you to tell me about the High Keep job," Sal said.

"What about it? You were there, weren't you?"

"I was there, and I know what I saw, I know what I heard and what I think. What I don't know is what you think about it all, but I would like to learn."

"The job was botched. Whole thing went south the moment those steel caps sprung their ambush."

Sal nodded. "Strange, that."

"Strange what?"

"That ambush."

Valla sat up straighter, her eyes narrowing. "What do you mean?"

"I mean it was strange. How did they know we were coming? Also, if they did know we were coming, why spring the ambush before we were all within the Keep? Wait a few minutes, and they'd have had us all cornered like rats."

Valla shrugged. "I'd not considered that, but you're right, half of us were still outside the walls."

Something occurred to Sal that he'd not thought to ask. "Val, who was still outside when the steel caps sprang?"

"Hard to say. We were all split up at that point, but from what I can recall—I was roof-side. Dellan, Vincenzo, and the big man were within. You," Valla said nodding to Sal, "were in the courtyard, and Anton was on the bailey wall. Which leaves—"

"Bartley," Sal said.

There was a moment of silence while they both seemed to digest the information.

Sal shook his head. "No."

Valla lifted both eyebrows and tilted her head, her eyes wide and her lips pursed.

Sal shook his head again. "You don't know him like I do."

"And you'd stake your life on that claim?"

"I would," Sal said without hesitation.

Valla shrugged. "If you say so. You know the Yahdrish better than I. Still, the fact stands, there was a rat in the crew. Someone talked to the City Watch."

"Any word on the rat?"

"Nothing as of yet. The big man says he's still working on an in with the steel caps. Regardless, someone told them we would be there. I have to wonder how much they knew. Did they know what we were after?"

"And just what was that, exactly?"

Valla looked at him skeptically, as though sensing a trap.

Sal shrugged, and nearly reached for the locket hanging about his neck. Just what did Valla know of the locket? "I mean that with all sincerity," Sal said. "I know what we were after, sort of, but I couldn't tell you why, nor to what end."

Valla took a swig from her mug and wiped at her mouth with a sleeve, glaring at Sal all the while.

Sal didn't like that look. It was the sort of look that told him he didn't have long to live unless he changed the subject. But this was what Sal had come to find out. He needed to know what Valla knew. He needed to know what had gone wrong that night, and why.

"I mean it, Valla. We pulled a job on the High Keep. Lady's sake, the bloody High Keep, and for what? A ring and a letter?"

Valla's look softened, and she put two fingers to her lips. She seemed to be thinking, a good sign. It was when she acted before thinking that she was truly dangerous. "He didn't tell you, did he?" Valla finally said.

"Who? Tell me what?"

"Anton," she said.

Sal's heart skipped a beat. Did she know? Had she known about the locket all along? Suddenly he saw everything in a whole new light. He'd thought he was the only one, but of course he wasn't. Someone else knew. Someone else was looking for it. Had Anton told Valla about the locket?

Sal clenched the edge of the table. It was all he could do to keep from bolting. "What did Anton not tell me?"

The way Valla looked at him was so catlike Sal half expected her to meow when she opened her mouth. "The ring and the letter," Valla said, before taking a long, slow drink from her mug. She was intentionally dragging out the moment. It was just like Valla to delay, if only to watch him squirm. "They both belong to the same man."

The ring and the letter, but no mention of the locket. Sal relaxed somewhat.

"They belong to the duke, yeah?" Sal said. He had assumed they must have belonged to the duke, but the hint of a smirk Valla showed made him think otherwise. "They didn't belong to the duke?"

Valla flashed a coy smile.

"All right, out with it."

"Andrej," she said. "The ring and the letter, they belonged to Andrej."

"Prince Andrej?" Sal asked.

"Do you know of another Andrej living in the High Keep?"

"But Andrej," Sal said. "That makes no sense. Why Andrej?"

"Why not? The letter and the ring belonged to Andrej, and we set out to snatch the pair."

"But why Andrej? I mean, why steal the letter and the ring? What good are they? Valla, what was in that letter?"

Valla shrugged easily. "Fuck if I know."

"It just doesn't make sense. I don't see what good it would do to —unless," Sal said as realization struck, "Luca means to blackmail the prince."

"Ah, now there's an interesting fucking angle, blackmail."

"So Luca does mean to blackmail the prince?" Sal asked. "But why Andrej? He's the duke's youngest son. Why not the duke himself?"

Valla arched an eyebrow, and Sal took a moment to think it through.

"Two reasons, I suppose," Sal said. "The duke would be a hard man to threaten, but his son, his youngest, weakest son, he might crack. The second: blackmail requires leverage of some sort, and it seems Luca found leverage on Andrej."

Valla shook her head, smiling. "Why ask the questions if you only mean to answer them?"

Sal returned the smile. "Right, then, here's the new sticking point. What does Luca mean to blackmail the prince for?"

"Another good fucking question," Valla said. "But you're not asking right."

"What do you mean?"

"Luca, he was only running the crew, he wasn't backing the job. He was just the point man."

"So, the backer," Sal said. "Who was that?"

"How should I know? Luca runs the crew, not me."

"And the High Keep job. It was all about blackmailing a prince?"

Valla shrugged. "Seems to me that's the case."

Sal shook his head skeptically. "And Anton—Lady's sake, Pavalo for that matter—why were they done?"

"Word hasn't come down so far as I've heard. But it's like I said, seems to me they were done outside Commission sanction. Why not ask that uncle of yours? If anyone knows something, it would be Stefano."

Sal sighed. "You don't think Anton was, you know, the rat?"

"Anton?" Valla said. "Antonio Russo, a rat? I don't see it. No, not Antonio."

"And what of Luca?"

"What of him?" Valla asked.

"Tying up loose ends," Sal said.

Valla fixed him with a level stare. "He wouldn't be the first crew-point to do that on suspicion. I'd not put it past him, either. Not after Fabian."

Sal nodded and stood.

"The fuck are you going?"

"I need to see a man about some wool. In the meantime, stay safe, Val. There's something in the works that we don't know about."

Valla scoffed and took a swig from her mug.

THE LETTER

INTERLUDE, EIGHT YEARS EARLIER

Five hundred krom. Just holding that much coin was a thrill. Sal had never seen a coin purse that size, much less been trusted to handle it himself. He tucked the purse inside his cloak, hoping not to attract attention. This was a big-time job, the sort of job Sal had waited months to get. It was a chance to prove himself, to show he had what it took to do meaningful work.

But once the job was under way, the glow of prestige that surrounded it quickly vanished, flitting away like morning dew beneath the afternoon sun. Sal spent the entire walk imagining what it could be that he'd been sent to purchase. A jeweled sword, a mythical beast, an exotic woman perhaps, but no, he'd been sent to buy a scrap of tattered old parchment.

Tattered parchment for five hundred gold krom hardly seemed a good deal. The Dahuaneze man that met Sal on the loading round of Harbor Nine appeared to be thinking the same thing. The look he gave Sal was one of sheer skepticism when Sal handed over the coin purse in exchange for the scribblings.

"Kellenvadra," he said in his heavily accented voice. "Kellenvadra."

"Kellenvadra," Sal said with a nod. Whatever that meant.

After the little Dahuaneze man had scuttled off, Sal scanned the parchment, but the writing was in some foreign script. He hoped, for his own sake, that he had not been duped, and that his uncle was interested in that scrap of parchment.

The rain had begun to fall just before Sal crossed South Bridge. Once in High Town, Sal slipped into a covered alley, the parchment tucked inside his cloak where it would stay dry and hopefully attract less attention.

The last thing he needed was to have some steel caps take their toll with his uncle's new purchase.

Eventually he reached home. To his surprise, Greggings was nowhere to be seen when he entered. Still, he wiped the mud from his shoes as the manservant would have instructed. Sal crossed the lavender tile and made for the stairs.

The house was quiet, nearly silent. He could hear his footfalls echoing down the hall as he walked to his room. The quiet was odd, and Sal couldn't figure the reason.

When he reached his room, he looked about. Nothing seemed out of the ordinary, nothing out of place, and yet Sal couldn't shake the feeling that something was wrong.

And then he saw it: a letter at the foot of his bed. A red wax seal, unbroken, stamped with something serpent-like. He picked up the letter. The wax seal looked to have been stamped with a dragon.

"M-Master Salvatori," said Greggings from behind him.

Sal turned slowly, the break in the man's voice setting his hackles on the rise.

"Greggings," Sal said. "What's happened?"

"Come with me," Greggings said, his eyes rimmed with red. "It's your mother."

UNCLE STEFANO

L illiana approached tentatively, looking all about before she took a step. From the rooftop, the gloves were only a blot on the ground, but Sal knew that indefinable shape to be a pair of indigo woolen gloves. He knew this because he had put them on the steps himself; he'd tied a red ribbon into a bow and slipped a hadrisk flower into the ribbon. Nicola had made the gloves. Sal had told her his vision and his sister had made it come to life.

Nicola had woven the gloves on a spider loom, dyed them with true indigo, and at Sal's request had worked meadowsweet into the wool to give the gloves the smell of spring. The gloves were the third gift he'd left for Lilliana since Fitzen, when she had purchased the indigo scarf. The first of his gifts had been a woolen cap, admittedly not the most fashionable accouterment, but warm, made with materials of the highest quality and dyed with true indigo to match Lilliana's scarf. The second was a pair of woolen stockings, dyed to match the scarf and hat. Sal had tied a red ribbon about the stockings and slipped into the bow a marsh lily, a purple variety that grew down by the riverside.

The indigo gloves that smelled of meadowsweet had been the climax to his crescendo of gifts, the final piece of his plan. With the gloves Sal had left a note, tucked behind the white petals of the hadrisk flower.

Leaving the note, Sal had felt the fool of a fool. Her acceptance of his gifts had been a true gamble, with longer odds than any sane man would bet on. The note was another matter entirely. If his gifts had not spoken his intentions loud enough, the note would be near impossible not to hear. Lilliana Bastian was the daughter to one of the wealthiest men in Dijvois. She was a maiden of marriageable age, desirable looks, and unfathomable promise.

She was entirely unobtainable.

However, in all the time Sal had watched Lilliana as he gathered information for Luca, there had been scant few suitors, and those who had tried had made attempts feebler than Sal's own.

Lilliana reached down and picked up the gloves. She looked around, as though feeling she was being watched.

Sal ducked out of sight.

He smiled to himself at his knee-jerk reaction. He hadn't needed to worry. No one ever looked up at the rooftops, apart from thieves looking for steel caps, and steel caps looking for thieves. When Sal resumed watching Lilliana, she was reading his note. His pulse began to quicken, his tongue sticky against his dry palate. He wished he were close enough to see the reaction on her face, to know whether she was pleasantly surprised or outright disgusted by the note. To know whether she would show up to meet him or not. To know whether he should bother waiting for her beside the limestone statue of the Lady White.

The anticipation plucked at his nerves. All he wanted was Lilliana's answer, yes or no, but it was an answer he would needs wait to receive.

Tomorrow, the note said, evenfall.

For Sal, the best parts of the past weeks had been those short moments he'd spent watching her. She seemed to be the only thing that brought him joy. Despite that, or perhaps because of it, he'd begun to feel guilty about spying on Lilliana, even unclean for the thoughts he'd had about her. He tried to convince himself it was not his fault, and that he should not feel guilty about watching her; after all, it was his job.

Sal knew Luca would be displeased about the gifts he had left for Lilliana, even more so about the note, but he assured himself Luca would never learn of it. He was Luca's scout. He was the eyes and ears of the operation. Luca only knew what Sal wanted him to know.

Or so he hoped.

Still, Luca wasn't the one Sal needed to be concerned with. Luca might not learn of his contact with Lilliana, but Luca's backer, whoever it was that had paid Luca to set up the operation, was a complete unknown, and was all the more dangerous for that. Sal would have no way of knowing when or if they'd found out about his contact with her. Might be the backer already knew.

Lilliana continued down the steps and was met in the driveway by her carriage. Damor Nev stepped from the coach, his bastard sword slung on his back. The bodyguard moved aside and held the door for his lady.

A smile crept over Sal's face as he saw Lilliana pause and slip on the indigo gloves before she stepped into the coach. When Damor Nev closed the door and the carriage departed, Sal stood. He checked the street below for steel caps, lowered himself to the cobblestones, and made his way to the South Bridge. He was still feeling quite hopeful concerning his prospects with Lilliana as he crossed the Big Island, when he saw Odie, a head and a half taller than everyone on the street, walking in his direction.

The big man lumbered directly toward him, and for an instant Sal tensed. He remained where he was, feet planted on the cobblestones.

Odie smiled, an unsettling sight by any standard. It reminded Sal of an oversized child.

"Oy, Salvatori," Odie said, hailing Sal with one massive hand. "Got a message from Luca."

"Let me guess," Sal said with a smirk. "The Crown?"

Odie nodded, and just like that moved on.

"Hey, Big Man."

Odie turned back.

"Whatever happened to the tattooed freak? I thought he was playing messenger boy for Luca."

"I ain't seen Dellan since Fitzen," said the big man. "Seems the Vordin's been busy with some job."

"You working this next job for Luca as well?" Sal asked.

Odie nodded, and began to move away once more.

At times Odie seemed cold natured, but there was something Sal could appreciate about a man of few words.

"Odie," Sal said, nodding toward the big man's hand. "The tracer."

Odie looked at his hand as though only then realizing he was carrying the folded square of linen. He nodded, opened his hand, and let go of the square of cloth as black ash drifted away with the breeze.

Sal turned around and headed back the way he'd come, only this time he followed the Kingsway up High Hill until he reached the Crown.

Each time Sal met Luca at the Crown, he noticed more and more just how out of place the man was. Luca was like a long-jaw swimming in a school of herring. Placed just outside the walls of the High Keep, the Crown was the sort of posh establishment frequented by newlywed gentry and lords of state seeking a night on the town.

But Luca had been a dock thug, and a dock thug he remained. After all, he couldn't merely wash the scars from his face, nor the tattoos from his skin.

Sal imagined the Crown had lost business since Luca had decided to make its back table his place of meeting. There were times when Luca had Sal meet him at the safe house, but that was rare, as the safe house was short of women in tight bodices serving roast capon and suckling pork with jugs of mulled wine and thimble glasses of sweet hippocras.

As usual, Luca was seated at his table in the back. There was no meal before him, merely a bottle of wine, a candle, a paring knife he used to trim his nails, and a look on his face that revealed he was in a sour disposition.

When Sal sat, Luca cleared his nail trimmings off the table. He did not let them fall to the floor, though. Rather, he swept them into a small swatch of his linen napkin, folded the cloth twice and set it afire on the lit candle. The flame glowed in Luca's eyes as he dropped the linen swatch to the tabletop and watched it burn.

Sal sat upright and did his best to keep his breathing steady. Luca's paranoid precaution had startled him more than he wanted to admit.

"Wine?" Luca asked.

Sal accepted the offer. It was a sour vintage, appropriate for a man in a sour mood.

"Well, what have you got for me? What news of the council's interests?"

"Little has changed since my last report. Lord Hugo remains quite entangled in the Shiikal trade tariffs, and his correspondence with Lord Vaughan and Lord Peaks suggests others in the High Council have opposed the proposition of a full embargo. They argue an embargo would not stop the trade, but merely move it to a black market where the crown of Nelgand will lose out on taxes and regulation."

Luca arched an eyebrow. "Opposition to the embargo in the High Council? This is news indeed. What are your thoughts on the matter?"

"I agree with Lord Hugo's opposition. If my interests aligned with those of the duke, I would oppose the embargo. However, as my interests are not aligned with the duke's, I support the embargo and intend to exploit the future inflation of imports from the Near East."

Luca smiled and tapped the side of his head with two fingers, the sour look all but scrubbed from his visage. "An enterprising mind, but what else have you for me? What of the sugar blossom?"

Sal hated when Luca mentioned Lilliana. Spying on her felt like enough of a betrayal of her trust, and relaying her movements and secrets to Luca seemed a betrayal of the highest order.

"Little and less has changed," Sal said, feigning nonchalance with a shrug. "She goes to East Market on Tiens, South Market on Sujens and Thorsens, Town Square on Leidens, Malens, and Sacrens. Soluns she visits the cathedral."

"And the hired sword, this Bauden creature, he's always with her?"

"More often than not. You'll want him to be far away when you make the move on the estate. Many of the house guards have gone soft with their leisurely posts. Not a man of them is worth his salt with a sword, but Damor Nev is another story."

Luca nodded. "I anticipate Nev won't be much of a problem with a dagger in his back and his life's blood spilling from his throat."

Sal shuddered. He knew no threat from Luca was an idle one, and despite not liking the bodyguard, he didn't think the man deserved a red smile. Besides, Damor Nev had saved him in that alley off Penny Row. If anything, Sal owed him a debt, and a dagger to the back was no way to repay that debt.

"Who will be guarding the gate come evenfall?" Luca asked.

"If the rotation remains consistent it'll be Dingle and Twitch." Sal had given all of the guards names to keep them straight; Dingle and Twitch were two of the softest and least adept of the household guards.

Luca nodded, poured them each a cup, and told Sal he'd done well. "There will be a big cut in this for you, my boy. Surely you of all people have earned it."

"You mean to do the job come evenfall?"

"Not something you need to worry over. You'll get your cut for work well done. Consider your part taken care of."

Sal nodded, took a drink of the sour wine, and wondered whether he should be relieved that his work for Luca was finished or terrified because Luca no longer had a use for him.

Luca flicked the back of his hand in the air a few times, as though shooing an animal.

Sal stood. Eager to leave as he was, he had little desire to turn his back to Luca. If Luca wanted Sal dead, he wouldn't let a little thing like a crowded tavern stop him from slitting Sal's throat then and there. Just ask the corpse of Fabian.

"The Lady's luck to you, then," Sal said, and turned.

"Hold," Luca said before Sal had taken a step. "You'll need to excuse me, kid. Incidents of late have been of an upsetting nature, and I fear it has left me in a disgruntled fucking state."

Luca stood and closed the distance to Sal.

Sal flinched as Luca wrapped him in a hug.

"You've truly done well, Salvatori. Truly."

Sal returned the embrace, moving his hands with the deftness of a soft-touch artist, his heart beating so fast it was difficult to draw breath.

"Be safe," Luca said, releasing Sal. "You'll have word of your cut soon enough, I assure you."

Sal nodded and turned for the door, his fist clenched tight about his prize. He felt the stares of the other patrons as he left. Once outside the Crown, Sal pocketed the hair he had plucked from Luca's doublet, feeling a tick safer knowing the hair was in his jerkin pocket.

B artley and Vinny had been waiting in the taproom of the Hog Snout for a full hour. Bartley didn't seem to mind, but Vinny was in a right state about something.

"That Sacrull damned singer needs be gone," Vinny said. "Surely Bessy could find one man in the city that can carry a tune and knows some new songs, for Light's sake."

"Before you go piddle," cried the singer, strumming his lute, *"consider you this: If not for that diddler, who'd diddle your sis?"*

"What news of Luca?" Bartley asked.

Sal shrugged. "Claims this was my last report, I am officially out of the job. Now I wait for the coin to come to me. That or the knives, there's no telling with Luca."

"He wouldn't dare," said Bartley. Not with your uncle being who he is."

Sal wasn't as sure as Bartley. After all, Anton was a made man, and he found himself with a red smile all the same. Sal wasn't made, he wasn't even connected, merely the nephew of a Commission underboss. By any measure, Sal was a nobody.

"Right. Well, it seems I find myself unemployed and without any coin to show for weeks of work," Sal said. "Anyone have a job in mind?"

Vinny's top lip curled. "Why don't you talk to your uncle? He should have work, and I'm certain he, at the least, is a man of his word."

The way Vinny spoke was like an assault, every word projected like the thrust of a dagger.

"Did I do something wrong?" Sal asked, taken aback by the behavior usually reserved for Bartley.

"Wrong?" Vinny said. "Clearly you've done nothing if naught comes to mind."

Sal looked to Bartley, but the Yahdrish only shrugged. Sal was incredulous.

"Something must be wrong. Elsewise your smallclothes wouldn't be in such a bunch."

Vinny snarled. "Might be I'm only upset because Antonio Russo's old route was filled, and it's not me that's working it."

Sal frowned. He'd forgotten all about his promise to speak to his uncle on Vinny's behalf. "Oh, Vinny, I'm sorry, mate. I'll speak with him, surely it can still be settled."

Vinny spat to the rushes. "Too late. The route's already been filled."

"Who?" Sal asked, in the hopes that it was a leg-breaker of little enough significance that he might be replaced without much fuss.

"One of Alonzo Amato's boys," said Vinny. "Bruno Carbone, I think his name was."

"Anything to drink, honey?" said Bessy.

"Nothing for me, thank you," said Sal.

"A vial of dredge" said Vinny sullenly.

Bessy frowned. "Anything for you, hon?"

Bartley blushed, something that still seemed to happen even

after he claimed to have coupled with the barmaid. "Another ale," Bartley said, winking to compensate for his rosy complexion.

"Luca say anything about Anton this time?" Bartley asked as Bessy moved off.

"Quiet as ever," Sal said. "If he had something to do with it, he doesn't want anyone to know."

"What did your uncle say about it?" Bartley asked.

"How should I know?" said Sal.

"Well, you did ask the man?" Vinny said.

Sal shook his head. "Haven't gotten around to it."

"Hold on," said Bartley. "You mean to say you haven't talked to your uncle since we found Anton?"

"Haven't seen him in a few months," Sal said defensively. "It's not as though I visit the man often."

Bartley stared at him slack-jawed. "You never bothered to ask your uncle whether he knew something about Anton's murder? Sacrull's balls, you never fucking bothered?"

"Lady's sake, Bartley, I've been a touch busy. What with Luca's job and worrying about my own neck and all. Besides, what makes you think Stefano would even tell me?"

Not deigning to grace Sal with a reply, Bartley simply shook his head, as though he couldn't believe Sal's behavior.

"You'll be off, then?" Vinny asked.

"Now?" Sal said.

Vinny nodded. "Now, and don't you bloody forget to ask about that route. I need this one, Salvatori."

Sal felt a twinge of irritation boiling up, but he swallowed his pride, knowing that at times the only way to win was to lose. Sal stood. He looked first to Bartley, then to Vinny. Something else was bothering Vinny, but Sal couldn't quite pin down what it was.

Vinny took a drink, pretending to watch the singer, the very same singer he'd said wasn't worth the toe-jam from an especially stinky boot.

"Right, then." Sal said. "Suppose I'd best be off."

Vinny's top lip twitched as he nodded. Bartley grunted and turned his attention to the singer as well.

At that, Sal turned and headed for the exit. The door of the inn swung shut behind him. Overhead, the crudely painted sign of the boar swayed listlessly in the breeze, the hinges creaking in a rhythmic cadence.

Sal reached for the locket at his collar, and the soft pulsating power coursed through his body, reenergizing him before he began his walk to High Town.

———

B eneath the fresh coat of lacquer the door was solid oak, and each rap of the brass falcon's-head knocker resounded with a heavy thud. Three knocks and he stepped back. Sal heard noise from within. The heavy door swung open, and a little brown man with a head like a spotted egg stood on the threshold.

"M-Master Salvatori," stammered Greggings, wringing his hat in his little arthritic hands.

"Just Salvatori. I'm no one's master, especially not yours."

The old manservant bowed deferentially. "How might I be of service?"

"My uncle, is he in?"

"Lord Stefano is in his solar. I could call on him and see if he can make the time." Greggings stepped aside, allowing Sal into the tiled foyer.

"I know the way, Greggings. There's no need for you to climb the stairs."

"But Master Salvatori, it wouldn't be proper."

"Bugger propriety," Sal said, giving the manservant a wink. "Consider this a homecoming."

"Will you be returning to us?"

"I meant it in a figurative sense. I'm only here for a visit."

The old manservant's relief was visible in his eyes, though he did his best to hide it.

"Worry not, Greggings, there will be no need to change the rushes and beat the curtains in the guest quarters."

Greggings paid him the hint of a smile. "Will you require

refreshments? I've some pickled herring in the larder to which his lordship has grown quite partial."

"Nothing for me, thank you. Why don't you find yourself a nice place to sit and put your feet up. I'll only need to speak with my uncle a moment, but anything he needs I can take care of while I'm here."

Greggings smiled and nodded, but Sal knew the man was too dutiful—and far too stubborn—to ever allow himself such a respite.

Each time Sal returned to the home of his uncle, he was reminded of how he used to feel, walking through that house as a child. He'd been like a mouse, scurrying this way and that, always trying to stay out of sight and keep from being crushed underfoot. It was almost surreal to him now, to walk beneath that same roof, on that very same floor. Only now, all he felt was sadness and loss.

Sal made his way across the pale lavender tile of the foyer, up the grand staircase, and along a hall. He took the third door on the right and entered the solar. He shivered as a draft swept through the room.

A magnificent gold and crystal chandelier hung at the center of the ceiling, refracting the light that penetrated the bay windows. Each wall was lined with shelves full of books, the floor carpeted with a massive, elaborately patterned Miniian rug. The one space on the wall devoid of bookshelves or windows was occupied by a quartered crest of carved wood and gilded bronze. Gold for Novotny, blue for Moretti, white for Scarvini, red for Dvorak. Bronze falcon at the center, upon the black of Svoboda.

The silver-haired man lounging in the armchair looked up as Sal entered the solar. He wore a double-breasted frock coat and reading lenses. In one hand was a thick leather-bound book, in the other a crystal glass of golden wine.

Stefano Lorenzo fixed Sal with a look of pure apathy, the placid expression unchanging as Sal crossed the room and sat in the armchair beside his uncle.

"Good day, Uncle."

"A good day, is it?" asked Stefano, not unkindly but certainly lacking genuine interest.

Sal shrugged. "I've naught to complain of thus far. How have you fared of late?"

Stefano frowned. "I've no patience to bandy words." Stefano placed his wine glass on the table between them and closed the book in his lap. He kept a hand on the stem of his glass to stabilize it as he slid open the table drawer. From the drawer he withdrew a leather cord and held it at eye level.

Sal's heart plopped to the pit of his stomach as his uncle's ring rocked to and fro upon the throng.

"When the man came to my door demanding his due, I thought him a liar. Surely this man was mistaken, my own nephew offering twenty krom for a ferry ride," Stefano said, shaking his head. "Twenty krom for passage across the Tamber, he says to me. If not for this ring, I'd have slit the man's throat and named him liar."

"Twenty krom? The crook! We agreed to eight."

"Eight or twenty, the coin is not the point," snapped Stefano. "Though you are not of my loins, you bear my name. I tell you, boy, a gift given can be taken. I'll not have you bantering about my city making mock of the name Lorenzo."

"Surely, Uncle, it is not so bad as that. I had every intention of returning to the ferryman—"

"The ferryman? The ferryman is not the half of it," Stefano said, shaking his head. "I ask you, boy, have I taught you so little? Did I truly send you out into this world so ill-equipped, with naught but stuffing between your ears?"

"Uncle, I—"

"What is this I hear of you working with Luca Vrana?"

Sal shrugged. There was little and less he could say in his own defense.

"First you frolic about with that fop Antonio Russo, then you take work with Luca Vrana? The man is a dockside thug. There is good reason he's not moved up the ladder. With a temper like that, he's not to be trusted. Not to mention the man's associates have a long history of disappearing."

"I've ended my working relationship with Luca."

"A sentiment hollow of reassurance. Do you think me simple, as well as deaf and blind? Fool of a fool, you don't think I know the job you took? Of all the asinine acts of a jackanapes, what would possess you to accept a job with such a man?"

"What do you know of the High Keep job?" Sal asked.

"Like as not, more than you, boy. Luca Vrana played point. Most of his usual crew, along with three stand-ins. The job was considered a failure by all accounts. Botched, as they say. City Watch interference, and bodies soon after."

"Commission-approved bodies?"

"No permission was sought of my don, nor any of the five families so far as I am aware."

"Who was the backer?" Sal asked.

"Backer," Stefano said. He frowned and shook his head. "There was no backer. It seems this Luca Vrana thinks he can back his own jobs."

"You're certain of this?" Sal asked. Valla had seemed quite certain otherwise.

Stefano wrinkled his nose and narrowed his eyes.

Sal felt a twinge of panic, a fear he'd not fully come to terms with, a truth that sank right to the pit of his stomach.

"Luca, he's the killer, yeah?" Sal asked. "Luca Vrana, he killed Anton?"

"The man is a dockside thug," said Stefano. "To think such a man would attempt a job on the High Keep. His pride is as big as the emptiness between his ears."

"But he's the killer?" Sal asked. "Luca Vrana. He killed Anton and Pavalo Picarri?"

"So far as I can surmise," his uncle said, confirming the suspicion Sal had held for weeks. "Luca Vrana has always been a killer."

BARTLEY AND BESSY

It had been Luca all along.

The realization sank in slowly, like rendering fat. The longer Sal considered the fact, the more questions arose. If Luca was responsible for Anton's death, how much did Luca know about the locket? For that matter, how much did Stefano know of the locket? He seemed well enough informed on the rest of the situation.

"Your sense has been lacking in the highest degree," Stefano said, as he pressed his reading lenses back onto the bridge of his nose. "You should never have involved yourself with Luca Vrana—with this High Keep business."

"Ah, hindsight truly is all it's made out to be, is it not, Uncle?"

"Now you mock me, boy. Do not do it again."

"I'm sorry, Uncle. You're right. I made a mistake. What can I do to correct it?"

"Correct it?" Stefano said, a hand on his chin. "What makes you think this can be corrected?"

"Because if anyone in this city could fix this, it's you, Uncle."

Greggings stepped into the solar with a knock on the open door. "M'lord, the evening meal is prepared. Will Master Salvatori be supping with you this eve?"

Stefano's face tightened. He hesitated a breath before speaking. "It would be rude of me not to extend the invitation, now that you have so blatantly announced the existence of a meal." Stefano turned to Sal. "Well, boy?"

Sal shrugged.

His uncle's nose wrinkled, his top lip curling back. Then he stood and nodded.

Greggings led the way down the stairs and into the dining room. It was an opulent room, from the grand walnut dining table, large enough to seat eighteen in plushly cushioned thrones, to the intricate designs of cherubs rolling in fields of flowers that were carved into the ceiling beams and baseboards.

An ancient tapestry from the Far Eastern city of Yardu hung upon the wall. It depicted a scene of a serpentine dragon coiling itself about some ancient city. A man in blue armor, a red banner streaming from a pole on his back and a thin, slightly curved sword in his hands, approached the dragon from the bottom corner of the tapestry. Though his uncle had long ago told him the unfortunate result of the conflict between the man and the dragon, according to ancient Dahuaneze myth, Sal liked to imagine the little armored warrior winning the fight against impossible odds, his slender curved sword cutting open the white underbelly of the dragon.

Uncle Stefano seated himself at the head of the table, so Sal sat in the cushioned throne at his uncle's right hand. Stefano's eyes narrowed, his jaw clenched, and for all Sal knew his anus puckered tight as a snapping bear trap.

It was not long before Greggings returned, balancing a tray full of steaming platters and bowls.

He started them with scallops breaded and fried in oil, then drowned in butter, with leeks slow-cooked in lemon butter and garlic, and a foie gras from one of Stefano's flock of fattened geese.

Greggings served a golden wine from Stefano's reserve stock, a fact Sal only learned due to the chastisement Greggings received from his uncle for wasting such a fine vintage on a palate so unrefined as Sal's.

The meal passed with little conversation. The dining hall felt empty, as it lacked the presence of Nicola. Sal recalled the last time his mother had sat at that table, and his appetite disappeared. As his uncle ate forkfuls of mince pie, washed down with mouthfuls of wine, Stefano seemed to loosen up, his hard edges softening.

"Your sister, how is she?" Stefano asked.

Sal covered his mouth as a belch escaped him. "Nicola is thriving. She has grown her business to thrice what it was. Bought a property off the South Market as well. She's already talked of expanding the home for her clothier's work, even mentioned buying the property next door, tearing down the home, and doubling the size of her own."

Stefano smiled, a look of pride shining in his eyes. It had always been blatantly clear, even back when Sal and Nicola were children growing up in their uncle's home, that Stefano preferred Nicola to Sal. He'd begun grooming her from an early age, taught her the secrets of his trade, equipped her with everything she would need to take his place when it came his time to leave this world. But Nicola had turned away. She'd chosen a new path, though not before spitting in the face of the man that had raised her, telling him she never wanted to see him again and blaming him for the death of their mother.

"I would that she visited sometime. It's rare enough I see this face of yours, but the face of my beautiful niece would suit nicely."

"Nicola is willful," Sal said, leaving the rest unspoken.

"There is too much of her mother in her. I'd have done anything for my sister, you know that, don't you, boy? In the end, she only had herself to blame."

Sal's fists clenched beneath the table.

Greggings cleared away the dishes from the main course and brought strawberry tarts.

Sal picked up his fork but didn't touch the tart.

"She did the best she could," Sal said, finding it difficult to unclench his jaw enough to speak.

"I told you, boy. The reason has never changed," Stefano said, scoffing derisively. "Coward's way out, I always thought."

Hands shaking, Sal threw his fork to the tabletop and stood.

"Thank you for the meal, Uncle. I am sorry your wine was wasted on me. It is always such a pleasure, but I do believe I will take my leave."

Stefano didn't show surprise, merely stared at Sal with eyes half-lidded.

Sal stalked out of the dining room and past Greggings, who tailed him to the foyer.

"Master Salvatori, please."

Sal about-faced on the pale lavender tile of the foyer, and Greggings shuffled close.

"Do be safe," Greggings said, a look of fear on his weathered brown face. "One hears of cloak-and-dagger work afoot."

Sal nodded, his anger leaving him as the words seeped in.

Greggings shivered, wringing his small hands. His eyes met Sal's as though there was more to say, but rather than speak, Greggings turned away and walked in the direction of the dining room.

T he heavy oaken door closed with a satisfying thud as Sal stepped out. The sky was a panoply of red, pink, and golden hues as the sun receded below the horizon.

As Sal walked along the cobblestone streets, he contemplated the manservant's parting words. *Cloak-and-dagger work.* It was enough to upset the confidence of any man. Even more so a man already in fear of such things, a man who'd spent weeks worried over just that. On the other hand, Sal told himself that the warning from Greggings was nothing new, he'd known there was cloak-and-dagger work afoot the very night he'd found Anton—hell, the very day he'd heard from Nabu about the fate of Pavalo Picarri. Only now he knew for certain who was behind it all.

Suddenly, Sal found himself worried about the well-being of his friends. He felt a pressing need to warn them, and doubled his pace.

He stood beneath the swaying sign of the boar. The taproom of the Hog Snout was almost deserted as he pushed through the door and made his way in. A man and woman sat at a rickety table with mismatched chairs, while an older man sat alone, calling for ale.

The man continued to call for ale, and yet Sal saw no sign of Bessy or the kitchen hand, Cooky. Blessedly, there was no singer in sight either. If Sal was going to spend another night in Bartley's room, he'd certainly appreciate a night of quiet.

As the lone man banged his empty mug on the table, shouting for ale, Sal made his way up the staircase. Apart from the man's shouting, the inn was quiet, and Sal could hear the creak of every step. The lighting was dim in the hallway atop the stairs; two of the three wall lamps had been snuffed out.

Sal inhaled the scent of meadowsweet as he reached for the handle to Bartley's door. He had never bothered to knock before entering Bartley's room; it was a sort of unspoken agreement between the two. The door was unlocked and opened with a click.

The smell of stale rushes wafted from the room, propelled by a gust of air from the open window. Bartley's room was entirely dark aside from a thin strip of moonlight that illuminated the dresser.

It seemed Bartley was out. Sal would need to search for him elsewhere. As much as he wanted to lie down and call it a night, he felt a need to warn his friends.

Before Sal headed back out, he thought he would smoke a cap, telling himself that Bartley wouldn't mind. Sal crossed the room and nearly fell flat on his face as he stumbled over something.

He managed to throw his hands out before him to cushion the fall, and landed on something softer than floorboards and wetter by far.

Something rather like—a body.

It took only an instant before realization and revulsion struck.

Sal scrambled backward, gagging and spitting his disgust, his forearms slick with warm blood. He fell on his back in his fit of panic, kicking and writhing toward the door.

He was sobbing, heaving, and shuddering. He tried to catch his breath. Snot and saliva streamed down his cheeks and lips and dripped from his chin.

He closed his eyes, allowing them to adjust to the dark, and did all he could to slow his breathing. His heart pounded like a drum of war. His hands shook like leaves in a tempest. Eventually he managed to steel his nerves enough to stand, wipe wet forearms on his trouser legs, and tentatively approach the body.

At a second look, Sal realized there were not one, but two bodies on the ground before him. A woman and a man, facedown, their naked bodies white as fish bellies in the faint moonlight.

She was closer, the larger of the two, the pale flesh of her back freckled and sagging.

The man was short and slender, a familiar tangle of black hair on his head.

Sal knew them both. Bartley and Bessy.

He knew them to be dead but couldn't help but check to be certain. He rolled first Bessy and then Bartley, checking for breathing or the beat of a heart, but found them both as he'd feared —throats cut clear across, jagged, deep wounds that had nearly drained them of blood.

The tears came on, an unquenchable flow that left Sal heaving and short of breath once more. On hands and knees he became sick, vomiting into the rushes.

His head was spinning. Why, who, how? Questions flooded his mind, and the shaking in his hands seemed to course through his entire body.

Sal needed a cap. He stumbled to the dresser, shaking and sobbing, and fumbled open the drawer. The carved ebony box was in its place snuggled among Bartley's most prized possessions.

Sal flipped open the lid of the box and removed a golden-brown cap and the pipe. He crumbled the cap into the pipe's bowl with thumb and forefinger. His sticky, bloody fingers became coated in a film of skeev dust as he worked.

Sal reached for the unlit handlamp on the bedside table, when a movement in his peripheral vision caught his attention.

He snapped around and realized he was not alone in the room.

The piercing blue eyes of a predator stared back at him hungrily, as a lithe figure separated from the shadows. Dellan wore all black, a layer of boiled leather armor and a hooded cloak. When the Kalfi-born Vordin smiled, he showed a set of teeth filed to wicked points.

Sal stumbled back. It was like staring into the face of a monster, a nightmare creature in its full corporeal form.

Dellan's knives were drawn, two jagged, ugly pieces of steel.

"All done blubbering?" Dellan asked in a voice like the crunch of a boot on gravel. "I was rather enjoying the show. Not so much as the one your little Yahdrish and his wench put on, but then there were two of them. Still, might be you'll prove droller in time. Up for a strip and a roll in the sheets before I slit your throat?"

"Why?" Sal said through quivering lips. "Why are you doing this?"

Dellan's smile spread to his eyes. "Only thing I've ever found worth taking the time to do."

Sal wanted to pull his pigsticker from his boot, but knew if he moved for the knife, Dellan would have him stuck full of holes before he even bent down. His finger-knife was handy, slipped up his sleeve, but the minuscule blade would do little against the daggers Dellan held.

"Was it Luca?" Sal asked, buying time.

"Luca?" Dellan asked, genuinely perplexed.

"He's been sending you after the rest of the crew because he never found the rat. First Pavalo, then Anton, now Bartley. Was I next?"

"Never found his fucking rat? What is it like to wallow through life in ignorance? Luca was never looking for a rat. Luca *was* the fucking rat."

"Luca, the rat?" Sal was incredulous. "How? Why?"

"Because Luca is a worm with shit for brains. Should have realized that steel cap was going to turn around and bugger him. That's what them City Watch are good for, cheating and buggering."

"But why? If Luca was the rat, why is he killing off the crew?"

"You think it's him done the killing?" Dellan said, chuckling and shaking his head. "Luca's been too busy with his little girl to be making no corpses."

"Little girl?" Did Dellan mean—but no, he couldn't.

The pale Vordin made a purring sound deep in his throat. "Soft-flesh noble bitch. Luca's going to have himself a bit of fun, I imagine. Might be I'll go for him next. Take his little prize off his hands. Claimed she was worth a sizeable ransom when he offered me the job. That was before he knew I had other work lined up. Still, think I'll take him up on the offer. Never tasted noble flesh myself."

"Lilliana?" Sal blurted.

"Might have been the cunt's name. Might be I'll ask her before I've had my taste."

Sal felt nauseous, his stomach twisted in knots. His gaze darted around the room, searching for a place to run, a way to escape.

Dellan stood between him and the door.

That left the open window. It would be a long drop, but he might survive the fall to the cobblestones.

"Why, then? Why Anton, why Bartley and Bessy?"

Dellan shrugged. "Antonio had something that belongs to my employer, or was supposed to. Inquires led me to believe your little Yahdrish had it, but now I've come to believe otherwise."

Sal's eyes widened.

Dellan's smile grew. "Where's the locket?"

Sal's hand went to the chain at his collar. The locket was warm, and sent a current of energy surging through him.

Dellan ran his tongue across his top lip. His eyes narrowed, and without warning he sprang for the kill.

Sal's legs went weak. He clutched the locket all the tighter and lashed out with his free hand.

He put all his will into the blow and saw, as much as felt, the blue lighting that surged from his palm with a boom of thunder.

The blue bolt struck Dellan square in the chest just as the Vordin punched a fist into Sal's ribs. Sal felt his breath forced from his lungs as Dellan flew backward and slammed into the opposite wall.

As quick as that, it was over.

There was the smell of burning hair. A soft thump as Dellan's corpse slumped to the floorboards, his back leaning against the wall. His chest was split wide open, boiled leather and dyed wool burned away, flesh and hair charred black. His heart and lungs had exploded. His filed maw was fixed in a permanent scream, the staring blue eyes sightless.

Even in death, Dellan was a terrifying sight to behold.

Sal's head was spinning. A flush of triumph washed through him. He had cast lightning from his hand—bloody lightning—but savoring that triumph would needs wait until he'd had a moment to sit down.

Dellan had punched him hard in the ribs, and it had knocked the air from his lungs, making it difficult to draw breath. He needed to take a seat, to rest and recuperate. He put a hand on his side where he had been punched. He assumed there would be severe bruising for a week at the least. Still, he was alive. He had faced Dellan and walked away with minor bruises to show for it. At least, he thought it was a bruise.

Only, when he removed his hand, it came away wet and sticky with blood—his blood.

A FLASH OF LIGHTNING

S al stumbled, hand clutching at his side as warm rivulets of blood slithered through his fingers and dripped to the floorboards. He had been stabbed. The pain set in like fire. Sal wanted to scream but didn't have the air in his lungs, each breath coming in a wheezing gasp.

There was no help for Bartley and Bessy, nor what remained of Dellan. Sal was the only one not beyond saving, and so, staggering, Sal fled the room. He stumbled down the stairs, leaning heavily against the wall as each jarring step sent a stab of pain into his ribs.

The taproom patrons craned their necks as Sal passed. The man who'd been banging his mug and shouting went quiet, the woman let out a muffled gasp, and her companion moved to comfort her.

No one so much as lifted a hand or spoke a word to Sal, as he pushed through the door and out into the night.

The walk to Beggar's Lane was a blur, his head foggy, his eyes unable to focus. Each sharp inhalation was like a punch to the chest. He focused on progress, nothing but the forward movement of his feet, ignoring the stares and catcalls that accosted him as he moved one foot past the other in a slow death shamble.

He coughed. The iron taste of blood filled his mouth, and when he spit his saliva was red.

Sal staggered into a deserted alley, leaning against a brick wall as he stumbled forward. Unable to stand any longer, he dropped to his hands and knees.

Thunder cracked, and lightning cut a jagged tear across the black sky. Heavy rain began to fall, slapping the cobblestones and splashing Sal's face. The stone under his hands quickly grew slick.

Sal drew in the deepest breath he could manage, put a hand upon the brick wall, and struggled to his feet.

In that instant, he saw them.

They spilled from the alcoves and out from behind the wooden crates and stacked barrels, like a colony of rats. The gang was at least twenty strong—urchins, the lot of them.

The pack crept closer, chittering and hissing words that Sal couldn't quite hear. The kid in the lead was holding a weapon of some sort, but Sal couldn't focus well enough to make out what it was. The kid said something, and Sal reached for his boot but was too weak to get the pigsticker loose from its sheath, and the gang closed in.

Just then, someone shouted. A man, not a child—a man.

The gang of urchins scattered and fled like so many rodents exposed to the light. They slipped back into alcoves and nooks, behind barrels and stacked crates.

Sal braced himself against the wall, letting it take his weight as he searched for the source of the voice.

A tall man, Norsic, stringy blonde hair, fleshy and pale. Eyes bloodshot, half-lidded and watery. His face was drawn, but it was a familiar face, one Sal knew well—Vinny's face.

Only this wasn't Vinny. He was too old.

The man helped him to his feet, but Sal found he was too weak to stand, and he dropped back to his knees.

The man spoke, but the words jumbled up in Sal's mind, and he was unable to decipher their meaning.

He groaned as a new bout of fire surged through his wound.

The man spoke again, and before Sal knew what was happening, he found himself being carried upon the man's shoulders. The ride was rough, and each jarring bounce sent a wave of pain bursting in his side.

Their journey could not have taken long, but the pain made it seem an eternity. The man pushed through a door, the hinges grating.

The man said something in a booming voice, and there was movement across the room. Sal was laid down gently upon a bed, and water was brought to him in a wooden cup.

He drank until he began to cough painfully, and sputtered water all over his chin and chest.

A familiar voice spoke in a concerned tone. Suddenly Sal realized who it was that had handed him the cup. Shoulder-length blond hair, and eyes like the calm before a storm.

Vinny put a hand on Sal's shoulder and spoke again: "Salvatori, can you hear me?"

"I can hear you, yeah. Not my ears that's bleeding."

Vinny flashed a strained smile. The other man, presumably Vinny's father, let out a sharp laugh.

"Even on your deathbed," Vinny said, shaking his head. "We need to get you to a mender. You're letting blood like a stuck pig."

Vinny's father scoffed. "Just where do you expect to find a mender? Talents don't go around the city advertising their trade. Be scant few left if'n they did."

Sal opened his mouth to speak.

"I'll find one," said Vinny. "There has to be someone that can help. What of the mender that put Antonio back together?"

"Look here," said Vinny's father. "Ain't no way you're going to find someone this time of night. It can't be done. Most you can do is give this man something strong to drink and let him enjoy his last hour in a warm bed."

Sal thought about telling Vinny's father to go and bugger himself over a wine barrel but reconsidered, as the old man had saved him only moments before.

"Luca—we have to stop—we have to stop Luca. Get Valla and

Odie, warn them. Bartley, he——" Sal tried to tell Vinny, but the words wouldn't form.

Vinny shushed him. "Mender, that's the first priority. We need to get you a mender."

"Bart—Bartley, he's dead," Sal blurted.

Whatever Vinny had meant to say next vanished in one sudden exhalation. "Bart, dead?" Vinny shook his head. "No, not now. We need to get you to a mender, fast."

"Alzbetta," Sal said, as the pain struck in throbbing pangs.

Sal's mind went hazy, as though a thick fog had set in, but he did his best to tell Vinny where to take him. When Vinny lifted Sal from the bed, the pain of moving overwhelmed him, and darkness consumed his consciousness.

———

A sweet, tangy smell of incense hung in the air. Sal blinked and quickly adjusted to the soft candlelight. He breathed easily as he processed his surroundings.

"A cruel place to stab a person," said Alzbetta. "Wanted you to die slow, I imagine."

Sal's hand went automatically to his side. He was naked from the waist up. Where earlier there had been an open wound, only a faint scar remained.

Alzbetta smiled.

"Where's my shirt?" Sal asked.

The old woman motioned to a table beside the cot. "The jerkin will be all right if you get it stitched and you don't mind a little blood; you'll want to burn the shirt."

Sal slipped two fingers into the hole that went clean through his wool jerkin, padded doublet, and blood-sodden linen shirt. All three layers of cloth had proved less than a match for Dellan's dagger.

Yet Dellan's wool and boiled leather had proved even less of a match for Sal's weapon, a bolt of lightning. It had been magic—true magic, a spell of storybook legend, and it had come from the locket. Like a miracle, the lightning bolt had been unleashed in the nick of time, and had it not been for that miracle, Sal would be as dead as Bartley.

Bartley—the thought of his friend tugged at his heartstrings, a twinge of sharp pain that dulled to a throbbing ache.

"Vinny, where is Vinny?"

"The pretty long-haired one?" Alzbetta asked. "Told me he had things to take care of after he dropped you off. Claimed you'd understand."

Sal put his feet on the ground and felt a strange stretching in the spot where he'd been stabbed.

"Not so quickly," said Alzbetta. "You ought to stay off your feet for a tick, give that wound some time to heal. I've stitched the flesh up tight, but that doesn't mean it can't tear right back open if you're not careful."

"I'll have to risk it. There isn't time for rest. Listen, I need another favor." Sal searched through his pockets and pulled out the hair he'd taken from Luca. "I need a tracer."

"I have that skill, but I will need time. I've not prepared the ingredients, you see, and I'll need to check that I have tellicumin," Alzbetta said, shuffling to a cabinet. "By the way, you wouldn't recall the pretty bauble I had on that shelf last you were here?"

"The, uh, flasher, wasn't it?"

Alzbetta nodded and continued to rummage through the cabinet. "Strangest thing. I've not seen the little bauble since I last saw you," Alzbetta said, and turned to fix him with a level stare.

"Strange indeed," Sal said. "Might you commission another?"

"Afraid not," Alzbetta said, turning back to the cabinet. "The last one was given me by my dear friend Pavalo, rest his soul."

"Pavalo Picarri?"

"Why, yes. Were you acquainted?"

"We crossed paths a time or two."

"Aha, here we are!" said Alzbetta as she spun and held up what looked like a pale root, shaggy like a spider's leg.

She crossed the room, root in hand, and took the hair from Sal. She then instructed him to cut a swatch of fabric from the linen shirt he'd been wearing, insisting it was going to be thrown in the fire by night's end regardless.

While Sal attempted to find a clean patch of linen to cut out, Alzbetta placed the hair and root together and began crushing them to a pulp with mortar and pestle.

"Do you know anything about Pavalo's death?"

Alzbetta paused, pestle in hand. "Poor man, he was found dead in his home. Murdered, if the rumors are true. I told him, more than once, mind you, never to get involved with princes and their affairs."

"Princes—what princes, what sort of affairs?"

"Oh, the ducal sort, I imagine. As to what princes, why, it must have been Matej, or Andrej, or any one of those royal bastards that is allowed to leech about the High Keep bearing that name and seal."

"Your depth of information is staggering," Sal said, his words dripping with sarcasm.

"The specifics hardly matter. Pavalo was always vague about those in any case. The specific prince, what this man wanted of Pavalo, none of that is of consequence. What is of true import is that Pavalo stuck his neck in ducal business, and now he's dead." Alzbetta gestured for the square of linen Sal had cut, scooped the gray pulp into the cloth, and slammed a palm upon the square, flattening it to the tabletop. She muttered a few words that Sal presumed to be a binding, and placed the swatch of linen into Sal's hand.

"How does a tracer work?"

Alzbetta only smiled.

Slowly the tracer began to warm, until he feared it would be too hot to hold in his hand. However, before the thing grew hot enough to burn, it started to cool until the little swatch of cloth was cold and damp with the sweat of his palm. Once the tracer had cooled, Sal felt an inkling, an urge, that tugged at him—guided him.

Without thinking, he began to move toward the door. As he left, Alzbetta wished him luck and reminded him to be careful.

The torrent of rain had not let up since Sal's encounter with the gang of street urchins. He found himself appreciating the storm as the rain slapped his bare torso beneath his jerkin, drinking in the rainfall as though it were life-sustaining manna. He felt energy flowing back into his body. The locket hanging from his neck pulsated with rivulets of electricity.

Touching the locket reinvigorated Sal's sense of urgency. Luca had Lilliana, and Sal would do whatever he must to make certain Lilliana was safe.

He gripped the locket tighter, the sixth sense provided by the magic tracer guiding his every step. He needed to move faster. His feet beat a rhythm of rolling thunder, rapidly slapping the rain-slicked cobblestones. He ran with all the urgency he felt, and still it was not enough. He needed the locket and the power of the storm stored within.

He had ridden the lightning in the past, used the locket to travel long distances in the blink of an eye. Still, there was much and more he didn't understand about the thing, including how to bend its magic to his will. He'd done it before but hadn't managed to unlock the secret, and there were plenty of times the locket had failed him when he'd tried.

He'd come to believe the locket had little concern for his own needs. His need for a magic intervention when facing Dellan had been no different than when he'd encountered the thugs in the alleyway as Nabu was being beaten.

What had been the difference? What was the one constant each time the locket's magic had been unleashed? Then it came to him like a flash of lightning.

Skeev.

The very first night with the locket, the night he'd ridden the lightning through his window, he had smoked a cap with Bartley, and it had been Sal that had crumbled the mushroom cap into the pipe. The night he'd blinked himself out of the river and up across the rooftops, he had once again been the one that had crumbled the cap of skeev. The one constant, the key to unlocking the power of the locket, lay in the skeev.

It was clear to him now. It mattered not what the stakes were, nor how hard he willed the locket to yield its power; it was the drug that made the difference. So simple an answer to a problem that had vexed him for so long.

He looked at his hands and realized they'd been scrubbed clean —by the storm or Alzbetta, he couldn't be certain.

Sal slipped the tracer into the pocket of his jerkin, forced his mind from the path where it had been guiding him, and set off in another direction.

When Sal reached the Hog Snout, he saw two men running from the front door, arms burdened with as much as they could carry.

Sal shouted at the backs of the looters, wanting to chase the thieves down and give them their proper comeuppance, but realized he had no time to waste.

The smell of meadowsweet did not give him a pleasant feeling as it once had. Rather it brought to his mind an image of two corpses, naked and lying facedown in pools of their own blood. As he climbed the stairs, he felt sick with the thought of going back into Bartley's room, knowing what awaited him within. Yet he had no choice; Lilliana's life depended on it.

At the top of the stairs the hallway was dark, all three wall lamps snuffed out. Sal felt for the door handle in the darkness, opened, and stepped in.

As of yet there was no smell of rot, though the overwhelming stench of cooked meat, burnt hair, and vomit lingered in the small room.

Sal doubled over, tears welling in his eyes and saliva steaming from his mouth as he heaved, over and over, but there was nothing left in his stomach to disgorge.

Somehow he found the strength to press on. He pushed himself upright and held his breath as he stepped into the room. It was dark, and difficult to see by the moonlight alone, but among the scattered belongings on the floor Sal spotted the carved ebony box and breathed a sigh of relief that the looters had not taken it. He went to the box and saw it was open, its contents nowhere to be seen. Frantically Sal looked about, but there was no trace of the pipe full of skeev, nor any of the golden-brown mushroom caps.

Sal's throat tightened and his heart sank to the pit of his stomach. He cursed and threw the ebony box across the room so that it crashed against the opposite wall. He dropped to his knees and pounded the ground with his fists, tears streaming down his cheeks, curses flowing from his lips.

He shouted until he was hoarse, his throat raw. How could his luck have turned so bad?

He slammed his fist to the ground once more, lying flat on his stomach, breath shortened by the grip of panic. Then suddenly, through tear-filled eyes, Sal spotted something golden-brown beneath the bed. He reached for it and felt a spike of elation as he realized what he'd found.

Sal crumbled a piece of the skeev cap between his thumb and forefinger, allowing the grainy residue to coat his fingertips. Putting the remains of the cap into his pocket with the tracer, Sal darted from the room, down the stairs and out of the Hog Snout as quickly as his legs would take him. The moment his boots touched cobblestones, Sal grabbed hold of the locket and focused upon the farthest rooftop he could see.

There was a crack, like a deafening clap of thunder.

Sal was pulled off his feet and tore through the sky like lightning. He landed feetfirst upon the rooftop.

Fingers stiff with the cold, Sal grabbed hold of the locket and willed himself to the next rooftop that caught his eye.

A jolt of lightning, vertigo, and his feet landed upon another roof.

Sal dropped flat to his belly, arms and legs splaying out upon wooden shingles.

He caught his breath and allowed his heart rate to slow. The night air was cold on his sweat-beaded skin. He crawled on his belly up the steep roof until he was able to sit straddling the ridge. He focused on another rooftop, the tracer guiding his direction. He grasped the locket and willed himself forth.

Lightning, vertigo, feet taking root only long enough for him to spot another target before he rode the lightning to his next destination.

He continued to bounce from rooftop to rooftop another four times until he found himself in the Lowers, looking upon Luca's safe house.

REQUIEM

W ith no windows, it was impossible to see what was happening inside the safe house. Luca must have wanted Lilliana for a ransom. Why else kidnap the daughter of one of the city's richest nobles? Surely Luca wouldn't dare hurt her, as that might decrease his chances of collecting the ransom.

The front door wasn't much of an option. It was too visible an entry. If Sal was going to get in without being spotted, he would need to use the cellar and hope that Luca had not barred the rear door.

Sal put his hand on the locket. Energy flowed into him, but when he willed himself to the alley behind the safe house, nothing happened. His fingers had been washed clean in the rain. Sal dried them as best he could, then crumbled some of the skeev between his thumb and forefinger. Again he grabbed the locket, and held his breath as he was ripped from his feet and shot through the air. A boom of thunder, a rush and a touch of vertigo, and his feet landed upon cobblestones.

The cellar doors were secured with an old brass padlock. To Sal's relief, the lock was of the single-arched swing-shackle variety. He pulled the pigsticker from his boot sheath and used the butt of the knife to bash upon the weak point of the lock where the pipe met the arch. It took time, but with steady, concentrated strokes, Sal managed to cave in the corner of the pipe. He wedged the blade of his pigsticker into the arch and pried until the old brass gave way with a click. Sal tossed the broken lock aside and opened the cellar doors.

There was a flight of stairs cut into the earth, which Sal descended into darkness. When his boots landed on the earthen floor, he was forced to find his way by touch. At the other end of the cellar, a glimmer of hope: a sliver of light at the base of the safe house rear door. He continued to feel his way through the dank, dark cellar, then up the flight of earthen steps which lead to the door.

Sal pushed on the door, ever so gently, doing his best not to make a sound. As the door budged, he breathed a sigh of relief. Luca had left it unbarred. By the Lady's luck, things were looking up. It seemed favor had finally turned a forgiving eye in Sal's direction. He pushed the door harder, but when the hinges creaked, Sal cringed and held his breath, listening for signs that he'd been heard.

The only sound aside from the rain was a wet, rhythmic slapping.

Sal pushed the door a bit more, and again it creaked, but Sal pushed on and hoped against hope Luca would not hear.

The rhythmic slapping noise was accompanied by muffled grunts like a man with labored breathing.

The elation Sal had felt the instant before at finding the door unlocked melted away as his heart jumped into his throat.

He pushed hard, and the door swung fully open to reveal Luca standing at the foot of one of the cots, naked from the waist down, pumping at the hips. A pair of slender legs hung over the cot, limp and lifeless.

Luca pulled back as the door slammed open, his member swollen and wet, a look of savage fury in his eyes.

Sal charged before Luca could fully grasp the situation. He closed the distance in a matter of seconds, throwing a punch while his feet still moved. His fist struck Luca's jaw with a dull thud. Sal threw a second punch, directly to Luca's nose.

Luca grunted and his head dropped back.

Sal grabbed hold of the locket, but just as his fumbling fingers clasped the cold metal, Luca's head whipped forward.

Blood spurted, and Sal cried out as Luca's forehead cracked into his nose with a sickening crunch. The blow jarred him so badly that he yanked the locket, snapping the chain and sending the locket skittering across the floorboards. His vision went black, and pain bloomed like fire as he staggered back.

He shook his head and blinked. When he opened his eyes, he saw the blur of Luca's fist just before it cracked into his jaw, buckling his knees and dropping him to the ground.

Sal rolled to his back and slipped his finger-knife loose just as Luca lifted a bare foot to stomp him.

Before the foot fell, Sal lashed out with the finger-knife.

Luca screamed and staggered back, both hands grasping his crotch as blood spurted.

Sal slipped the pigsticker from his boot and stabbed up hard as he rose, putting all of his strength behind the thrust. The long, thin blade penetrated deep into Luca's naked torso, just beneath the arch of his ribs.

Luca huffed and Sal pushed the blade deeper, twisted it, and cut down toward the man's navel with both hands.

The pigsticker was ripped from his hands as Luca slumped to the floor, gasping and moaning as he writhed in the bloody rushes.

Sickened by the sight of the dying man, Sal rushed for the cot where Lilliana lay, her delicate legs still hanging lifelessly over the edge of the cot, her sex exposed, her face a bloody, swollen mess.

And yet she breathed.

Sal covered her nakedness with a sheet and did his best to steady his breathing as he laid a hand on her brow.

Slowly Lilliana opened her eyes, one of them bruised purple and black, so swollen it opened only a sliver.

"You're safe," Sal said, pinching his nose to stanch the bleeding. "It's over—it's all over."

Lilliana breathed through swollen, cracked lips, dark red with smeared blood. She didn't speak. Instead, she closed her eyes and laid her cheek against Sal's hand. They stayed that way for a time, until Lilliana found the strength to sit upright.

"We'll get you home, I promise. We'll get you home, and all of this will be behind us."

Lilliana gasped and shuddered in pain with the effort of standing, despite Sal's help. She clenched her jaw, teeth gritting with every step. It was going to be a long, painful walk to the Bastian estate—unless Sal could find the locket. He scanned the rushes as they tentatively progressed, each step seeming to cause her more pain than the last.

A muffled moan caused Sal's attention to shift to Luca. The man continued to writhe, slower than he had, his movements more rigid, his breathing strained.

A loud crash sounded at the front door.

Sal whipped around to see a long crack splitting the center of the pine door. Another booming crash, and bits of the door splintered away.

With the third crash, an iron wolf's head burst clean through the door. The fourth crash sent more of the pine splintering away, leaving a hole big enough for a man to slip through.

The first man through wore a tabard of midnight blue over a chain mail hauberk, and a coned helm. The steel cap was followed by a slew of companions. They were eight in all, some wielding spears, others poleaxes, and one a battering ram bearing an iron head in the shape of a snarling wolf.

Lilliana looked at the company of steel caps with eyes that seemed sightless, but Sal could see clearly despite the swelling around his nose. When he caught sight of the steel cap with the gold band about his arm, Sal nearly loosed his bowels.

As their gazes locked, the lieutenant's burn-scarred face showed surprise, a look that swiftly shifted into one of pure malevolence. It was the same lieutenant that had nearly arrested Sal in High Town, and would have, had it not been for the flasher.

But Sal was fresh out of flashers. He had only his pigsticker, his finger-knife—and the locket!

Sal put a hand to his collar, but remembered he'd lost the locket in his fight with Luca. It had fallen somewhere in the rushes.

A wicked smile crept across the lieutenant's face as his focus moved from Sal to Luca and back to Sal. "Well, lads, seems we've missed the fun," said the lieutenant. "The pair of you look out of sorts. Might we be of assistance?"

The steel caps circled Sal and Lilliana, making a sort of human net that closed in on them like the tightening of a noose.

"We came expecting Luca Vrana, but it seems someone has gone and killed him. As much as I would like to reward you for your good deed, the law prevents me. If we allowed everyone to go around sticking steel in men's bellies without so much as a slap on the wrist, it would only be a matter of time before our duke lost his head to a peasant mob." The lieutenant clicked his tongue and slowly shook his head. "No, I am afraid we cannot allow such crimes as murder to go unpunished."

Sal knew he needed to act, and quickly, but in his state of fear no plan came to mind. If only he'd kept hold of the locket. With the locket, there would still be a chance. He scanned the floor, and to his amazement he spotted it, a glimmer of gold in the rushes.

When Sal looked up from the floor, his heart stopped as the lieutenant met his gaze.

Sal looked quickly away, but it was too late; the steel cap had followed his eyes.

"Gregor, the floor there," said the lieutenant, pointing a finger. "Be a dear and pick that up."

One of the steel caps walked to the spot that the lieutenant had designated and removed a lobstered gauntlet. The steel cap bent down and scooped up the locket, flinching as his fingers closed about it.

"Hold on to that for me, won't you, Gregor," the lieutenant said, chuckling. "This is most fortunate indeed. Kid, you seem to be my lucky charm. That slimy bastard Luca had it the whole time, did he?"

The lieutenant walked over to Luca and kicked him in the chest.

Luca squirmed, a gargled wheeze escaped him, and blood spilled from the corner of his mouth, viscera bulging from the gash in his abdomen.

For an instant Lilliana seemed to snap from her shocked state. "I am Lilliana Bastian, daughter to Lord Hugo Bastian, Fourth Seat of the High Council. You and your men will escort my companion and me from this place, or you will answer to Duke Tadej."

"My Lady, by all means," said the lieutenant, his eyes widening in surprise at the outburst. "My men and I will do just that. Only you must understand, to keep men such as these in line working for the common good and all, they must be compensated for their hard labor."

The steel caps slowly moved in ever closer, and Sal knew his chance for escape had passed.

"Looks to me like she's been warmed up already," said the lieutenant. "Who'll have the first go?"

Two of the steel caps grabbed Sal by either arm, while two others caught hold of Lilliana.

Sal expended what little energy he had left trying to fight free. He managed to slip out an arm, until one of the steel caps put an armored fist in his gut, doubling him over.

"Got more than one hole don't she?" said one of the steel caps who'd grabbed hold of Lilliana. "Don't see why we can't go two at a time."

The sheet was ripped from Lilliana, exposing her nakedness. The two men wrestled her onto the cot, and a third steel cap began to unbuckle his breeches.

"I'll kill you!" Sal screamed. "Every fucking one of you, I'll fucking kill you!"

The steel caps only laughed.

Lilliana kicked and thrashed until one of them hit her in the mouth with a steel gauntlet, and she went still as a corpse.

"What'd you go and do that for?" said the man unbuckling his breeches. "Ain't no fun when they got no fight in them."

"Gentle, now, boys," said the lieutenant. "We want to collect the ransom on the little cunt, her face is going to needs be recognized by someone."

The full attention of all eight steel caps seemed to be on the cot, but Sal thought he heard the creaking hinges of an opening door. Muffled footsteps closed in behind him, and as Sal turned to see who or what it was, he heard a whoosh and felt the brush of wind as something whizzed past his face.

There was an unmistakable crunch of steel on steel. The man gripping Sal's left arm went limp and dropped to the floor.

Without thinking, Sal used his left hand to grab hold of the long knife scabbarded at the hip of his remaining captor. With one swift motion, Sal pulled the blade free and stuck it deep into a gap in the steel cap's armor, just below his ribs. Sal ripped out the knife and stabbed again, and again, until the steel cap dropped to his knees and then flat on his face, armor rattling as he fell.

Newly freed, Sal took a moment to absorb the situation. The steel cap that had held Sal's left arm lay dead in the rushes, helm driven in by a war hammer. Odie's war hammer.

The big man swung again, caving in another coned helm and dropping another steel cap to the ground.

Valla was there too. She was near the cot. Two steel caps lay dead in pools of their own blood; a third defended himself from Valla's attacks, sword in hand and breeches about his ankles.

Vinny fought another, fending off sword blows with a chair. The steel cap pressing the attack used only one arm, his other rendered useless by the dagger planted in his back.

The steel cap continued his one-handed attack, backing Vinny up until the half-Norsic tripped over his own feet and fell backward.

Sal attacked from behind, dashing to Vinny's aid, driving the long knife swiftly into the steel cap's neck just beneath the lip of his helm.

Blood sprayed, and the man slumped to the ground.

Vinny shouted Valla's name.

When Sal looked, he saw she was bleeding. Despite the breeches about his ankles the steel cap had managed to defend himself from Valla's attack.

Vinny picked up the sword of his fallen foe and closed the distance to Valla's attacker.

Sal realized in that instant that Lilliana was no longer lying on the cot. He looked to the floor, then swung his gaze about the room. He managed to catch only a glimpse, but it was enough to see the lieutenant leaving through the front door, Lilliana slung over his shoulder.

Sal gave chase. He stopped only to pry his locket from the dead fingers of the steel cap Gregor.

A flush of energy rushed through him with the contact.

When Sal reached the door, he saw the back of a carriage as it sped through the rain. Quickly he shoved a hand into the pocket of his jerkin and crumbled what remained of the skeev cap between his fingers.

With a crack of thunder, Sal jolted through the air and onto one rooftop and then the next, moving like a bouncing bolt of lightning.

The carriage sped through the street below. The lieutenant urged the horses on, running pedestrians off Beggar's Lane as he made for the Bridge of the Lady.

Sal kept pace, ripping and tearing through the sky, bouncing from rooftop to rooftop, hardly giving his feet long enough to land and slip on the rain-slick shingles before he bolted for the next roof.

Just as the carriage passed under the façade of the Low Town tower and onto the bridge, Sal leaped and willed himself for the driver's bench. A boom of thunder, a rush, and Sal landed feetfirst on the driver's seat beside the lieutenant.

He squeezed the locket and lashed out, willing the magic. A bolt of ethereal blue lightning burst from his palm, but only grazed the lieutenant's shoulder plate.

The lieutenant jerked the reins, and the horses cut hard, pitching the carriage sideways and throwing Sal from his purchase.

Sal tumbled across hard paving stones until he came to a stop flat on his stomach. His head felt like to burst, but he somehow found the strength to gather his hands and knees beneath himself and push himself back to his feet.

Slowly he approached the toppled carriage. He called for

Lilliana but received no answer. The horses shifted nervously, whinnying and champing at their bits. People all around him on the bridge spoke, but Sal couldn't make sense of the words. As he rounded the carriage, his heart sank.

The lieutenant had backed up to the parapet. He held Lilliana, with one steel-clad arm about her chest and a dagger pressed to her throat. "I'll cut her fucking head off," said the lieutenant as Sal approached. "Take your black magic and go, or the bitch dies."

Sal took a deep breath and closed his eyes. When he opened them, he focused on the dagger and only the dagger.

"Back off!"

Sal squeezed the locket.

A crack of thunder and he burst across the distance to the steel cap, planting his feet right in front of the man. In one swift motion, Sal wrenched the dagger from the steel cap's hand and shoved.

The lieutenant tripped backward over the parapet, but grabbed hold of Lilliana's dress.

Quickly Sal drove the dagger into the lieutenant's side, then wrapped his arms about Lilliana.

They were both dragged bodily over the parapet.

As they fell toward the black water of the Tamber, the steel cap's grip slipped, but Sal managed to keep both arms wrapped around Lilliana.

Sal looked up, grabbed the locket, and willed the lightning to take them.

He and Lilliana bolted upward, flashing through the air high above the Bridge of the Lady. Sal held her tight and focused on the paving stones below, willing the lighting to take him one last time.

They landed awkwardly atop the bridge, rolling across the paving stones in a heap of tangled limbs. When they came to a stop, Sal gingerly untangled himself. Once he was certain Lilliana was alive and whole, Sal breathed a sigh of relief and rose to one knee as tears welled in his eyes.

24

THE HIGH KEEP

Interlude, Three Months Earlier

S al felt a twinge of guilt. It wasn't the lying, but the fact that what he was doing could altogether botch the job. The rest of the crew likely thought he was in the courtyard right about then. No doubt that tattooed Vordin would be expecting him any moment.

But Dellan would have to wait. Anton's side job was going to pay nearly as much as the rest of Sal's cut, and there was no way he was going to put it off. Dellan would be outright furious, but there was no helping it now. Besides, what was the worst thing that could happen?

He crept along the stone hallway guided by the light of a lone torch, the rest of the sconces as empty as the castle itself. End was not for another two days, and until the return of the duke and his retinue, the High Keep would be scarcely occupied, minimally staffed, and scantily guarded.

Even so, Sal's nerves were on edge. This was the biggest job he'd ever been hired for, and he didn't want to muck it up. To compound the pressure, there was the side job to consider.

West tower, the top room. Sal hadn't really considered whose rooms they were until that moment. More important considerations had come to mind as he had prepared. He bought a minor counter-ward from Pavalo Picarri, but he wasn't certain he would be able to activate the binding. Wards had always been more Vinny's thing. Sal hoped he wouldn't even need the counter-ward, but it didn't hurt to be prepared. More often than not, his lock picks and pigsticker had been all the tools he needed. With the right finesse they could get Sal into just about anything.

Sal peeked around the corner, and finding the way clear he continued down the shadowed hall. He had once lived in the High Keep, though he had no idea where they had roomed. Sal had been so young when they'd left that he didn't have a single memory of living in the place. His mother had been a serving woman of some sort, and then one day they had up and left. She had never explained it to Sal, why they had moved from the High Keep to his uncle's estate. She'd simply not gotten around to it before—

The double doors at the end of the hall were a towering nine feet tall. Upon them was a carved relief of a lion doing battle with a three-headed dragon. The wood was gilded, as were the massive twisted ring handles. Sal grabbed one of the rings and pulled; the heavy door yawned slowly open like some waking beast.

Sal stepped inside and closed the door quickly behind him. Everything from the baseboards to the furniture seemed to be gilded. The room was vast, the vaulted ceilings giving a cathedral-like impression, as did the massive windows which allowed a view of the entire city below. He looked out on Dijvois for just a moment, soaking in the vista of the lighted city. He recalled a time when he'd looked out upon a similar view nearly every day from his uncle's estate, but in those days he never knew what he had, and it was not until he'd moved away from the High Hill that he developed a true appreciation for what he'd lost.

The rushes smelled freshly changed. There were makings upon the bed and tapestries hanging on the walls. Clean and furnished, the room seemed to be awaiting an occupant. Rushes crunched under his feet as Sal crossed the room to a small steel lockbox atop the mantel of the great fireplace.

Right where Anton had said it would be.

The lockbox itself was steel, Sal could tell just by the weight of the thing. The steel was likely unbreakable without something like Odie and his war hammer, and even then the big man might do little more than dent the lockbox. The padlock was a beastly thing, black iron, heavy as sin and twice as tough. There was no breaking black iron, at least so far as Sal knew. Even worse, Sal could tell by the sliver of gray pig iron that the lock had a trip tumbler, if he tried to pick the lock the trip tumbler would trigger, shattering, and jamming the lock for good and all.

Faced with an invincible box and an unpickable lock, Sal unsheathed the pigsticker from his boot and raised it high. He brought the butt of the knife down hard against the lockbox, right where the clasp was forged to the lid. He bashed the clasp several times more, striking the forged seam harder with each successive blow until the clasp dented slightly, cracked, and finally popped free of the lid altogether.

While the clasp remained secured by the unpickable black iron padlock, the steel lid of the lockbox was free to open.

Slowly Sal lifted the lid, revealing a padded red velvet interior. At the center of the box, atop a small velvet pillow, was a tarnished yellow gold locket, three parallel lines etched upon its face.

Sal reached out and grabbed hold of the locket, then leaped backward and threw the thing back into the box, feeling as though he'd been stung. He looked at his palm, but when he could see no visible damage he reexamined the locket. There was nothing special about it, merely a piece of old gold with some strange rune carved into its face. Surely the sting he'd felt had mostly been in his head.

Cautiously he reached out and prodded the thing with a finger. Feeling stupid, he looked about, took in a deep breath, and snatched up the locket once more.

Tendrils of electric energy surged through his entire body. He shoved the locket into his pocket and sighed with relief as the uncomfortable feeling dissipated.

Just then he heard shouting, and a scream that rang through the night.

25

MERELY A BEGINNING

The Tamber had swelled so much with the late fall rains that it threatened to overflow the cobblestones. Sal walked along the river's edge, watching the fast-flowing current and the spray of breaking whitecaps. It was the first time he'd left his bed in three days. Another day in, and he might have gone mad. Supposing he wasn't mad already.

When his nights weren't sleepless, they'd been filled with fever dreams, night terrors of the worst sort. He'd killed four men with his own bloodstained hands. Before that night, Sal hadn't known himself capable of such a thing. Yet when his back was pressed against the wall, he had chosen his own life over theirs. His life, and Lilliana's.

He'd not seen or spoken to Lilliana since the day at the safe house. He could only imagine the sorts of terrors she'd experienced over the past three nights.

After they had landed on the bridge, the lieutenant falling to his death, Sal had somehow found the strength to get to his feet, lift Lilliana, and carry her up to High Hill. He'd been shirtless, only a jerkin over his bare chest, streaked with blood that had streamed from his broken nose, a half-naked noblewoman in his arms. No one had stopped them on the Bridge of the Lady, nor on the Kingsway. Not until they had reached the black iron gate outside the Bastian estate had anyone dared question him.

The guards would have likely killed him when they realized the woman in Sal's arms was their lord's daughter, but Lilliana had managed to croak out enough of an explanation that the gate guards had sent Sal off with no more than cross words.

That had been the thanks he received for what he'd done, and it had been no less than he deserved.

Sal followed the Tamber until he reached South Market. He was supposed to meet with Vinny and the others at the Rusted Anchor but needed to head home for his coin purse. As he stepped inside, the smells of lavender and of pottage simmering in the hearth set his mind at ease.

Home was a place where he could be happy, a place where he could leave behind the worry and sorrow of the outside world. He walked over to the kettle of pottage and spooned out a bite.

He was savoring the taste when he saw Nicola seated at the table with the lord's get she'd fancied of late, Oliver Flint. Sal frowned and nodded to them, and was headed for the stairs when Nicola called his name.

"Someone's come by looking for you," Nicola said.

Sal's throat tightened, his mind imagining the City Watch. "Who?" he asked.

Oliver Flint smiled. "A girl, mate. Good-looking lass, to boot. Even despite the—the, uh, bruising."

"Lilliana Bastian?" Sal asked.

"Was that her name?" said Nicola.

"Lilliana Bastian?" asked Oliver. "Was that Lilliana Bastian? No, truly?"

"I don't understand," said Nicola. "Who is this Lilliana Bastian?"

"The daughter of—"

"What did she say?" asked Sal.

"Not much," said Nicola. "Asked if you were in. When I told her you'd gone out for a bit, she asked me to give you this." Nicola held up a cloak. Black wool with sable fur trim.

Sal ran his fingers over the tight weave of the wool and felt the softness of the sable lining. "She left this for me?"

"I don't think she meant it to be mine," said Nicola with a smile. "You must have done something nice for this girl?"

Sal shrugged and took the cloak up to his room. He laid the cloak on his bed, took a few krom from his coin purse, and slipped them into the pocket of his jerkin. He opened the drawer of his dresser, moved aside a linen shirt, and put a hand on the locket. It was cold to the touch, and he shivered as tendrils of electricity trickled into his hand. Sal dropped the locket back into the drawer atop the parchment letter with the red wax seal. Then he slipped into his new sable-lined cloak and walked downstairs.

Before he left, he turned to Nicola and her nobleman. "I'm headed out to meet some friends," Sal said. "I wish the pair of you an enjoyable evening."

Nicola opened her mouth, but Oliver spoke first. "Of course, mate. You take care, now."

Nicola looked from Sal to Oliver and back to Sal. "I suppose we will, then."

Sal smiled, nodded, and turned for the door.

"Black sable, eh?" the big man said, stroking Sal's new cloak with the back of a massive hand.

"Sable?" said Vinny. "Lord Salvatori has a new sable cloak, does he?"

"A man can treat himself, can't he?"

"I see," said Valla. "And rather than treat yourself to a whore, you've gone and treated yourself *like* a whore. But I'll tell you what. You make sure I'm the first you come see when you're looking for a nice stable to settle down in, and I'll take good care of you. I don't pay so well as some, but no one puts an angry hand on one of my whores and lives to touch his next."

Sal smiled and shook his head as he looked about the taproom. There was never a singer in the taproom of the Rusted Anchor, merely the clicks and clacks of rolling dice and the quiet mutterings of men at cards, accompanied by shouts from some of the rougher drunks. The floor needed sweeping, and the tables were topped with a sticky residue from years of spilled drinks. Still, it was comfortable enough, a place to stay warm and dry.

"I'm surprised they even let you in this place anymore," Valla said, giving Sal a knowing look, "and not just because you dress like a whore."

Sal shook his head. "I didn't come here to talk about that," he said seriously.

"Well, now we're all here," said Vinny, "what's the word on the City Watch?"

Valla elbowed Odie, who had been staring at Sal's new cloak. The big man stirred, blinked twice, and arched an eyebrow.

"The steel caps, you big oaf," Valla said.

Odie grunted.

"The source," Valla said, dangerously quiet. "You said you had a bloody source on the fucking City Watch."

"Oh, right," said Odie, shaking his head. "Well, you're not going to believe it, but word is, Luca was the rat on the High Keep job."

"Goddamned Norsic," Valla cursed. "Big as an ox and twice as thick. Of course he was the fucking rat."

Odie looked at them each in turn, wide-eyed and innocent as a child. "And no one told me?"

Valla shook her head contemptuously. "And what of our end? Does anyone know we were involved with those steel caps at Luca's safe house? Has anyone put our names on the street?"

Odie shook his head. "No one left that safe house alive, apart from that lieutenant. And, well, Salvatori took care of him before he went spreading any names. Though that's just the thing."

"And just what thing would that be?" said Sal.

"Your name," said the big man. "Seems you were seen on the Bridge of the Lady when that lieutenant took his little fall."

Valla arched an eyebrow, and the big man shrugged.

"You're going to want to lay low for a while," Valla said. "And you'll want to talk to that uncle of yours. Might be he can smooth some things over."

"I might well do that," Sal said. "I do appreciate the forewarning. Never been fond of the look of those crow-cages."

Odie nodded.

"Well, that's nothing to worry over," said Vinny. "Surely your uncle can take care of it. He could put word out that you were never even near the bridge that night."

"I take it your source would have told you if any warrants were issued?" Sal asked.

"She would," Odie assured him.

"Well then, it's nothing we need worry over. For now, I say we drink to the fact that we're all still breathing." Sal held up his ale, and the others joined him.

"To life," said the big man.

"To not fucking dying," said Valla.

Vinny scoffed, and they drank.

"Well then, now Luca's gone, you all are going to be needing a crew to run with," said Valla.

"What's your point?" Vinny asked. "You saying you've got something lined up?"

"I'm saying I'm to be made before the next moon. I'll have the backing. All I need now is bodies to fill the roles."

Sal and Vinny shared a look.

"I'm going to run a full crew," Valla said. "I want the three of you to fill the first half." There was a moment of silence, and Valla shifted uncomfortably in her seat. "Well, don't you all fucking clamor to be the first."

The big man shrugged, and Vinny pursed his lips.

"I'll need to think on it," Sal said.

"Fuck you," Valla said, standing. "Fuck all of you."

"Vallachenka Smirnichezk," said the big man, nodding toward

Valla's empty chair, "there's no need for tantrums. Take a seat and—"

"No, fuck you and your seat. I don't drink where I'm the only one with at least half a set of these," Valla said, grabbing her crotch and snarling like a mad cat.

"Sit down," said Vinny, shaking his head, the hint of a smile playing at the corners of his mouth.

"Fuck you too, Vincenzo, you half-Norsic mutt."

Vinny put a hand on his chest as though Valla had damaged his delicate sensibilities.

It was all in good fun, but Sal thought it best to stop it before someone got hurt. No good ever came from poking at sharks with sticks. "Val, don't forget what we came here to do." He reached across the table and put a hand on the bottle of fire-wine.

Something in Valla's eyes changed when she saw the fire-wine.

Sal nodded as Valla met his gaze, then she sighed and took a seat.

"That fucking Yahdrish," Valla said, shaking her head. "I never even liked the little weasel."

"As bad a thief as he was at everything else," said Vinny, taking the bottle from Sal and uncorking it. "A bad thief, but a good friend."

Vinny took a swig and passed the bottle to Valla.

"I never much liked any of their breed," Valla said, "and that Bartholomew was no different. But he sure as Sacrull's hell didn't deserve what he got, and neither did that barmaid was with him." Valla closed her eyes, wiped at a tear, and took a drink, then passed the bottle to Sal.

"He was the first real friend I ever had," Sal said, then he too took a swig right from the bottle. The fire-wine burned like Sacrull's hell all the way down. He really never could understand why Bartley liked the stuff so much. He took a second drink, for Bartley, and passed the bottle to Odie.

"To Bartholomew Shoaly," said Odie, raising the bottle. "For Pavalo Picarri, Fabian Abrami, and Antonio Russo,." Odie drained what remained of the fire-wine in one fell swig.

"To old friends," said Sal, clearing his throat and raising his ale. "To us."

Thus ends
The Hand That Takes
Fall of the Coward, Book One

FREE BOOK

A FOOL OF SORTS

FALL OF THE COWARD, BOOK TWO

ONE
OUT FROM THE SHADOWS

Rainfall pounded the weatherworn limestone of Knöldrus Cathedral. A pair of adjacent spires protruded endlessly heavenward as they pierced the black storm clouds and vanished beyond. Between the two towers, a rose window of brilliant stained glass, illuminated by flashes of lightning. Gargoyles perched about the façade, glaring down in judgment, runnels of rainwater pouring through their open maws, splashing upon the cobblestones below.

Hidden beneath the shadows of the cathedral, broken down on all fours, Sal felt the wet stone underhand. Acid burned his throat as he heaved forth another spurt of bile. A shiver racked him, pain so severe it felt as though a hole had torn through his stomach.

Too weak to stand, he crawled, fingertips digging into mud-sheathed cobblestones until the massive doors of the cathedral loomed before him. Sal reached a trembling hand and grasped the oversized bronze knocker, using it to right himself. A resounding creak echoed through the nave as the heavy door swung open.

Candlelight cast flickering shadows to dance across the limestone walls.

Still shaking, Sal took a cautious step into the cathedral.

His racing heart slowed as a sigh escaped him. He'd made it. He'd not been caught, not been seen. A miracle, no doubt. He wouldn't have been hard to spot, dropping into the mud and vomiting as he had. Still, it seemed he'd not been pursued.

Sal walked farther into the cathedral but rested at the first pillar, allowing it to support his weight. He looked back over his shoulder. The door had swept shut behind him. No one had pursued, not the man, nor his victim, nor the blood-curdling scream the victim had unleashed. The scream swallowed by the storm and the night. Sal doubted anyone had heard, anyone but himself.

He had to press on, had to find someone to help. His wet boots were slick on the floor. He reached for the next pillar, staggered, and slipped on the flagstones.

Sal put his hands out to catch his fall, but it was too late. His face hit the floor with a wet smack.

———

"Another skeever?" said a man with a rather shrill voice.

"A lost lamb seeking shelter from the storm," answered a deeper voice.

"You should have thrown him out," said the first man. "See how he sweats, his body craves the substance."

"Is it not our responsibility to care for the sick? Give me your destitute, your—"

"Do not quote scripture to me. I know the book as well as you, Jacques. But these skeevers cannot be trusted. Stealing and lying are but second nature to their kind."

Sal was parched, sick to his stomach, and exhausted. He wanted to be out of the damp sheets, but he dared not move should they notice he'd woken.

"By the Light, the young man has yet to commit any acts of

sacrilege," said the man with the deeper voice. "As for the stealing, how can one steal what is gladly given?"

"You make mock, but take note when I tell you no good comes of keeping company with this sort. Where did you find the creature, looting the larder?

"Far from it. Phillip here found him in the Cathedral, searching for a place to pray."

"I'd name you fool did I not know you for a liar, Jacques. Phillip, you're young, new to the order, you do not yet understand how things work. The election is coming. You would do well to distance yourself from men such as our Master Infirmarer. Wiser, place yourself favorably among men of import, men who may soon occupy positions of influence come the casting of the votes."

"I'll keep it in mind," piped up a young voice. "Though, the election is a fortnight away and nothing is certain as of yet. I am young as you say, but even initiates have heard the stories. When the brothers of Knöldrus Abbey cast the stones, there is no telling where the votes will land."

"You dare threaten me?" said the man with the shrill voice.

"The boy meant nothing by it, Brother Leobald. No one here doubts your political ambition. Though, one might wonder as to your interest in this young man."

"I care not for the skeever nor your bandying of words. If you wish to say something to me, Jacques, say it to me now."

"I would say only this. We are in the infirmary. I am here because I am Master Infirmarer. Phillip is here because he brought in the patient, and the patient is here because he is in need of my arts. Remind me, Brother Leobald, why it is that you are here?"

Sal heard a loud scoff. "When I am abbot, we may find we have a new Master Infirmarer."

"I thank you for the warning, and it shall be duly noted. If a time truly comes when our brothers name you abbot, you may find I will not be difficult to remove. Now, if you don't mind providing me the same courtesy, as I see the patient may not be so asleep as we had assumed."

Sal cursed to himself, wondering what had given him away.

"Remember what I said, Philip," said the man with the shrill voice. "You do yourself no favors backing the wrong man."

"You may leave as well, Philip," said the man with the deeper voice. "Idle hands make waste."

Sal peeked when he heard the door close, but the exposure to light sent his head spinning, and he quickly closed his eyes.

"As I suspected," said the man with the deep voice. "I shall leave you to the dark. The door will be locked from without. Do try to get some sleep. I'll return come dawn's break."

<hr />

Waking in sheets dampened by sweat, Sal took in his surroundings. The space was spare, adorned with a single stained glass window and a sconce holding a lone beeswax candle that had melted to little more than a stump. Morning's light shone through the stained glass, casting resplendent hues of red and yellow on the adjacent wall. Three other beds, identical to the one he occupied, were crammed within. The clothing he'd worn the night before hung atop a rack near the hearth.

The door crept open, and a man entered. He had a tonsured pate and wore the drab, brown robes of a brother belonging to the Vespian Order. He was tall, thick-chested, and broad of shoulder, built more like a soldier than a man of the cloth. His features were strong, rigid, as though chiseled from the very stone of the cathedral.

"Ah, you're awake. Are you well?" The man's resonant tone rang of familiarity, one of the monks from the night before, the Master Infirmarer.

"Better, though my head feels like it's to burst."

"No surprise," the monk said with a slight chuckle, "you took a nasty spill. I had feared you would be addled. It's good to know you still possess the ability to speak."

Sal felt his brow. A sizable knot had formed above his left eye. A slight tremor coursed through his body. Would that he had a cap of skeev to soothe the throbbing in his skull. "You're a Master of the Vespian Order?"

"I am," replied the monk. "My name is Jacques. I am Master Infirmarer of Knöldrus Abbey. What might your name be, my son?"

My son. The words cut deep. He was no man's son. "My name is Salvatori Lorenzo."

The monk gave him an inquisitive look. "Lorenzo, you say, who might your father be?"

Sal hesitated, then smiled in hopes that the heir of humor would soften the awkwardness of his reply. "Would that I knew myself."

"I see," said Jacques. "I only thought because of your look that you might have been—well, it's of no import. Do you hail from Dijvois?"

"Listen, Jacques, I don't mean to be rude. But my throat is parched, and my lips feel dry enough to crumble. You wouldn't have something on hand that I might drink, would you?"

"I fear I come empty-handed. Though, my brothers have only just finished their morning prayers and gather this very moment to break their fasts. If you would join us, you would be welcome to your fill."

Sal's insides turned over, as if answering the monk's inquiry. "I would greatly appreciate a fine meal."

The monk smiled. Despite the man's hard features, it was a comforting smile that put Sal's frayed nerves at ease. "I dare say, no such thing as a fine meal has been served within the walls of Knöldrus frater since the passing of our dear abbot. That is not to say it is not passing fare. It does serve to fill the belly. Although, the first man to suggest a more palatable menu would have my vote in the upcoming election, that he would."

Sal couldn't help but smile. He liked Jacques. Speaking with the man was rather like sitting by a warm hearth on a rainy day.

"When you've dressed, join me in the hall, and I'll guide you to the frater." After placing Sal's clothing at the foot of the bed, the monk turned and stepped from the room.

As Sal dismounted the bed, he felt unsteady, weak with exhaustion. A meal would serve nicely, but what he truly needed was a cap. He dressed quickly and joined the monk in the hallway.

Motioning for him to follow, Jacques headed for the opposite end of the hall. They crossed a lawn and entered a high-ceilinged building.

"The frater," said Jacques.

The frater was the size of a great hall, more suited to a king than men of the cloth. The ceiling was timber, blackened by years of oven smoke. It was filled with tables and benches that seated row after row of monks.

"Knöldrus is the largest monastery in the kingdom of Nelgand" Jacques said proudly, gesturing to the rows of monks seated at the tables. "There are over four hundred brothers in service of our holy order living within these walls."

"Ahem," coughed a slender monk standing in Sal's immediate path. The man was tall, his close-set eyes and hooked nose resembled a predatory bird. "I see the skeever lives," he said in a shrill voice. "How long must we suffer his presence, Jacques?"

Jacques crossed his thickly muscled arms. "Such coarse terms are beneath a brother of the order, Leobald. Now make way, we are ready to break our fast."

The hawkish monk narrowed his eyes to thin slits. Sneering in disgust, he shouldered past Sal and exited the frater.

"Never you mind Brother Leobald," said Jacques reassuringly. "Amid the politics of the monastery, some of us forget our order exists to serve. Even though Knöldrus Abbey is within the city walls, we tend to remain isolated from the general population, and isolation will brew fear in the bellies of suspicious men."

Sal unclenched his fist, wondering what would have happened if he had punched Leobald in the back of his tonsured head. Instead, Sal gritted his teeth and adjusted his shirt. When something suddenly occurred to him. His hand snapped to his collar. The locket, it was gone. With everything that had happened, he'd not even thought to check for it.

"Jacques," Sal said, doing his best to keep the panic from his voice, "when you took me in, was I wearing a locket?"

"Ah, yes, I'd nearly forgotten. I put the little pendant in a safe place while you slept. When we've finished breaking our fast, we shall return to the infirmary." Jacques led him through the vast hall, nodding to those who greeted him. "Good morrow, my brothers," said Jacques, taking a seat across from a pair of monks. He patted the empty spot next to him on the bench, signaling for Sal to follow suit. "What news from the brewery, Brother Tanao?"

A podgy, red-faced monk looked up from his porridge. He had a nose of burst purple veins and eyelids that drooped, giving him a melancholy look. Wiping his thick, grey mustache with the sleeve of his robe, he said, "A new harvest was brought in just this morning. With this new batch finishing later in the week, I presume the abbey stores will be full come winter."

"Supposing Tanao doesn't drink it all first," said a mousy, buck-toothed monk seated across from Sal.

Tanao scoffed and puffed out his chest as he fixed the mousy monk with a withering look. "I seem to recall I was not the only one in the brewhouse before dawn's break. On more important business, have you heard the morning count?" the podgy monk asked, turning back to Jacques. "They are saying Leobald has acquired ten new votes."

"Another ten votes won't win him the office," said the mousy monk. "The man is still a horse's ass."

"Still, it is troubling news," said the red-faced Tanao. "It shows he is gaining support. I need not remind you, if Leobald becomes abbot, it would spell trouble for us all."

A young acolyte arrived at Jacques's signal. On his tray, he carried a stack of wooden bowls and a pot of porridge. Rich, buttery aromas wafted from the steaming pot. Jacques took two bowls and filled them with the cream-colored slop, then handed Sal a bowl and a wooden spoon. Sal was no stranger to breaking his fast with porridge. Still, he'd never much liked the stuff.

"And who is Leobald's opposition?" Sal asked, growing rather interested in the talk of the monastic elections. After all, abbots served for life, it was a rare thing for any citizen of Dijvois to witness more than one election for the abbot of Knöldrus Abbey.

"Brother Martin and Brother Henry," said Jacques.

"Martin is too old," said the mousy monk, "and Henry has the wit of a dung heap. Neither will gain more votes than Leobald. Jacques here is the best fit for the job. Though, he has shrugged off our best efforts at persuasion. I have begun to suspect his mother is a mule. After all, he certainly bears the look, does he not?"

Tanao looked at Sal as though he had only just noticed him. "And who might this young man be?" said the red-faced monk.

"This is Salvatori Lorenzo," said Jacques, "a guest of the infirmary."

"Found him praying on his face in the cathedral, I did," said the young, mousy monk.

"You—I mean, thank you. I owe you a great debt."

"Pay your gratitude to the Lord that is Light. It was *he* that saved your hide, not I."

"Right," said Sal, a touch uncomfortable.

"The names Philip, by the way. Salvatori Lorenzo, did you say?"

Sal nodded. Like Sal himself, Philip looked to be of Pairgu stock. Nineteen, if he was a day. Philip was short and slender, with a pair of bucked-teeth that gave him a somewhat rodent-like appearance.

The pudgy, red-faced monk, Tanao, squinted his droopy eyelids and looked Sal up and down. "Gentle-born, I've no doubt."

Jacques looked at Sal with one eyebrow cocked, as though asking a silent question.

"Not of the Dijvois gentry," said Philip.

"You know every noble in the city, do you?" asked Tanao.

"Aye, well, I'm one of them, aren't I?"

"Not any longer," said Jacques. "You took our vows, and now you bear but one name."

Philip looked abashed, his young face turning nearly as red as that of Brother Tanao. "Noble or initiate, I've sense enough to know Lorenzo is not a name of the Dijvois gentry. They're merchant class."

"Ah, but by his features, I would have thought—but no matter," said Tanao.

Philip snapped a finger. "Lorenzo, Stefano Lorenzo, no?"

"My uncle."

"Ah, but I knew the name was familiar," said Philip.

The mention of his uncle cast a spell of silence over the table, as it always did when the name Stefano Lorenzo was spoken aloud.

"Why is it you're not running for abbot?" Sal asked Jacques in an attempt to break the silence.

"A sorted answer is the best I can give. I've never been much of a man for leading. It's true, I garner the respect of some, and the position of abbot is an honorable post, but many and more know my true passions lie with my work in the infirmary and my work for the Lord that is Light. If I were to be elected, my life would be filled with bureaucracy and beadledom, long days and short nights. When it is all considered, I feel my life is better spent where I am."

"And if you don't enter your name in the running, the lives of the men at this table could very likely be filled with emptying chamber pots," said Philip.

"Surely that couldn't happen," said Sal.

"Ah, but it could," said Philip. "You see, abbot is an elected position. As the highest authority within the abbey, it is only appropriate that my brothers and I have a say as to who will wear the collar of office. Aside from our abbot, the rest of the positions of the Enlightened Council are appointed and revoked by the abbot himself."

"Therein lies the rub," said Tanao. "All the power lies with he who wears the collar of office, and as such, it is imperative that Jacques enters himself in the election."

"What you men seem to forget is that Leobald must first win the election. As you said, young Philip, abbot is an elected position. Leobald seems to think that, as prior, he will simply step into the position of abbot as though it is his rightful inheritance," said Jacques. "I'll admit, there are fools among our order who would vote for such a man, but do you truly believe the fools outnumber those among us with sense?"

"Many men of sound mind have pledged Leobald their votes," said Philip.

"Pledges mean nothing. They are only words," Jacques

snapped, the first crack in his limestone demeanor. "Until the stones are cast, nothing is set. Keep in mind, when the last election was held, our brothers did not elect Leobald. They chose abbot Tarquin, who proved to be one of the most amiable men to ever wear the collar."

"Aye, it's true, our brothers ought to elect a man worthy of the position. A man of strong will, good sense, and a humble heart," said Tanao. "Yet, no such man has put forth his name, and when there are no good options, men will reach for the familiar. You know this as well as I, Jacques. As prior, Leobald has naturally been looked to as the transitory abbot and will remain so until the election. If things go smoothly until the time of the election, the brothers may say to themselves that things should stay as they are. They may know in their hearts Leobald is rotten to his black core, but they may forgive this fault if he can give them more of the same."

Jacques sighed and put his face in his hands dramatically. He drew in a breath, sat up tall, and turned to Sal. "Master Salvatori, I must apologize on behalf of my companions. It seems they forget themselves, even in the presence of an honored guest. Let us be done speaking of politics, my brothers."

Sal spooned another mouthful of porridge, his hand shaking involuntarily, his body weak and craving something with a hunger that food could not fill. What he wouldn't do for skeev was anyone's guess. "Forgive my ignorance, but what happened to the last abbot?"

Jacques took on a somber expression, and Tanao busied himself with his food, but Philip scooted to the edge of the bench, elbows on the table as he leaned close to Sal and rubbed his palms together. "Sickness of the belly, consumption, wasn't it, Jacques?"

Jacques looked away, his eyes seeming to have welled up. "It began as a sickness of the belly, but when he developed a persistent cough, I knew what I was dealing with. Though, by then, it seems it was too late. Soon after I relayed my discoveries to the Enlightened Council, the sickness took our abbot swifter than anything I've experienced in my years as Master Infirmarer."

"Well, there've been rumors," said Philip conspiratorially. "In the initiate housing, some of the other boys—"

"Philip!" said Tanao, placing his spoon on the table and fixing the mousy monk with a leer like a mad dog. "You do forget yourself in our company. Put a hand on that shaved spot atop your empty skull and keep in mind, the Lord that is Light sees all from above. Would you profess your servitude to our Lord with your talents as rumormonger?"

Philip opened his mouth, but whatever he was about to say, they would never know. At that moment, commotion spread through the gathered monks like the rush of a storm over calm water.

When the message reached their table, it was delivered by a little monk with a lazy eye. "Prior Leobald has asked that the masters of the Enlightened Council gather at the orchard."

"A most unusual request," said Jacques, arching an eyebrow.

"Does the prior not know this is the hour at which we break our fast? I will join him when I've had my fill," said Tanao, raising his hand to summon one of the serving boys.

"I'd not keep the prior waiting," said the little monk with the wandering eye. "It seems to be a matter of urgency."

"Very well," said Jacques, standing. "Come, Master Brewer. It seems we are required in the orchard."

Tanao stood, scowling. "Would that I'd broken my fast in the brewhouse, where dodgy eyed imps seldom come with summonses from their master."

"Light's blessing upon you, Brother Tanao," said the little monk with the wandering eye.

As the two monks began to walk away, Sal felt a pang of anxiety. He wasn't going to let Jacques out of his sight until he got his locket back. He stood, and when no one stopped him or said a word in protest, Sal followed the two masters out the frater doors.

Jacques and Tanao joined another cluster of three monks. The group crossed the yard and made for the orchard, where they saw another group of seven monks some ways into the trees. The others were gathered about the massive trunk of a pardimon tree. Soon to be twelve strong, they made up the entire Enlightened Council.

As they neared the massive tree, its gnarled, leafless branches spotted black by carrion birds, a distant scream sounded in Sal's head.

He nearly dropped to his knees. Terror gripped him by the throat with an icy hand. His heart set to racing, his legs weak and shaking. There was something familiar about the pardimon tree, something horribly familiar.

The monks nearest the tree had begun shouting, and it sounded as though a scuffle might break out.

"What is the meaning of this?" said Jacques.

The gathered monks began to part in order to make way for Jacques, who, it seemed, was a rather big deal, even amongst the Enlightened Council.

Sal had never wanted a cap of skeev more than at that very moment. Everything inside him said to run, to be as far from that place as he could get, but he couldn't move. His feet were planted to the spot.

As the monks made way for Jacques and the other newcomers, Sal caught a glimpse of what they'd gathered about. A black heap lying on the ground. No, not black, brown, a man in drab brown robes—a monk.

"Brother Dennis," said Tanao breathlessly.

Jacques knelt to examine the body closely.

Others gasped, one man's breath caught, another began to break down and sob there and then.

Sal felt a tightness in his throat and a hollow pit in his stomach. Something nagged at him, a familiarity he could not pinpoint. A terrible sinking feeling, ominous as black storm clouds on the horizon.

"A demon walks amongst us, brothers," said Leobald in a loud, shrill voice. "I have summoned you here today to witness for yourselves, and so, there can be no denying the truth. Before you is the victim of a violent and senseless act."

"Strangled," said Jacques. "A garrote."

"Brother Dennis," said a tall monk. "One of the initiates reported him missing at the morning prayers."

"This was not brought to my attention," said Leobald.

"I'd not thought it to be of import," said the tall monk defensively.

"It is not uncommon for an initiate to miss the morning prayers," said Tanao. "As they are often undisciplined."

"Your failure to recognize authority is not the issue at hand," said Prior Leobald. "Someone has violated our laws of sanctuary, despoiled holy ground."

"My concern lies, not with the ground, but with the taking of a life," said Jacques. "This boy was our brother, a member of our order. We should not concern ourselves with the theological implications, but those that pertain to corporeal matters. Our concern, my brothers, should be for the safety of the flock."

The collected group began to mutter their ascent.

"The only way to guarantee the safety of the flock," said Leobald bitterly, "is for the shepherds to beat back the wolves. Our path is clear, brothers, it has been illuminated for us by the Lord that is Light. We must hunt for this wolf that has infiltrated our walls. We must kill this wolf and hang his pelt above our gates as a sign to others who would think our sheep ripe for the taking."

"But how can we know?" said one of the monks.

"A servant of Sacrull cannot conceal himself among the righteous for long," said Leobald. "We must be vigilant. We must be aware of all that which may seem queer, if only in the slightest. We must—" Leobald stopped speaking as his scanning gaze fell on Sal. "What in Light's name is this creature doing here?"

The others seemed only then to notice Sal.

"Salvatori is my guest," said Jacques. "He has come at my invitation."

"He has come to view his night-work in the light of day!" said Prior Leobald, his eyes burning with something like realization. "I want him seized."

No one moved. The eleven others seemed as shocked as Sal.

Yet, an instant later, two of the monks began to close toward Sal with the clear intent of subduing him.

Before anyone else answered the prior's call, Sal ran for it.

He fled the orchard, crossed the yard, cut through the cloister, and burst through the transept of the cathedral. Taking a sharp turn, he sprinted, disregarding shouts of protest that rang through the nave.

Once he'd pushed past the cathedral's oak doors and out the Abbey Gate, Sal felt the elation of freedom, but he didn't stop. He ran down the cobblestone street, fast as his feet would take him, giving no regard to where he went, so long as it was away from Knöldrus Abbey and the corpse beneath the massive pardimon tree.

AFTERWORD

This one has been a long time in the coming. I feel incredibly fortunate to reveal it to the world. I want to thank everyone who helped along the way. To my family and friends who provided invaluable feedback, I love you all. To my parents, who provided me with the confidence I needed to complete this project, and support whenever that confidence waned. To my editor George, and my cover designer Stuart, thank you both for your professional manners and expertise in your chosen crafts. A final thank you, to you, whoever you are, for reading this far and allowing me to occupy the space between your ears for so long. It's difficult to express the depth of feeling I hold for this series, but I hope that it will someday come to mean as much to the rest of you as it does to me.

Taylor O'Connell
Bennington, Nebraska
June 30, 2019

ABOUT THE AUTHOR

Taylor O'Connell is the author of *The Hand that Takes*, *A Fool of Sorts*, *and The Man in Shadow*. And very much looks forward to presenting the final pieces to the series: *Fall of the Coward*; *A Throne for Thieves*, and *For All that Ascends*.

Taylor primarily writes fantasy, but loves books of all genres. When not lost within the city of Dijvois, he spends most of his time with his beautiful wife and children.

For more information or more novels by Taylor O'Connell, visit
Tayloroconnellbooks.com

Made in the USA
Columbia, SC
01 November 2019